Telomere

L. J. Williams

TELOMERE
A Novel

Published by BBV Publishing
We print our published books on demand and digitally to save paper, trees, energy, and our Earth for our children.

TELOMERE
A Novel by L. J. Williams

Layout and design by Belenna M. Lauto.
ISBN 978-0-9844797-0-2
ISBN 978-0-9844797-3-3 (digital edition)
Library of Congress Control Number: 2012931808

All work done in the United States of America
www.bbvpublishing.com

For additional copies of this book either in print or digitally, please visit:
Amazon's web site
OR
For a possible autograph copy, visit BBV publishing's web site page:
www.bbvpublishing.com/bbv_index/suspense/telomere.html

Contents

Author's Note:

I altered some physical locations and modified the names of the municipalities. While the characters are fictional, the rumor that ignited the realization of reasons for this story is real. The scientific terms are true. The theories will lend a non-conceived hypothesis to the world of science and present a vortex cognizance to mankind.

DEDICATION:

TO MANKIND LIVING IN PEACE.
FOR THAT IS THE GREATEST AND MOST NOBLE PRIZE.

11/15/02 - 02/02/03

THE LAB, Chapter One

The last evening of the year had already begun, but few people in America noticed. Everyone went about their lives as if the lingering effect of a strong sedative persisted upon them. Emotions were fickle and fear became an unwanted companion. Anger would surface from time to time in many minds, but this feeling offered no immediate solution. The day was Wednesday, December 31, 1941. The New Year did not look promising and a link started to be forged that would slowly manifest itself sixty years into the future.

As the last evening of 1941 grew colder, a perfect looking neighborhood peacefully reflected the moonlight on the West Side of Cold Creek Harbor. Not a single porch light had been turned on. A few dimly lit windows lined the shore. Victorian style houses were dressed with yellow window shutters. A church, post office, and library completed the little neighborhood snuggled between the harbor and leafless tree-covered hills rising in the background. However, one odd element stood out about this community. At the only land entrance, next to Route 5A, were large evergreen bushes trying unsuccessfully to hide a wooden entrance gate and security booth. The gate and booth were highly unusual, but a more peculiar feature for this charming neighborhood in suburbia USA remained. The peculiarity belonged solely to the cloaked personnel inside the entrance booth because of their uniforms, which represented the newly formed U.S. Military Police Corps of 1941.

Slightly after midnight, the last neighborhood light went out as the moon set behind the horizon. On schedule, at two that morning a small periscope broke the surface of the Harbor's water. By half past two, the submarine that the periscope belonged to sat on the surface of the water with two capsized rowboats secured to the deck. Ten minutes later, three men in black jumpsuits were upon the shore of Cold Creek Harbor. Quietly they pulled their rowboat ashore.

The only other crafts in the Harbor that night were some small private fishing boats. All were in dry dock on the opposite side of the Harbor for the winter; all except a small fishing vessel still in use by the owner. His craft now floated precariously close to the submarine. The elderly captain slept below deck under a bulky pile of old navy blankets. His eyes opened wide when he thought he heard voices. Voices in the cold dark night that brought back memories of World War I. He made no mistake about the language heard in the night. He threw off the blankets and stood in his wool socks, Long Johns, and the uniform shirt of a Captain. His scrubby unshaven gray chin whiskers and the torn material on his captain's shirt from the First World War reflected the living conditions aboard his ship. As he struggled in the darkness to find his old helmet a deep chill caused him to shudder briefly.

His abrupt entrance on deck reflected his determination as he fastened the strap to his helmet. The resulting noise and image of an old man in a WWI helmet offered an easy and immediate identification by one of the three lookouts on top of the submarine. Two backup sailors in the second rowboat received orders through hand signals as the old man searched the shoreline for people talking. Fear then struck the old Captain upon perceiving that the voices possibly originated from a vessel behind him. He turned around to look at the waters of the harbor. In horror, the captain looked upon the outline image of a submarine with the painted flag of an old enemy anew. Hidden in the shadows, less than twenty yards away floated the rowboat. Instinctively, the old Captain turned toward his ship's bell. As he went to grab the rope of the bell, a harpoon shot through his cold and fragile body. His unfurling fingers induced the bell to rattle off two frail rings as he fell dead to the deck.

The upstairs bedroom in one of the Victorian style houses remained dark as a tall lanky man rolled out of his warm bed toward the window. George Mannuso wore a long white night shirt and had a bushy black mustache. He tossed his nightcap onto the bed revealing his balding head as he approached the window in a crouched position. Slowly, he pushed back the curtain ever so slightly to investigate the questionable faint sound of a bell. There, in between some tree branches outside his window, he saw Captain Wayne on the deck of his boat. Bell ringing sound solved, until he took a second look. The dark figure lifted a lifeless figure from the boat's deck. Quickly George raced to his armoire. Feeling for the handles he swung open the doors and grabbed his binoculars on the top shelf. By the time he focused them through the curtain and tree branches, he saw that the limp body wore a World War I helmet. Like garbage, Captain Wayne's body went overboard, leaving someone else standing on the deck. George scanned with his binoculars rapidly as he started to breathe heavily.

"Mamma Mia, a submarine no less," George proclaimed to himself in an Italian accent. He ran from his bedroom to the downstairs kitchen in a state of panic. Fearful of turning on an electric lightbulb, he fumbled through kitchen drawers finding a box of stick matches. Locating the icebox, George pulled down a candle in a holder from the top. He nervously lit the candle on the floor and scrambled to the twenty year old Automatic Electric wall telephone. Squinting to see the numbers around the dial that were just below the Transmitter, he managed to dial 009 for the military police in the security booth at the front gate. Impatiently he waited for each number to click around the dial and the last number nine became an excruciating wait expressed in his reply.

"Yes, yes this is Doctor George Mannuso in Victorian sixteen. We have a code red by sea! I know who... I am not dreaming, I assure you! They want Victorian Seventeen, I'm going there now!"

Dropping the receiver to dangle by its thick black wire, George ran over to the other side of the kitchen after picking the candle up off the floor. He did not hear the soldier on the phone yelling, "Doctor Mannuso stay where you are. Do not leave Victorian sixteen!"

A Gurney Potbelly stove stood next to a brand new Chambers Gas Range. The Potbelly stove no longer functioned, except for pulling open a passage hidden behind the brick wall. With candle in hand, George hunched over and went down a small slope. Through a rock hard dirt tunnel, only five feet high, George moved as fast as his six foot two inch frame would allow. At each turn or new direction in the tunnel, George checked for carvings in the dirt wall that had arrows with V 17 under them. Within a minute, he headed up a slope to a dead end. The number 17 had been painted on a brick wall in front of him. After putting the candle down, George gave one long push on the brick wall. Reaching back for the candle another kitchen lit up as he raced through. Leaving the swinging kitchen door behind, George went through the parlor and up the stairs.

"Gabrielle! Doctor Maida! It is I, Doctor Mannuso. Please wake up we must leave now!" George shouted out as he shielded the candle with his hand so the breeze created by his running would not cause the flickering flame to go out.

At the top of the staircase, the bedroom door banged open. Footsteps then raced back to the stairs. The huge banister made of dark maple wood gradually glowed from top to bottom as the candle, again shielded by George's other hand, traveled the distance downward. On the way down, the barefooted Doctor started a frantic conversation with himself.

"My God, my God this woman is insane! Morning of the New Year and she is still working! She is addicted to work! Yes, she is and I will tell her you are crazy woman. Oh, oh! Hot wax, very hot wax."

Back through the parlor, down a long hall, a left turn and upon a wooden door with a glass doorknob. As the door swung open, the candle blew out with the exchange of air. Frantically, Doctor Mannuso moved his hand through the darkness until he found a large round toggle switch mounted on the wooden plank wall. A steep, dirty wooden staircase without any railing became visible as one incandescent lightbulb came on at the bottom of the stairs. After descending the steps, Doctor Mannuso deposited the candle and holder on one of four large empty barrels that once held wine. Taking ten more running steps, he came upon a metal door. Quickly, he turned the combination lock above the doorknob and slid the metal door into the wall. A massive laboratory came into view that had several Pan shaped fixtures hanging from a twelve foot high ceiling. The bright illumination came from 250 watt incandescent bulbs in each fixture.

* * * * *

Meanwhile, in the security booth at the front gate, absolute panic fell upon the young face of a nineteen year old MP as he struggled to crank up a Field Radio. "Answer...answer...damn it answer. Yes, sir! This is the front gate checkpoint for Mistress of Cold Creek. I need to speak with Colonel Boyd immediately... I know the time and I'll have very little time left if you don't get the Colonel on the telephone now. It is imperative! We have a code red by sea here!"

Now the voice on the other end raised several decibels, "Flying crab crap soldier. I'm going to wake him and if this is full of crab crap, I will come down to your little Mistress checkpoint and crush the crap out of you."

Silence came over the telephone and utter stillness filled the air of the neighborhood in a furor. The MP then heard over the radio a muffled sound of an older man yelling in the background. Next, he heard some vigorous moving of furniture and finally, "This is Colonel D. Boyd! This had better be damn real. We just had a false air raid report here this past ninth day of December! The damn day after we declared war on Japan!"

"Yes, sir, I know and I..."

"You know! Then you know we performed beautifully! We got two hundred eighty planes in the air and over seventy-five hundred men at their ground stations within twenty minutes! Next we have to have some..."

"Oh God," exhaled a distraught nineteen year old.

"Some damn fool reporter describes our siren going off high and thin like some anguished nightingale in his newspaper!"

"Oh God, sir I..."

"I do not need that crap..."

"Oh God, with all due respect Colonel, please shut up and let me talk! I... I mean... I mean shut up sir."

* * * * *

Gabrielle's old lab coat had a strong yellowish tinge from the incandescent light bulbs throughout the lab. Her laboratory boasted state-of-the-art and pushed through the envelope of technology for 1942. Newly invented equipment were throughout the lab: electron microscopes, centrifuges, refrigeration units, freezers, incubators, autoclaves, rotators, rockers and a computer that prominently operated, occupied three walls of another room. Each section that made up the computer stood just five feet shy of the twelve-foot high ceiling. This well illuminated room had a meeting table with eight chairs in the center. The large walk-in entrance proudly exposed the giant computer and the genesis of a new age.

Gabrielle removed her eyeglasses as she turned around to face the heavy panting she heard from behind, "Oh dear Jesus, Mary and Joseph! Doctor Mannuso are you drunk?" She had a strong and proper English accent.

"Doctor Maida, I wish I was."

"Well, do make yourself some tea. I have hot water on that asbestos pad next to the Bunsen burner, just help yourself."

"Gabrielle, you don't understand."

"Yes, I do Doctor Mannuso. You had too much Eggnog to drink last night."

"Gabrielle they are here for you. They are on the property!"

"And you say that to me in your bare feet! Poppycock! Am I to believe the Japanese are now after me? What is this, first Pearl Harbor, second Doctor Maida? I am not such a person to be so high on their list."

"No, Gabrielle, the Nazis are here."

Doctor Maida looked away and pulled out her hairpin letting her gray hair fall to shoulder's length. "To them I am dead," she finally said in a now exhausted tone of voice.

"I beg to differ. They seem to believe otherwise. They just killed... No, they murdered Captain Wayne. I know what I saw, we have to go."

Doctor Maida's eyes swelled just a little for she knew Doctor Mannuso would not fool with murder. She turned to shut off the first of three Bunsen burners that were on at her lab station. "I will shut down and call the MP at the gate," Doctor Maida said calmly.

"That, Doctor, *vill* not be necessary." The thick and uninvited accent mispronounced 'W' each time.

"Oh my... I don't have anything close to what you think I have," Doctor Maida quickly responded to the intruder's pre-conclusions.

Three men in black jumpsuits had entered the lab. The soldier leading the way carried a Luger and he pointed the pistol directly at the two doctors. Two other soldiers behind him, held harpoon guns.

"Our Fuhrer *vill* be the judge of that." The soldier spoke again as he waved his gun to motion both doctors closer to the end of a lab station's counter top. However despite the soldier's concentration, the massive computer panels with blinking lights in the other room acted like an addictive drug, thus dividing his attention.

"He is your Fuhrer, not mine," Doctor Maida snapped back.

"Don't provoke him," Doctor Mannuso requested of her.

The commander then spoke in German and directed his order to the two other soldiers. Immediately the soldier closest to the exit left the lab.

Turning his attention and gun back to the two doctors, the commander unbuttoned his jump suit and systematically stepped out. A big smile slowly grew as he enjoyed watching the fear build in the eyes of his prisoners who stared at his uniform and gun.

"I told him to signal our ship and inform them that we have you, the Mistress of Cold Creek. Yes, I am afraid you *vill* be coming with us." The commander gave an additional order in German as he kept his eyes upon the two doctors. When finished he spoke in broken English again. "You both go to sleep now, yes. By the time your colleague *vakes* up here at your laboratory, you *vill* be halfway to the Fatherland."

The other soldier put his harpoon gun on top of an opposite counter and turned his back to them as he followed commands by removing items from a container that hung around his neck.

"You both move over to that counter now," the Commander ordered as he pointed his pistol to where he wanted them to go.

Fortunately, the German Commander who kept stealing looks at the massive computer did not notice that his gun hand hovered by one of the lit Bunsen burners near the counter's edge. However, Doctor Mannuso did notice that this Burner, permanently anchored to the counter, stood directly under the gun. Instinctively Doctor Mannuso yanked the rubber hose that supplied the gas to that Bunsen burner. First the black quarter inch diameter hose whipped off the Burner's connection and toward the two doctors. The German Commander looked from the computer to the gas hissing rubber hose snapping back toward him. Instantly the gas escaping from the hose exploded in a ball of flames when contact occurred with the hot flameout of the Burner. The Commander yelled as the skin on his wrist along with the shirtsleeve of his military uniform burned.

The gun fell to the counter top and Doctor Mannuso used his whole body to slam the Commander to the floor. Doctor Maida closed all the gas valves at the end of the workstation's countertop causing all flames to extinguish.

"Run, Gabrielle run!" shouted Doctor Mannuso.

From the floor, the Commander roared in German an order to stop them. Gabrielle ran out of the lab as the other soldier with a filled syringe in one hand reached for the harpoon gun with the other. Doctor Mannuso grabbed the hand with the syringe and stuck the needle right into the neck of the soldier. Immediately excreting the contents into his blood stream and threw him to the floor causing the harpoon gun to fire. The spent harpoon shot harmlessly across the lab and Doctor Mannuso made his break for the exit.

Within a second, that seemed to be an hour, Doctor Mannuso heard a clear and precise gunshot. He stumbled through the open doorway, leaving some of his blood on the doorframe.

* * * * *

"Corporal, where are you?" called the nineteen year old MP.

"Private, keep it down," the corporal angrily answered. "Over here in the bushes before the path."

"Sorry, sir, I did get through to Colonel Boyd himself."

"Now tell me the better news," the more experienced Corporal said as he peered through his binoculars at Doctor Maida's house.

"Better news it is sir. He is sending all available B-25 Bombers that are overnight visitors at Mitchel Field to take out the sub."

"Damn, you're telling me that the First Air Force is on the way?"

"Yes, sir and Colonel Boyd is coming himself with ground troops. Also sir, the Colonel gave us orders to fire flares over the harbor once we hear the bombers approaching. I brought the only flare gun we have with six rounds. What's the situation out here?"

"Not good, Victorian Seventeen has the front door wide open and no lights are on. We can't wait any longer, we have to go in and stop whoever is in there. The trick is to do that without the lookouts on the sub spotting us."

"Corporal what do they want?"

"All I know is because of a rumor, we guard this place. A rumor that this place will be Hitler's first stop in America if he wins the war and I don't know why, so don't ask. Damn... The rumor must be true and Hitler isn't waiting. Cover my back and move out."

As the two MPs with their pistols drawn reached the open door of the house, a woman's cry emerged from the dark interior. Quickly, their bodies hit the floor of the front porch.

"Oh my God, I surrender! Oh my God, George... George you are bleeding!"

At the edge of the rug in the parlor, Doctor Mannuso laid on the floor holding his shoulder. Doctor Maida knelt next to him, but could not attend to his wound. She stopped moving to stare at the harpoon gun pointing directly at them. The German soldier who left earlier to signal the submarine from the upstairs bedroom window had come back down and stopped Gabrielle in her own parlor. Doctor Mannuso collapsed when he finally caught up to her.

The two MPs were now in the house and focusing in on the three dark figures, one standing, and two on the floor. The Corporal called out, "Halt, you are under arrest."

The German soldier did not understand anything past the word halt, but he understood he had trouble. Swinging his harpoon around to face the MPs, he took three bullets. One bullet came from the Corporal's gun and two bullets came from the Private. A third bullet from the Private missed and crashed through an empty vase on top of an upright Bentley piano against the wall.

The Private rushed toward the two doctors and dropped to his knees. A gunshot sounded from down the hall as he felt a bullet whiz by his ear. Doctor Maida screamed and huddled over Doctor Mannuso as he shuddered from the sound recognition of the gunshot. The Private fell sideways to the floor cupping his ear with his left hand. The Corporal hit the floor and unloaded his Pistol into all areas of the dark hallway.

"Are you all right, Private?" the Corporal wanted to know.

"Yes, sir, I feel no blood," came the Private's shaky answer.

"Give me your gun, reload mine and get them out of here."

"Yes, sir."

The Corporal slowly headed down the hall. A miniscule amount of light came from the lightbulb at the bottom of the stairs to the lab. In the shadows of the hallway, the Corporal saw the outline shape of a body on the floor. Holding his pistol outward, he slowly reached down to check the neck for a pulse. The Corporal felt no pulse at all, just the blood that now covered his hand as he froze upon turning his head upward.

"Sir," cried the Private from the parlor. "The bombers are already here!"

"Throw me your flare gun!" ordered the Corporal. Running as fast as he could into the parlor, the Corporal barely caught the tossed flare gun in the dark. The sack of extra rounds followed as he continued out the front door.

The lookouts on the submarine had heard the B-25 bombers before the MPs inside the house did. The German sailors started scrambling on deck of the sub so they could submerge. The Corporal still could not see the bombers, but they were getting louder and closer. Running down the house's private driveway, over some bushes and down through trees growing on the embankment, he saw the dark slow moving outline of the Nazi submarine. Cold Creek Harbor, then and now, isn't of any significant size. The supply came in from the body of water called the Sound about two miles north. The harbor's widest point spanned three quarters of a mile, thus the distance between the twenty Victorian homes on the west bank and a smaller number of two bedroom Ranch houses on the hills of the east bank. The harbor's water ended seventy feet from the embankment going up to route 5A on the south. Stopping just two feet from the edge of the water, the Corporal sent the first flare high over the water. As the flare exploded with light, the sound of the bombers' engines from above altered in pitch. Upon seeing the signal, the pilots adjusted their course.

Two men in robes now raced from another Victorian house to the front porch of Doctor Maida where she and the Private were attending to Doctor Mannuso's wound. The Private heard the men running up the walk and went for his gun.

"We know them, we know them!" Doctor Maida proclaimed as she held the Private's hand holding the pistol.

"Oh my God what is going on here?" the first gentleman stated with utter fear in his voice.

"Doctor Mannuso was shot trying to save me. Please get blankets from inside my house. We have to get him to the medical lab in Victorian one."

The young Private turned and gave an intuitive order to the gentleman scurrying into the house, "Keep the lights off looking for those blankets or we'll get bombed!"

"Private, let me see the wound," announced the second gentleman. "I am the Director here and a medical doctor. Another flare...perfect timing to help me take a look."

The Corporal now stood in cold water up to his knees as he tried to get closer to the sub that slowly moved further away. He fired off the third flare before the second one had completely extinguished itself. Then, from the heavens came the sounds of one falling bomb after another. Only to be surpassed by the deep bass sound of the exploding bombs. Trapped between the hills around the harbor, every thundering explosion echoed repeatedly. Splash after splash, water stretched upward to reflect the starlight and crashed downward creating a multitude of consecutive waves. Plane after plane continuously dropped bombs that began to pulverize the sub as well as the entire harbor. Captain Wayne's boat took a direct hit, sending pieces in every direction. The corporal knew that the time came to leave, when parts of the boat almost hit him. He started running for his life back up the muddy embankment. Soaking wet, holding his ears and freezing, he turned to fire one more flare over the harbor allowing more planes to make their pass. Screeching metal sounds etched outward among the bombs. The sub began sinking fast. Citizens sleeping in their homes on the opposite hills were abruptly thrown from their beds as the bombardment shook the very foundation of their world. This had become overkill. Waves were hitting the shore now, bashing small fishing boats, windows were breaking, dogs were barking, people were screaming and men were dying. War arrived in America's front yard, yet the Military did not officially record the event as such.

"My God, Private, when will they stop? My front porch and house are shaking!" Doctor Maida shouted.

"When that Nazi sub is at the bottom of the harbor for good!"

"I can't believe this is happening," screamed the gentleman coming out of the house with several blankets.

"Quick, cover Doctor Mannuso!" the Private shouted over the relentless bombing. "He's freezing and he's lost a great deal of blood. I have to go find Corporal Rogers! He may need my assistance! Can the three of you carry Doctor Mannuso over to your medical building?"

"Yes, go!" Doctor Maida stated as loud as she could.

The Private dashed off to the water and could not get down the embankment with all the noise, dirt, water, and debris pounding the shoreline. The entire harbor gradually turned upside down. Finally, the pandemonium on earth stopped. With scrutiny, the Private searched the embankment for any sign of his Corporal. Slowly he slid halfway down toward the water through the turned up mud, weeds, and dead fish. Nowhere could he find the Corporal. Just as he started to give up, he could hear truck engines coming. Not just one, two or five, but a truck convoy. Headlights were now all over and still circling the harbor. Squeaking brakes brought truck after truck to a stop. Orders yelled out and hundreds of soldiers were unloading from the trucks and charging about to complete their commands. The reflecting headlights from the trucks and now roaming flashlight beams gave a glimpse of something moving by the edge of the water. Carefully moving closer, only a fish stuck in the mud became visible. The Flounder struggled to get free. Half covered with mud and getting colder by the minute, a Private decided to save a fish as if to make up for everything else that happened. Upon tossing the fish back into the water, he turned to head back up the slope.

"I hope you aren't go...going to leave me here. I'm... I'm freezing. You helped the damn fish."

"Corporal? Where the hell are you?"

"Yer... Your left, under this mud."

"Damn, I thought you were a goner."

"Me too. I'm... I am free...freezing. Help me...me out of this muck."

"Yes, sir!"

They both started laughing after pulling free of the wet mud. The suction noise sounded just like farts and splashes of mud flew into their faces. "God, wha... What was that?"

"Flying crab crap, sir. Flying crab crap."

"What a way...to bring in the New Year, eh Private."

"Yes, sir, a hell of a way."

From above the embankment they heard, "Sergeant! Two soldiers below need assistance."

Before daybreak, soldiers dispatched to every home in the town of Cold Creek Harbor. They provided comfort to the homeowners and put to rest any fears, concerns, or assumptions. By daybreak, the most obvious evidence that detailed what occurred had been removed. Within two days, broken windows were replaced and embankments cleaned up. By the third week, the appropriate division of the United States Navy discreetly removed all the remains of the Nazi submarine from Cold Creek Harbor. The Navy's 'practice maneuvers' were over and all official vessels left the harbor. However, all these efforts could not prevent the sustained rumor.

THE AWARD, Chapter Two

Few people in the United States were preparing to celebrate the holidays as usual. The jubilant New Centennial ceremonies the world saw two years earlier were now a distant memory, for the world had changed. The day was Friday, December 14, 2001. Everyone knew that the year was almost over, but few people were conscious of the fact. This time our technology brought the horror into everyone's living room as events happened. The world stood acutely aware that the calamity which unfolded in front of everyone's eyes did not come from a fictional movie production. There were no glowing, joyful promises for humankind this New Year. Emotions were fickle and fear became an unwanted companion. The American people were again in a state of mind that had not been known since Pearl Harbor.

Principal Browne stood center stage in front of the entire student body of Cold Creek High School. She wore business attire and acquired a plaque from her assistant. Leaning toward the podium and microphone, she looked out over a very respectfully quiet audience.

"I know this school assembly has been difficult. This has been a time for condolences, support, and hope. The community of our school, seriously touched by the recent events, will continue to take productive steps to help us all in the healing process."

"Now before the dismissal bell rings I would like to conclude on a happy note. As most of you know, our own senior class student body president won the State's Science Fair First Place Award. At this time, I would like to extend, with this plaque, our congratulations from all of Cold Creek High School to Addie Erickson. Addie, would you please join me on stage."

The student body applauded as a young woman of seventeen demurely stood from her reserved seat in the third row of the middle section. Her chestnut color hair, tied up and pulled back, emphasized her cheekbones and blue eyes. She wore blue jeans, a loose fitting white shirt, and a hand crocheted light blue vest. Upon reaching the stage, she did not hesitate to save some time getting to the podium. First she faced the audience, then lifted herself up into a sitting position on the edge of the stage. Effortlessly she swung her feet around and stood, thus avoiding the longer walk to the staircase in the corner of the auditorium. A modest young individual, but not bashful.

"Congratulations Addie," Principal Browne said as she shook Addie's hand and offered the plaque that Addie accepted with a big smile. "Thank you for representing our school so well."

The last school bell of the day started to ring and students began to stand and talk as they applauded one more time. Over the microphone the Principal added, "Please follow directions from your teachers in the aisles so that we have an orderly exit. I will see all of you on Monday!"

"Thank you Mrs. Browne," said Addie. "This plaque is a great honor."

"You are very welcome Addie. Winning the Science Fair is no small feat. Ah, before you go I have something else for you. I had hoped to announce this in front of your classmates, however the almighty dismissal bell has spoken."

"You don't have to give me anything else, this plaque is more than... I mean, this plaque says it all."

"Oh no, this is different. I'll explain as I walk with you to your locker so you don't miss your bus."

* * * * *

Addie swung her solid green backpack on as she ran to her bus with her blue ski jacket in her arms. Once on the steps of the school bus, Addie expressed her appreciation to the bus driver, "Thanks for waiting Jake."

"No problem with me Addie. It's my job to wait for any student running toward the bus. If you were walking, well maybe I wouldn't wait.

Take a seat now. Attention everyone, seat belts on. We're leaving! And due to the fact that Addie was late I don't believe we have enough time to make that First Friday Stop for the usual end of the week French fry treat."

A loud objectionable moan came from the occupants of the bus, including Addie. As she sat down next to her girlfriend, Addie voiced her opposition, "Oh no, don't blame me Jake."

"Only fooling ya," laughed Jake. "Get in those seats or I really won't stop."

"So girlfriend, let's see the award," requested Addie's friend sitting next to her. Addie's girlfriend had a solo earring dangling three brown leather strips from the lobe of her left ear. A black pullover fleece sweater with gold trim around the hood, cuffs, and pockets matched the gold stitches on her jeans.

"Oh, I don't want to take it out here," Addie said as she looked about to see if anyone else heard.

"Then you are showing it to me tomorrow when I come over."

"You're not coming over tomorrow, you're coming over next..."

"I am now, unless you show me that hunk of wood on this bus...in front of everyone!"

"Jannelle!" Addie emphasized her girlfriend's name as she pulled the plaque out of her backpack. "Will you please stop that!"

"Nice... Oh man a gold boarder with sparkling...whatever those chips of sparkling glass are."

"Thanks, so why don't you come over anyway tomorrow," Addie said as she rubbed her thumb over one of the glass clusters in each corner of the plaque.

"All right, I'll check with my mom and call you tonight about the time."

"Plan on late tomorrow afternoon," suggested Addie. "It turns out that I was invited to some lab tomorrow morning due to this award."

"No problem."

The school bus drove out onto the main road by the school and went just twenty yards before pulling into a parking lot known as the unofficial First Friday Stop. Students were already out of their seats and heading toward the exit before the bus even parked. Addie started to put the plaque away, as some friends passed her seat and received a close up look.

"Hey, cool Erickson."

"Yeah, nice plaque. Did us proud."

"Thanks Matt, thanks Kosy," Addie replied as the two boys headed off the bus. Addie then turned to Jannelle to whisper, "I don't care what you think, Kosy likes you."

"Knock it off Addie."

"Hey... Addie, Jannelle. So that's the plaque?" said another girlfriend exiting the bus. She wore narrow black framed glasses that disputed her rounded appearance. She held back her long jet-black hair with an elastic band. She carried her small white vinyl backpack that doubled as a pocketbook and book bag.

"Yeah, that's the plaque," answered Addie. "How you doing Yasu?"

"Fine, hey that plaque design is just like one of the plaques my dad has hanging in his office. Only difference is my dad's plaque is in Japanese...eh stop the pushing! I'm talking here."

"And I'm walking here," declared a tall thin boy with short red hair. He had a gold ring pierced through his lower lip and wore several gold rings on his fingers.

"Cut the crap Frankie," Yasu shot back.

"Ain't you never going to put away that damn bling bling, so people can get by for food?"

"Fine Frankie, just go," Yasu said as Addie put the plaque away. "Anyway, congrats on the plaque. Are you guys getting something inside?"

"No, I'll pass," said Addie.

"Then move aside so I can pass," said Jannelle. "Wait up Yasu, I'm getting some. You sure you don't want me to hook you up with something Addie?"

"Yeah, I'm sure. Thanks Jannelle."

"So Yasu it's cool the way you did your hair, I wish I could do that with mine."

"Your hair is beautiful the way you have it and you know I think Kosy really likes you."

Addie watched her two girlfriends leave the bus along with fifteen others. Jake, the bus driver, started wiping down his windows while the other students that stayed on the bus were talking or trying to do homework. Addie eyed Jannelle's empty window seat next to her and migrated over to rest her head on the window. She then heard and saw her boyfriend's car, with the top down, pull along side of the bus. Christopher Wilkins stood up on the front seat of his dad's old 1988 black Mazda convertible. Carefully he perused the bus windows for his girlfriend. Addie ended his search by standing up herself and lowering the top half of her window on the bus.

"Chris, hi Chris!"

"Addie where were you?" shouted Chris from his car. "After the assembly I waited at your locker, but you didn't show."

"Oh I took a slow walk to my locker with Mrs. Browne. I figured you left already by the time I got there."

Chris hopped over the closed car door and out of his car. Dashing onto the bus, he wore brown cargo pants and the baseball team's dark blue jacket with white leather sleeves. Sewn on the left side of his jacket were the letters of the school. He had dark brown hair and styled with a short cut. His blue denim shirt and Adidas sneakers both matched his eyes.

"Hey, Jake," said Chris coming in the bus' open door.

"Ah, no visitors allowed. Unless you hook me up with some fries."

"Jake I just drove here, I didn't go inside. Can I just say hello to my girl?"

"Course you can man, don't you know when old Jake is just giving you a hard time."

"Cool."

"Hey Chris," Addie said with a smile as Chris sat next to her.

"Hi, you know I drove around the school looking for you, but I missed seeing you getting on your bus. So I came here, knowing about Jake's FFS."

"I hear you!" Jake yelled out from the front of the bus. "The First Friday Stop is for you kids. All you kids begged me for this stop at the beginning of the year. I only do it out of the goodness of my heart, and that you kids hook me up with some fries or a burger every now and then. Not that I ask for that! They do it just as a thank you for stopping, you know. Because they want to."

"We know Jake, it's cool!" Addie said to end the rambling and turned to Chris with a smile.

"So what was the slow walk with the principal about?" inquired Chris.

"She received a letter from the assistant director of some research lab here in Cold Creek Harbor. I was invited for a private tour of the place since I won this Science Fair."

"What lab is around here? And why was the letter sent to our principal and not you?"

"I don't know," Addie said with some thought. "The assistant director only knew the school I attended from the write up in the newspaper."

"Oh I see... Hey do they mean that building over by the pond?"

"Oh yeah, that building by the lake and the church where everyone ice skates in the winter."

"That's no lab," Jake interrupted as he sat in his seat and looked back three rows to where Chris and Addie were sitting. He obviously eavesdropped on their conversation. "Didn't they give you an address?"

"That's right," realized Addie. "They did in the letter, let me see."

"My God, the woman wins the State's Science Fair and can't think to look for an address on the letter."

"Jake got ya Addie," said Chris.

"Yeah, good one Jake," Addie said with little concern.

She started reading the letter again after she pulled the paper from her pocket. Finally Addie looked up and said, "Actually Jake, I never read the letter. Mrs. Browne gave it to me and only briefed me on it. The address is zero one, twenty, Route Five A. Where is that?"

Jake turned in his seat to face the couple and as he rolled his eyes he said, "Oh boy, I tell you. I lived here since I was born back in nineteen fifty. That address is for those houses at the bottom of the hill and at the end of the harbor's waters. That's your lab."

"Those are just houses Jake," Addie insisted.

"No, they are not, Addie. Them houses are research labs. Haven't you two ever heard the rumors about that place?"

"Rumors?" Addie asked with some concern.

"Oh shit no," Chris said with some excitement.

"Jake don't start with your jokes. Those are just old houses. No more, no less."

"That's what our government wants you to think," explained Jake. "Just like they set it up some seventy or eighty years ago so to make Hitler and the Japanese believe the same thing. I heard that they even have a fake Post Office, Library and church to complete the look."

"Jake what are you talking about?" questioned Addie. "My family has lived here just as long and I never heard anything about that neighborhood being a lab."

"I'm just telling you what I know Addie," Jake said casually. "I don't know anyone who lives there. Have you guys ever met a student who lives there? I think not. The rumor is that if Hitler won the war, this would be his first stop in America because of the research going on in those innocent looking houses. One story goes by way of once Hitler realized he wasn't going to beat America he sent his bombers over here to blow up the lab. It was supposed to happen at sunrise, but they arrived too early and the sun wasn't up yet. So because the bombers didn't have enough light to see the target, they missed and blew up the harbor waters really bad. The U.S. Navy had to come into the harbor and it took them three weeks to clean out all the debris and bombs that didn't go off."

"Jake, nice try, but I'm not buying today." Addie said as she slowly shook her head and gave Jake a look from the corner of her eyes, "Hitler never had long-range bombers."

Three students bounced back on the bus with some food and blew past Jake while talking, laughing and eating. Jake immediately leaned on the horn of his bus for three seconds before complaining, "Look at the time. What is taking everyone so long today?"

One of the boys that came back to the bus turned around after hearing Jake's complaint and yelled, "Jake! Steve is coming out with something for you. Don't worry, we all chipped in to get you a mega meal and we double sized it."

"Oh that is unnecessary, but oh so nice. I thank you. And to you young woman I ask this. Explain to me the security gate at the only entrance to that place."

"So big deal, many places have their own security today."

"Yeah today, but these houses had a security booth there since World War Two!"

"Oh my God, he's right Addie!" Chris injected into the conversation. "About five years ago I went with my older brother and some of his friends to spook the guard on Halloween. We climbed the fence and we all got caught because out of nowhere three more guards surrounded us before we even made it to the security booth. All I remember is that they had cheesy uniforms on, but they were no mall security. They had guns! They scared the crap out of us. Everything was 'yes, sir' or 'no, sir,' I will never forget that night."

"You see," said Jake. "Your own boyfriend confirms this. I'll show you, we'll drive right past the place before I drop you off... Ooh Steve you are my main man. Thank you, thank you all. Now sit down so I can see that everyone is here. Chris get off, you drove. No offense."

"None taken, hey Addie I'll drive you home," Chris said as he stood up to allow Jannelle to sit back down.

"Great," Addie said as she collected her belongings.

"Hi Jannelle," Chris said as he walked to the front of the bus.

"Hey Addie were are you going?" asked Jannelle.

"Chris is driving me home. Hey Chris can you drive Jannelle home too?"

"Sure," said Chris from the front of the bus.

"Whoa, wait one minute space cowboy with your top down. I not fooling here. You can't drive them home. They got on my bus and I'm responsible for them. If you were to have something happen, I would not be able to explain why I let them get off my bus and into your car. Sorry."

"No way you can see around that Jake?" asked Chris.

"Sorry, no way in crab crap," said Jake seriously.

"Ha, crab crap, good one Jake. I've never heard that before. Sorry Jannelle, Addie. I'll call you tonight Addie."

"Okay," Addie said softly as she went to the window she left opened. She watched Chris jump into his car and wave.

"Hey Addie," Chris called out. "I want to see your plaque so maybe I can come over after I call tonight."

"Sounds fine, maybe we can rent a DVD," Addie said hopefully. "See you later!"

The school bus made its way through the quiet neighborhoods southwest of the harbor dropping off students at the appropriate bus stops. Every house had an American flag on display one way or another. After dropping off most of the students the bus turned onto Route 5A and started a long downhill drive toward the water of Cold Creek Harbor.

"Addie, here it comes," Jake called out as the bus approached the bottom of the hill. "It's coming up on your left."

Addie slowly turned and looked across the bus and out the opposite windows. The property across the street had only trees. A few feet in, she could sometimes get a glimpse of a hurricane fence. Next came a driveway entrance that led up to large evergreen bushes and a security booth. A heavy metal gate blocked the driveway entrance and Addie saw nobody in the booth, but there were several beautifully kept Victorian houses in the background, each with an American flag flying outside. She did not see any buildings marked Post Office or Library and if the property had a church, she didn't see one now. As the bus reached the bottom of the hill, Addie sat back and shook her head in denial. Route 5A continued past the water's end before heading back up a much smaller hill east of the harbor. Due to erosion, the harbor's water now came within ten feet from the railing by the road. At the closest point to the water, large boulders now retard nature's eroding effects. The bus came to a traffic light that offered only a left or right turn. Going straight went into the rising incline to the hillside east of the harbor. When the light turned green, the school bus made a left turn and drove along the rising road that traveled north next to the harbor. Houses down by the water were the oldest. Most of these houses dated back to the Revolutionary War and early 1700s. The rest of the harbor hills on the east side now had houses completely up the slopes. The small ranch houses of the 1940s were still there, as well as a few other Victorian style homes.

The road curved toward the right passing by the town's Firehouse. Addie's school bus continued into town along Cold Creek Harbor's half-mile long Main Street. All the appropriate prerequisites accumulated made this an authentic small town USA. There were old quaint gift shops, some buildings dated back over two hundred years, a Post Office, library and several churches all worshiping differently in harmony. Different sizes of American flags were everywhere. Passing this small town, Jake made one more turn to the right and drove down to Addie's bus stop.

"So you keep me posted on your visit to that place," said Jake. "I always wanted to know what was going on inside there. I'll talk to some of the old timers down at the barbershop and see if I can dig up some more rumors."

"Aah, that's okay Jake," Addie said as she stepped off the bus. "I think I had enough rumors for now. Enjoy the weekend." Addie rolled her eyes as she walked away from the bus. "God, why would Hitler make my small town his first stop in America?" She rhetorically mumbled with no concern.

THE FAMILY, Chapter Three

Gabrielle Erickson plopped a bowl of assorted peeled and sliced fruits on the breakfast table and in front of her daughter, Addie. Phillip, Addie's younger brother sat next to her. Gabrielle pulled out a chair across from her daughter and sat down. She wore her work uniform for the office supply store in the mall.

"All I'm saying Addie, is that you have to realize other people live in this house. Your father and I didn't mind you asking Christopher over to see a movie last night, but why didn't you check with us first? Your father and I were planning to watch a movie we had rented on Wednesday."

"Well, if we had a second TV, then this..."

"Oh, now you are avoiding the real issue here young lady. Yes, we only have one television, so get over it already. That's the way it is."

"I think our needs are changing," Addie stated. "Phillip will be thirteen in two months and I'm going to be eighteen in five days."

"Yeah Mom, you'll then have two teenagers in the house," Phillip added as he started to serve himself some fruit.

"I know, I know. So Phillip can see all the PG-13 movies now and you will have a regular senior driver's license. I heard this how many times and yes a second TV is in the future budget plans. Nevertheless! You still did not face the real issue or answer my question. Especially since this unexpected meeting for you today has turned all our morning plans inside out. On my way to work this morning, I was supposed to drop you off to visit Grandma and my girlfriend Ann, who works at the Nursing Home, would bring you home. Your father was dropping your brother off at his Dojo to take his test and then going to the Hardware store. Now he has to drive you to this lab."

While chewing some fruit in his mouth, Phillip supplied a few additional facts that his mother failed to cite, “My four hour long brown belt exam!”

“Please finish chewing before you speak,” instructed Phillip’s mother. “Yes, four hours long, thus giving your father all the time he needs to buy whatever at the Hardware store in town.”

“Wasn’t he there last week?” Addie quizzed as she put some fruit into her dish. “I think he loves that place.”

Her father Stewart, walked into the kitchen just in time to hear his daughter. He wore jeans with a rip over the left knee and printed on his sweatshirt were the words:

My daughter wants to go IVY!
Scholarship PLEASE!

Stewart just stood in place with his hands on his hips and finally answered his daughter’s inquiry. “Last week I needed the lawn mower tuned up and ready for next year before I put it away for the winter. Today is so I can hang up the Christmas decorations outside. The two of you said that you wanted some more decorations outside, right?”

“Yeah,” Phillip immediately answered as Addie just looked at her dad with a wrinkled up nose and nodded yes.

“Now as far as loving that place...” Stewart sat down next to his wife and blurted out, “Yes I do! I love Al’s Hardware store, I love it more than your mother.” He started kissing his wife to the objection of both his children.

“Oh look Stu, both our children are making faces.”

“Well, I would have kissed your mother last night like this while watching our movie, but someone...”

“Okay, I’m sorry about last night,” an exasperated Addie said. “Yeah, I should have checked with you guys first instead of just blowing your plans. But, I could drive myself to this lab if we had a third car.”

“Oh no young lady,” Addie’s mother said as she laughed. “We are not getting a third car. Besides we want to see this lab and meet this woman giving you the tour."

"Addie, I just want to make sure everything is safe," Stewart added. "Your mother and I had no idea these houses were a research lab."

"I'm sure it's fine or Principal Browne would have said something," Addie pointed out.

"I'm sure everything will be fine also," said Stewart. "But, I am still going in with you."

"Yeah," Addie returned. "I guess I can still visit Grandma for a little while, if Phillip doesn't care that we drop him off at the Dojo a little earlier."

"No problem with me," said Phillip.

"That will be nice," said Addie's mother as she gave a look to her husband. "Your dad can get to say hello also, since both of you haven't seen my mother since Thanksgiving."

"That is true," said Stewart. "Okay we leave in five minutes."

* * * * *

The Nursing Home had the typical smell of a geriatrics ward. Addie sat by an empty bed, as her father quietly kept busy by cleaning up the private room. Some voices echoed in the hallway as the door to the room remained wide open. In came an elderly woman wearing a shapeless Housedress with her hair up in a bun. She walked with a cane and had an old style pair of glasses on.

"That will be fine Judy," the elderly woman said before looking up. "I will see you at lunch. Ooh, look who is here to visit me! Addie how are you?"

"Hi Grandma, I'm doing fine."

"Good, good and Stewart can you leave my things where they are? Your father is such a neat freak."

“Hello Mom, you are looking well.”

“Thank you, thank you. How long have you been waiting for me?”

“Only a few minutes Mom,” Stewart said as he gave his mother-in-law a kiss on the cheek.

“Addie get up and let an old lady sit.”

As Addie stood she gave her Grandmother a hug and kiss. She then went over and leaned against her Grandmother’s dresser by her father.

“My, look at you,” grandma continued. “Almost eighteen and with a senior driving license. Hot dog! Are you going to pick me up so we can paint the town red?”

“Mom, please let’s not go crazy here. No painting towns for people who are eighty-three and eighteen years of age.”

Addie smiled and slowly stopped smiling, “Grandma why did you want to come live here? You would have been happy living with us.”

“I know my dear, but here I don’t get in anyone’s way and besides I’ll be sleeping over your house during the holidays, soon enough. You see, I have the best of both worlds.” Addie’s grandmother gazed out the window in thought and with a smile.

“Grandma?” Addie said trying to bring her back to real time.

“I also get to see someone I wouldn’t be able to see if I lived at your house.” Her gray hair sparkled as she shook her head briefly because she realized that her thoughts were elsewhere.

“Who’s that Mom?”

“Oh... Aah. Oh...you know. My friends, like Judy in the next room.”

Stewart could not tell if his mother-in-law corrected herself or had to manage a memory loss. Either way, her reaction surprised him because of the way she stumbled for the explanation.

“Dad, we have to get going or I’ll be late,” said Addie.

"Oh that's right!" Addie's grandmother said with a bang of her cane. "Congratulations on winning the State's Science Fair. Oh so smart like your, your... Your Mother. Give me a kiss goodbye." She then whispered in Addie's ear, "I know you'll love your tour."

"Thanks Grandma," Addie said after kissing her Grandmother goodbye.

"Goodbye Mom, have a good day. I'll pick you up for Addie's Birthday party next week."

"Very good, bye. I'll see you then."

In the car on the way to the lab, Addie looked at her dad perturbed, "Dad, did you or Mom tell Grandma about me taking this tour?"

"No, why?"

"Then how did she know?" Addie first mumbled to herself and then spoke normally to her dad, "No nothing, Grandma just seemed odd. Like when saying I was as smart as Mom. Seemed she wanted to say someone else."

Traveling south on Route 5A in their silver minivan, Addie and her dad approached the entrance driveway to the Research Lab's security booth and gate. Immediately a guard stepped out in front of the car and a second guard walked up to the driver's side while signaling to open the window with the rotating movement of his hand.

"Good morning," Stewart announced as his car window opened all the way.

"Sir, please state your reason for entry."

"Ah yes, my daughter was invited for a private tour of your facilities by... Addie let me see the letter."

"Doctor Barkly, Dad." Addie handed the letter to her father.

Looking at the bottom of the letter, Stewart first confirmed the information before speaking any details to the guard, "Doctor Janet Barkly. She's the Assistant Director." As an afterthought, he showed the letter to the guard.

The guard took the letter and stepped back into the security booth. Stewart watched the guard pick up a telephone and then a clipboard. He also noticed an open staircase leading to a lower level behind the guard.

"What are you looking at Dad?" A slightly embarrassed Addie put to her father.

Addie's father turned to face his daughter. "I just noticed that inside the guard's booth are some stairs going down. There must be a whole underground room to this security booth."

"Sir, may I have your daughter's full name?"

"Oh," Stewart reacted with surprise because the guard already stood by his car window. "Yes, Addie Lisa Erickson."

"Okay sir, your daughter will be allowed to enter upon Doctor Barkly's arrival. The Doctor will be here momentarily."

"That's fine, however I would like to meet the Doctor and receive some assurances before allowing my daughter to take this tour."

"Understood sir, you will have an opportunity to discuss that with her. She is coming now."

The two guards stepped back into the security booth as the metal gate started to open. The full picturesque view of the development presented itself once the gate moved out of the way. A small golf cart with one occupant drove toward them. Quietly the cart pulled up and stopped. A woman in her early forties with short blond hair stepped out. She wore a brown turtleneck sweater under a white lab coat with black slacks. Walking over to the minivan she took off her earmuffs and extended her hand through the open car window.

"Good morning, you must be Mister Erickson."

"Yes, and this is my daughter Addie," Stewart responded.

"Why of course, Addie wonderful to meet you," Doctor Barkly said as she reached forward to shake hands with Addie. "Congratulations on winning the State's Science Fair this year."

"Thank you very much," Addie said.

"Mister Erickson, I apologize for only obtaining clearance for your daughter. After reading in the newspaper that a local girl won the State's Science Fair we thought a tour would be very intriguing to her. At first, we wanted to arrange a tour for her teacher and entire science class. However, due to the holidays starting, and certain research conducted here, the government would not approve a large group. They only gave clearance for Addie. So yes, parts of the lab are off limits with the tour, but that is only for some long-term research projects. What Addie would be interested in, we will be happy to show her. As you can see, your daughter is under excellent protection here. The tour should take at most two hours."

"Hey Dad, did you hear that?" Addie asked of her father. "If I'm here for two hours, you'll have time to go to the Hardware store, come back and pick me up before going to get Phillip at his Dojo."

"That sounds good," said Stewart. "Where do I go when picking up my daughter?"

"Just pull in over here and the guards will allow you to park on the side. They will contact me when you arrive and you will not have to wait long."

"So the government runs this whole place?" asked Stewart.

"Yes, this is your tax dollar at work," Doctor Barkly said with a smile.

"What projects are being done here?" continued Stewart with his line of questions.

"The Human Genome Research Project is our top project. That has the ultimate goal of reading the complete genetic script by the year two thousand and five. In the long run this will help develop new molecular medicine in areas of diagnosis, treatments, and in the same area that won your daughter first place, prevention."

"Wow, that sounds great. What do you think Addie?"

"I think this is great," said Addie.

"Addie you can ride with me in my golf cart."

"Oh, Dad this is so cool, thanks." Addie gave her father a big kiss on the cheek and started to get out of the minivan. "I can't wait to see this place..."

"All right, have a good time. Be safe, I'll see you later." Stewart called out of his car window.

* * * * *

From a second floor window, a woman peered through the center opening in the full-length drapes. She stringently watched the golf cart with Addie slowly approach her house.

"Do you see her?" a male's voice came from the background.

"Yes, yes. Look at her figure, so pretty. Oh such a beautiful specimen of a human being she makes."

THE TOUR, Chapter Four

Opposite the Research Lab, on the east side of Cold Creek Harbor, a gravel lot existed by the water's edge. All the used RV units and Trailers on the parcel were up for sale, except for one large trailer closest to the water. A pathway had been outlined with stones painted white and they went from that large trailer all the way to the street. A sign covered with blemishes hung over the trailer's door and said: **SALES OFFICE**. Yet, this trailer looked uninviting and contagious neglect could be seen throughout the lot.

Between the dirty old blinds covering the trailer's windows facing the harbor, were reflections off shiny new silver metal and thick round glass. These objects were inside the Sales Office looking out. The reflecting sunlight bounced off telescopes and binoculars on tripods. No activity existed outside for selling trailers, but plenty of activity took place inside for spying. Methodically the lens of a telescope migrated to keep the golf cart in view that traveled up the path toward one of the old Victorian style houses across the harbor.

Doctor Barkly drove under the leafless trees to the front porch of the Victorian house. There the golf cart came to a halt. A wooden swing for two hung in the corner of the porch and a woodpecker struggled for the last insects of the year high up in the naked branches of a tree. As a cold breeze blew, Addie zippered up her ski jacket before getting off the cart.

"This is where your tour will start," Doctor Barkly said as she stepped off the golf cart. "The Director of our facilities lives here and she will take you around."

"You're not coming?" Addie surprisingly asked.

"No, I thought you knew. I'm sorry. I have other responsibilities today." Doctor Barkly began walking up to the front door and Addie followed. "I'll pick you up here when the tour ends and drive you back up to the front gate to meet your father."

The front door opened and in the doorframe stood a middle-aged woman. She had on a faded and wrinkled lab coat, the opposite of her smooth and radiant skin. She wore glasses, but her blue eyes were brilliant. Some gray hair sparkled amongst her chestnut color hair. Only her ears were slightly disproportionate to her face due to their ample appearance. The morning sunlight emphasized her cheekbones and her smile. A bursting smile, so jubilant, so revealing, so incorporated with her eyes and cheekbones that you would think this smile had waited years to be communicated. Under the long lab coat, she wore blue jeans, a hand crocheted light blue turtleneck sweater, a dazzling brooch, and a human heart that had been deprived of so much joy.

"Good morning, good morning," said the woman standing in the doorframe with a hint of an English accent. "Oh what a beautiful day. You must be Addie. I am so happy to meet you!" Veracity echoed in her voice, but her thinking commanded restraint. She kept Addie at arm's length as her hands held each of Addie's arms. Again, her heart denied by her reasoning. Finally they only shook hands, much to the relief of Addie who thought this crazy lab doctor wanted to give her a bear hug.

"Addie," said Doctor Barkly. "I would like you to meet the Director of our facilities. This is Doctor..."

"Oh just call me Gabbie. Doctor Barkly is always so formal and I want this to be an enjoyable day. Come in, come in."

"All right Doctor, I'll stop by in two hours or so to pick up Addie. You have a great tour."

"Yes, thank you Doctor Barkly. Come in Addie, have a seat in the parlor and I will make us some tea. Make yourself at home and I'll be right back."

"Excuse me Doctor... I mean Gabbie. Do you mean this room here?"

"Yes, the parlor... Oh I am sorry. Old habits never die, I mean the Sitting room, Family room, Living room or whatever you wish to call it."

"Okay sure..." Addie said while looking away from Gabbie who seemed to be exhibiting some eccentric tendencies. Addie then squinted in thought as she turned to look at Gabbie and her smile, "Excuse me Gabbie, one more question?"

"One more question? Sweetheart, by the end of your tour I expect you to have a thousand questions. Moreover, I hope my answers help to make you a better scientist. You do want to go into the field of science, right?"

"Why yes, it is at the top of my list," Addie said to the enormous relief of Gabbie.

"Oh you don't know how happy that makes me," Gabbie expressed with enthusiasm. Abruptly she throttled back on her emotions. "I mean, that I know this tour will not be a waste of time. I am so sorry, what was your question?"

"Oh, yeah...aah," Addie hesitated before making direct eye contact with Gabbie. "Have we met before, you look so familiar?"

Several very long seconds went by as Gabbie stared back into Addie's eyes. Finally, this woman of such high intelligence verbalized, "Oh I am not sure. Did I ever give a guest lecture at your school?"

"Not that I know of."

"Well, maybe we saw each other in town, passing each other at the bank or drug store."

"I guessss..." Addie dragged out in order not to persist, yet she knew none of those suggestions were the answer.

"We'll figure it out soon enough. Go ahead now, make yourself at home and I'll be right out with some tea."

Addie entered the room through opened double French doors. Overall, she saw no resemblance to a family room at all. The room didn't even have a television, just an old fashioned radio as a piece of furniture in the opposite corner. Addie took off and placed her ski jacket on the dark green and brown sofa by the front windows. Slowly she sat down in the middle of the room on one of the two high back armchairs that had ottomans in front of them. The two chairs faced the fireplace, as they should since the chairs had wings on each side where a person's head would feel the heat caught from a fire. Lion faces were hand carved into the dark mahogany wood of every armrest. The room had dark colors and long drapes over the windows. The large table lamp between the two chairs, one of which Addie sat in, stood on top of a tall mahogany End table. The old lamp fixture used a modern energy saving bulb. Addie took a closer look under this gigantic lampshade and read the label:

Compact Fluorescent
15,000 Hour life
40 watts equal to 200 watts

Doilies made of cloth and in various sizes were everywhere in the room. Under the lamp fixture, over each armrest of the sofa, on the coffee table in front of the sofa and every doily matched the Persian area rug on the floor. The majestic marble mantelpiece over a beautiful marble fireplace lacked all décor. Not even one doily laid on the mantel. Oddly, the entire room had no pictures or photographs. An upright Bentley piano stood against the wall behind her. On top of the piano stood only one vase, resting on top of a doily.

Boredom started to set in for Addie as she waited. Since her visual experience of the room concluded, she decided to stand and stretch. She detected a cardboard box on the side of the piano and against the wall in the corner. Wooden picture frames stuck out of the box and a few large doilies covered them. Curiosity lured her slowly toward the piano.

The teakettle finished whistling as Gabbie poured hot water into two cups. However, she had more concern over the conversation occurring through her brooch.

"No, I will not have this taken away from me," Gabbie spoke firmly to her chest and into her brooch.

From a small plastic piece in her right ear she heard a man's response, "I don't think this is a good idea. She said you looked familiar. She may just figure out too much. She's smart, you of all people know that."

"She has no reason to think there is anything to figure out."

"Oh Gabbie why do I... Gabbie! Did you put the box with all the photographs inside the parlor's closet?"

"On my God! Stop talking to me now. I have everything on the serving tray and must hurry in."

"Oh nooo! If she sees..."

"Stop talking!"

Addie started to examine the vase on top of the piano. Several cracks ran through the painted flower pattern and upon quick inspection, she realized that the vase had once broke and someone glued the pieces back together. Next she turned her attention to the box filled with picture frames. Just as she started to bend over to look, she stood straight up again.

"Here we are, some fabulous tea for us! Oh did I leave that mess in the corner?" Gabbie first took note that Addie did not see any of the items in the box. Next she put the silver tray with the teacups, sugar bowl, spoons, milk, and a small jar of honey on the table in front of the sofa.

"Really, what mess?" Addie asked with puzzlement and started to walk slowly away from the corner.

"That box filled with Knick knacks in the corner," Gabbie replied.

Addie came around and sat on the sofa, "Gabbie, if you think that box is a mess, you should come over my house. I'd hate to hear what you'll call my brother's room."

"I am sure your mother keeps a tidy house." Gabbie wasted no time with putting the box inside the closet that had the only solid wooden door in the room.

"Keeping house is more of a joint family effort," explained Addie.

"Yes, I can see that today," Gabbie said as she closed the closet door and went to sit with Addie. "How do you like your tea?"

"I'll have a little milk in mine."

"Wonderful, that is how I like my tea. Oh my goodness! Did you make that yourself?" Gabbie said as she referred to the hand crocheted light blue vest Addie wore.

"Yeah, I enjoy crocheting."

"On my, so do I! I made this turtleneck myself."

"Wow, it's beautiful."

"Thank you, thank you," Gabbie said as she smiled ear to ear while taking a sip of tea.

Addie felt the ice had broken and became more relaxed. After a sip of tea she said, "Mom showed me how to make the Granny Square when I was eight and I was hooked from then on."

"That is wonderful, before we go over to the main lab I have to show you the collection of sweaters that I made."

* * * * *

The house had a side door with a stone path leading to the backyard and driveway. A carport protected a golf cart parked beneath. The two women came out that door and headed over to the golf cart. Addie held onto a blue turtleneck sweater.

"Are you really sure I can have this sweater?" asked Addie.

"Of course my dear, I would not give this to you if I wasn't sure. Besides, isn't light blue your favorite color?"

"Yeah, it is."

After starting the golf cart, they drove upward on the hillside toward the entrance of a building that looked like a small auditorium. The two pairs of double doors had smoked glass that prevented anyone from looking through. The building didn't have a back since the design placed the structure into the hill.

"This is the main entrance to the lab," explained Gabbie. "We never use it. Actually, it is locked up because everyone uses the entrance from the parking garage."

"I don't see any garage. Where is that?"

"Underground, right here between these bushes and trees."

The golf cart dipped downward and into an underground parking garage. Parked throughout the garage were a few cars and several golf carts. An empty space by the elevator doors awaited them. A sign on the wall stated: **DIRECTOR**.

The elevator ride ended with one stop and the doors opened allowing Addie to gaze upon a spectacular oval shaped lobby. In the center stood a peanut shell-shaped desk. An elderly man with a white lab coat attended to one of several containers he labeled with various code numbers. The man had a physical challenge due to contracting Polio when young and kept busy despite being beyond retirement age. All around the oval room were photographs of cells, molecular structures, and different people wearing lab coats standing by microscopes from different years. The ceiling had a honeycomb shape pattern where light poured out from above. Along part of the wall behind the desk were three sets of smoked double glass doors.

"Good morning doctor," said Jim who attended to the containers.

"Good morning Jim," said Gabbie. "This is Addie Erickson who will be touring with me today. Addie this is Jim, he is semi-retired and has been with us for five years. He works mostly weekends."

Addie lingered behind Gabbie as she continued to view the photographs all along the oval wall. When Addie realized that Gabbie had just introduced her, she responded abruptly, "Oh, I'm sorry. Good morning Jim."

"Good morning," said Jim. "I have your temporary clearance pass right here." Jim opened a drawer and pulled out a plastic coated ID card with numbers, a square silver image, and Addie's name. "Miss Erickson, here is your ID for today. You will need to clip it on."

"Oh sure, thank you very much," Addie said as she took the ID and continued looking over at the photographs. "Gabbie is that you in those two photos?"

"Yes," Gabbie reluctantly responded. "Thank you Jim, we will be going into the main Lab, center doors. Please approve entry for us."

Jim moved his wheelchair over to a computer keyboard on the end of the desk. After typing for a few seconds, a double click at the center doors sounded.

"All right Addie," said Gabbie. "Just hold your ID like this in front of this electric eye so your RFID tag can be read."

The doors opened automatically and a long white hallway with the same type of lighting as the lobby came into view. This hallway led deep into the hillside.

"Gabbie those photos of you didn't do you justice. You look much younger in person."

Concern dragged across Gabbie's face. As they started to walk down the hall, she turned around to see the photos in the lobby and the doors automatically closing. The photos showed her with gray hair and more wrinkles. In addition, Gabbie did not have a response to Addie's comment. However, she knew how to buy some thinking time.

"I'm sorry Addie, I had something else on my mind. What did you ask?"

"Oh no it wasn't a question and I don't mean to pry. I just noticed that you look much better now than in those old photos of you."

"Oh my goodness, well yes. I never colored my hair until now, I did lose some weight, and I am using a new skin moisturizer twice a day. Something you don't have to worry about for many, many years." With that, Gabbie smiled in relief, unknowingly to Addie.

Accidently Addie noticed a small object in Gabbie's ear. "Excuse me Gabbie, is that a speaker in your ear?"

"Oh this," Gabbie said surprisingly as she touched the speaker in her ear with her index finger. "Actually, I really do not need this," she emphasized speaking toward her Brooch. "It's a hearing aid."

"Really..." a surprised Addie commented. A few seconds of silence went by before Addie spoke again. "This is some long hallway. By the way, what lights are being used in these ceilings? I don't see any fixtures or lightbulbs."

"Ah Addie, welcome to the real world. Above us is technology that has probably been shelved, phone number no longer in service."

"I'm afraid I lost you," said Addie.

"Sometimes when something better comes along you are unable to replace the old antiquated stuff. The reason is that the conglomerates will not allow you. If the new is endangering the old and all the money it makes, they will buy you out and put all your hard work on a shelf."

"How come the bulb in your lamp by the fireplace wasn't squelched out of the market?"

"Oh you saw that. Well, you are thinking those bulbs are brand new. They are not. The first one was sold in the United States back in nineteen eighty-two, nineteen seventy-nine in Europe. So twenty plus years had to pass before those bulbs became readily available.

"You see, why sell a lightbulb that will last fifteen times longer and save oil, when you can sell one that burns out in three months with a much higher profit margin."

"What can we do about that?"

"Well, around here when we can't do anything about something, we just say, 'flying crab crap.' I will admit saying that is not very proper for a young lady like yourself. I don't want your parents to think I'm teaching you foul words."

"That's cool, I think I can handle flying crab crap." Addie said with a big smile.

"Okay we have to scan our ID cards one more time to get in through these doors."

The smoked glass doors opened and a modern multilevel facility presented itself. A sitting area for casual discussion could be found immediately inside the doors. Chairs, coffee tables, note pads, calculators, all strategically placed. Coffee mugs were neatly stacked on a counter to the left. A cafeteria could be seen on the right through a glass wall with an automated sliding glass door. Images hung on the walls of this sitting area that illustrated members of our human microscopic world that few people are acquainted with. Other displays consisted of automated models that protruded twelve inches out to complete a three dimensional appearance.

Addie followed Gabbie up three rug covered steps to another level with two rows of computers.

"Is anyone working here today?" asked Addie.

"Well, it is Saturday, mostly everyone is home," said Gabbie.

"Does every scientist who works here live in one of the houses on the property outside?"

"All the long term top scientists do. That is why you will see more golf carts than cars around here. I do not drive myself... All right, let me tell you a little something about what is going on here."

"Okay I'm all ears."

"Splendid, have a seat. These computers are collecting data from around the world on various research projects. They are preprogrammed to download any new data recorded from a live feed or a project's web site. Some sites are available to the public, some sites are not."

"You mean like Top Secret?"

"I would have to say...not really. I am terribly sorry to disappoint you, my dear. These web addresses are shared amongst our colleagues. Now, the information updated here is on antibodies. A method to grow antibodies on one type of plant has led researchers to study the possibility of producing antibodies on an agricultural scale. This will cost a thousandth of current prices. Think of this for a second." Gabbie exhibited serious passion and looked into Addie's eyes before continuing, "It's possible that we can have proteins to counteract foreign substances in the human body, help in the treatment of diseases, including cancer."

"What's on this screen?" Addie inquisitively requested.

Gabbie smiled at Addie and continued to look at her as she went closer to the monitor. "Let's see what we have here," Gabbie spoke with her eyes still on Addie. "Now look on this screen," commented Gabbie as she turned to read the computer screen. "Today's report announced the ending phase of the study. This phase determined what plant would work the best and thus be used for growing a crop of antibodies."

"Is that the plant down here?" Addie pointed to the lower corner of the screen.

"Oh!" claimed Gabbie. "How ironic? A plant that killed so many may now save some lives." Next to Addie's finger, the bold lettering in the bottom corner of the screen read: Nicotiana tabacum, Tobacco Plant.

"Unbelievable, eh Gabbie?" Addie noticed Gabbie holding back some emotion. "Are you all right?"

"Yes, I will be fine. I lost someone I loved very much to this blasted weed."

"I'm sorry to hear that," consoled Addie.

"Thank you, that's okay. Let's move on, shall we?"

About ten minutes later, Addie and Gabbie stood on an observation platform watching three scientists working below. Wall freezers, computers, microscopes, and all the equipment necessary to do a job well had been placed at their disposal.

"Do any of them know that we are watching from up here?" asked Addie.

"I doubt that very much Addie. They are involved with their work and unless you tap them on the shoulder, they will not know you are in the room. They are concluding our contribution to the Human Genome Project."

"Concluding? What do you mean?"

"As you know from your work for the science fair, the project started in nineteen ninety. That was the official and formal start. Unofficially, I will just say that things started a long time ago. The US Department of Energy and the National Institute of Health originally planned the official start. Many people are working on this, not just us.

"Now due to rapid technological advances the expected completion date has been moved up to two thousand and three from two thousand and five. Most of the project goals, such as to identify all thirty-thousand genes in human DNA and store everything in a database, are accomplished.

"My lab is now in a deteriorating budget mode. Since hundreds of scientists are working around the world on this project, my lab is not needed for the 'official' completion."

"You say that as if the project has been completed unofficially already."

"Addie, it has been completed for decades."

"What? I don't understand."

"The old methods used to complete this project years ago may have contributed to possible human errors. Also computers in yesteryear were not what they are today, so, yes, errors may have been incorporated into the data."

"Do you believe there are errors?"

"Addie, just between you and me. I don't make mistakes."

"Oh my God. I don't believe this."

"Yes, and nobody will believe you. So please, that information is not for public conversation. Moreover, do not act so surprised that this project was concluded in yesteryear. If you do, you will sound like those who cannot imagine how the theory of relativity came about in nineteen hundred and five. Did you know that back in nineteen fifty-five, Einstein said in a letter to Seelig, 'There is no doubt that the special theory of relativity was ripe for discovery in nineteen hundred and five...' did you know about that?"

"I'm not familiar with his letters," Addie answered as Gabbie absorbed the frantic voice in her ear.

"Well, where was I? Oh yes, some of our projects are not completely successful, so our budget will adjust downward. Therefore, I have to make cutbacks."

"What are you telling her?" Gabbie heard over the speaker in her ear. "The purpose of me listening was to help you avoid these topics. What are you up to?"

Gabbie and Addie slowly walk around the observation platform as Gabbie continued speaking despite the voice in her ear. "Nevertheless we must now look at the gene more closely. We must look at the proteins such as the one in the photograph on the wall behind us."

Addie turned to view a photograph with a black background. A blue and white ribbon that looked like the coils in an old telephone wire were at the top. The bottom arrangement of blue and green scribbles connected the top grouping with one single flat band.

"Addie, what we have here is the green fluorescent color signaling proper folding of a protein. The top was altered to correct improper folding."

"So to treat disease and to prevent diseases," Addie surmised, "we need a better understanding of all the ways proteins can fold. That is some daunting identification task."

"Yes, and now here it comes, the big but. It has been estimated that there could be more ways to fold up an amino-acid protein than there are atoms in the universe."

"Oh my God!"

"I know if you think of this in depth, your mind will reel."

"Gabbie, this is impossible. This tells me that humanity will never know the fundamental level to the basis of life!"

"No, I do not agree with that. Yes, printing out all this data will probably fill a thousand phone books. However, there is another big but! Nature has helped us out in attaining answers. Proteins use different folding patterns to attain a three-dimensional structure. In biology, there are only certain forms. Stability and function, have conspired to limit the permitted variations of folds to just thousands."

"I'm afraid this is over my head," Addie reluctantly stated.

"That is perfectly all right. Shall we enter this next lab?"

"Sure, what's in here?"

"This is our protein library and VR room. This project shall continue, because this is apart from the Human Genome Project. No budget cuts here."

The dark room's illumination emitted only from nightlights. These nightlights were along the floor's perimeter every ten feet. They gave off a soft, soothing green glow across their two inch square surface. The solid metal door shut behind them and the lights came on in the lab. Powering up over shelves along the walls were 3D images of proteins. There were holographs of proteins slowly rotating to show all sides. Computer stations were in the center of the twenty by forty room. Solid glass made up the back wall with one glass door. Full-length drapes hid any view of what may be within.

Gabbie tapped her earpiece before putting her arm around Addie's shoulders. "This is our VR room, Virtual Reality as you may know it. We have identified over fifty-thousand protein families so far. The 3D holographs you see are the proteins we are working on now. The data library is in these computers."

"I do not believe this, oh I just don't believe this."

"Now Addie, listen to me very carefully. If you have not already construed what I am about to say, then make sure I have your undivided attention."

"Sure, okay. I'm listening."

"Officially the outside world has only identified seven thousand protein families. We not only have fifty-thousand plus, we have Holograph VR. This technology will help us assess how altered versions of proteins might behave, thus avoiding the dangers of bio-engineered proteins. Addie, this room does not exist."

"Okay, I know." Addie said with a slightly nervous voice and wondered why Gabbie would show her this room that wasn't supposed to exist.

"Addie, listen to me. The numbers I just told you do not exist outside this lab. This is not any major top secret project, but we have rules and reasons. Addie this room does not exist."

"Gabbie, I understand. No discussion with anyone." Addie stated determinedly, as she looked Gabbie in the eyes and saw her rubbing her ear.

"Wonderful. That is how I wanted to hear it. Now, how would you like to have a part time job here? I will get you government clearance so you can start on Monday right after school. Before you leave today, we will need to get a photo of you and a set of fingerprints. So what do you say?"

Addie's eyes opened wide and a smile lit up her face. In just a few hours, Addie came to admire Gabbie, a scientist and director of an obviously renowned lab facility. The level of excitement and possibilities Addie felt with this offer of an actual position at this lab were boundless. Addie knew that she would love to have Gabbie as her role model. Visions of working at a lab with different scientists and state-of-the-art equipment is a dream come true for Addie. She envisioned this since twelve; the year Addie's friend had passed away. A deep desire to contribute to the world of science and the elimination of such needless deaths, obsessed Addie where that desire plotted the course for her future.

As Gabbie waited for Addie's answer, she pulled on her ear that had the speaker. She raised one eyebrow and closed one eye.

"Thank you," Addie exhaled all at once.

Gabbie smiled and continued to endure the hyperactive voice blasting from the speaker in her ear... "You have crossed the line showing her the VR Room! The only explanation is that you are preparing her for your own use!"

THE FRIENDSHIP, Chapter Five

The yellow school bus turned onto Route 5A and started down the long hill toward the water of Cold Creek Harbor. Addie slowly turned and looked across the bus at Jannelle and smiled.

"I cannot believe you," said Jannelle. "How did you land this job? I'm telling you now, I expect a much better Christmas gift this year since you are now a W. W."

"A what?" Addie's face showed caution.

"W. W. is a Working Woman." Jannelle responded with dismay, because Addie did not know what she meant.

"Oh, cool, I thought you meant I was whacked whacky or something."

"Addie, here it comes," Jake called out as the bus approached the bottom of the hill.

"Thanks Jake," Addie quickly said as she grabbed her backpack and walked up to the front of the bus.

"Remember, wait 'til my flashing lights on the bus stop traffic in both directions. Cross in front of my bus. This can be a busy road and technically I shouldn't be dropping you off here."

"I know Jake, and I really appreciate this."

"I know you do, but just remember you owe me the scoop on everything going on in there."

"Okay Jake," Addie said with an innocent smile.

The bus came to a stop a few feet before the security booth as the safety lights were blinking. "Oh, oh look! You see that idiot blowing right by. Get his plate number!" Jake yelled as he looked out his window.

"Jake, Jake it's okay," Addie said as she noticed the Lab's security guard taking serious note of the situation.

Jake turned back toward Addie in the bus, "I tell you, no respect for the law and endangering human life like that is a sin. Did anyone get the plate number?"

"No, Jake, he was going too fast." Someone shouted out from the middle of the bus.

"Why the hell are we stopping here?" Frankie, with the red hair yelled from his seat in the back.

"Damn. All right...all right. Now Addie are you sure your father will be picking you up here after work?"

"Yeah, Jake. Thank you for caring, but you are starting to sound like my mother."

"Oh, oh no I don't want to do that. Get off, get off!"

"Much better Jake, see you tomorrow."

The school bus pulled away as Addie stepped onto the driveway entrance of the Lab. A black Mazda came up from two cars behind the bus and pulled into the entrance next to Addie. Chris Wilkins had his window down and his elbow resting on the car door.

"Hey Addie!" Chris called out.

"Chris hi, what a great surprise!" Addie said and rushed over to Chris' car.

"I had to wish you good luck for your first day on the job."

"Thanks Chris," Addie said and gave him a kiss. "But you wished me good luck this morning in English class and again at lunch."

"Yeah I know, so?" Chris asked and they kissed again. "Hey Addie, why is that security guard giving us a strange look?"

"Probably because we are kissing on his watch."

"I'll talk to you tonight." Chris looked up and down route 5A and then backed his car out.

Addie stepped up to the guard by the security booth and smiled, "Addie Erickson reporting for work."

"Welcome Ms. Erickson," the guard said. "Please place your right hand on this electronic scan for entrance approval... Okay, you're clear. I have your lab coat and credentials. When you leave the lab, these credentials are to be returned here every...single time. Do you understand?"

"Yes," Addie said cautiously as she placed the new lab coat under her left arm. "Do I keep the lab coat?"

"Yes, you may. Now you will have to walk up to..."

"I know where to go, thank you. I received all those instructions on Saturday. I'll see you at five o'clock." Addie began to head toward the small walkthrough entrance in the gate.

"Very good. Ms. Erickson, there is one more thing."

Addie stopped and turned around to look at the guard before saying, "What is that?"

"Give this to your bus driver tomorrow."

Addie opened the small folded piece of paper the guard gave her. The paper had a license plate number. Addie looked at the guard and commented, "Oh, you guys are good, real good."

From her second floor window, Gabbie peered through the center crack of the full-length drapes. She watched Addie walking toward the house.

"Is she coming?" a male's voice murmured in the background. "I don't think this is a good idea." There lingered a subtle Italian accent in his voice.

"Yes, you made that perfectly clear," Gabbie said with some annoyance in her voice. "I am not wearing the brooch again just so you can double check everything that is said. So please don't start or I'll give you a swift kick in the bone."

Gabbie turned to face a tall man of six feet and two inches. He wore a white lab coat just like Gabbie. He had a bushy black mustache and a full head of hair. The sufficient size of his ears and nose were in disproportion to his face. He also wore a smooth profile of sympathy and concern.

"Well, I don't think my bones can take any more kicks."

"Oh George," Gabbie said as she placed her hand on his chest. "I know you're just trying to protect me, but please let me spend some time with her without any awful debate. I lost all my time with everyone else I love."

"We have our time together," George said with some hesitation and disquietude of the answer.

"Yes, that is true, but that only comes after operating the lab and our research. Anyway, with all these budget cuts we may not even have a Cold Creek Harbor lab to worry about in six months." Gabbie paused and slowly shook her head while saying, "Quite frankly, if that happens, I don't know what will become of me."

George hugged her and stared out the window until he said, "There's the doorbell. I guess you should answer it."

"Oh thank you Love," Gabbie said as she started to leave their bedroom.

Gabbie swung open the front door, "Good afternoon Addie!"

"Hi Gabbie," Addie said as she received a one-arm hug.

"We are going to have a great first day on the job," Gabbie insisted. "I can't wait, so leave your backpack and coat inside here."

"Did you enjoy the rest of your weekend?" Addie asked as she dropped her stuff just inside the front door.

"Yes, very enjoyable, thank you. Two days filled with heavy debate and a great deal of kicking someone's bones. In the end, I won the debate... Oh my, you are wearing the turtleneck I gave you, how sweet of you dear. Please put your new lab coat on, I don't want you to catch the death."

"Gabbie, are you from England originally?"

"Why of course my dear. Now we will go over to my golf cart. I don't see any problem with you driving, do you?"

"Really?" said a surprised Addie. However, she quickly adjusted her tone, so not to miss out on the opportunity. "Oh no, no problem at all."

"I trust your day at school went well and you had a healthy lunch?"

"Gabbie, I had lunch in the school's cafeteria. Get real."

"I see, well we can address that over the next few days."

As they approached the carport, Addie saw two golf carts parked under the roof. Each one had a sticker on the rear bumper saying: God Bless America. "You have two golf carts Gabbie?"

"The one on the left belongs to my husband."

"I didn't know you were married."

"Yes, here are the keys, go ahead get in. My husband is Doctor Mannuso and he also works here."

"Why that's very nice."

"Yes, it certainly can be. Nice that is. At least I have someone that I can give a swift kick in the bone every now and then. Okay, start it up and back us out."

* * * * *

The next day Addie's school bus turned onto Route 5A and started down the long hill again. Addie sat in the aisle seat next to Jannelle.

Upon site of the approaching entrance to the lab, Addie started to collect her CD player, backpack, and coat.

"Addie do you think I can stop in to visit you at work one day? You know, just to see you enjoying yourself as you play with a real chemistry set. Unlocking the deep secrets of humanity."

"Jannelle, I wish you could, but I seriously doubt that. They are really strict with IDs, credentials and..."

"Addie," Jake called out from up front. "Coming up on your stop."

"Okay, I'll see you tomorrow. Thanks Jake, I'm coming."

The bus came to a stop as Addie arrived at the front of the bus. "Addie is that the same guard from yesterday who gave you the plate number?" asked Jake.

Addie squinted to look out of Jake's open window. "Yeah, that's the guy. See you tomorrow Jake."

"Sure thing Addie," Jake said, as he turned to stick his head out his window. "Yo! Thanks for the plate number." Jake waved the small piece of paper. "To get that number I know you weren't trained by an ABC security company. Are you or were you in the service? I mean, I can tell. I was in Nam."

Addie jogged onto the Lab's property by the security booth and waved to the bus as a horn blew from a car behind the bus diverting Jake's attention.

"Keep your shirt on!" Jake yelled as he looked toward the rear of his bus. "Thanks again man," Jake said to the security guard still standing there with an emotionally free face. As Jake pulled away, he saluted the guard.

Addie worked alone at a lab station that had a large venting hood mounted overhead. She wore her lab coat, goggles, thick black rubber gloves, and a respirator. Brown bottles stood under the hood next to an empty four by two foot fish tank. A smaller fish tank filled with a clear liquid sat in the middle of the workstation with three glass beakers submerged inside. The right side had another four by two fish tank with neatly stacked glass beakers and test tubes inside. The exhaust fan in the venting hood operated very loudly, so Addie did not hear or know that someone had come up behind her. Until she felt a light tapping on the shoulder.

"Ms. Erickson, can you hear me?"

"Yeah," Addie said after she turned to face another scientist working at the lab.

"Doctor Maida asked me to tell you that she would like to meet with you when you finish getting this glass scrupulously clean with that sulfuric acid."

"Doctor who?" shouted Addie over the exhaust fan.

"You know, the Director!"

"Oh, Doctor Mannuso."

"I guess you can call her that too."

"What?"

"Never mind, just go to her office when you are done here! Remember to be careful with that acid. In case of a spill or splash, use the buffer solution in that jar. That acid will eat through almost anything."

"No problem, I just have three more beakers to do!"

"Very good. I'll see you around."

Addie finished her task at hand and started to remove her safety equipment. She shut off the lights under the hood and the noisy exhaust fan by flipping two switches on the wall. She paused to view her work while slowly shaking her head.

"So much for unlocking the deep secrets of humanity," she mumbled to herself. "Jannelle if you only knew that all I am here is a glorified glass washer." A slightly depressed young lady slowly walked away from her workstation.

Addie knew the location of Gabbie's office from her tour on Saturday. After she obtained this part time employment, they went to Gabbie's office to discuss the details. A small modest office with walls that had no diplomas, photos, or certificates of any kind. There were no windows except for a false window directly behind Gabbie's swivel leather chair. Three of the four walls had rows of neatly stacked books from the floor to the ceiling. From the length of the office walls, Addie estimated at least one thousand books were along the walls and Gabbie said she read every one of them.

Gabbie sat behind her desk signing off on some papers when a barely audible knock came from her door. She clicked twice on her computer's mouse and a view of Addie outside her office door came on the monitor.

"Come in Addie, come in," Gabbie called out as she buzzed Addie in.

"Hi Gabbie, I was told to see you here," Addie said as she sat down in one of the two armchairs in front of Gabbie's desk.

"Yes, yes," Gabbie looked up and smiled. "So tomorrow is a special day for you."

"I'm not sure what you mean?"

"Oh sweetie, I know that tomorrow is your birthday and I met your father at lunch time today. I invited him for a short tour and lunch with me in the lab's kitchen. You should be very proud of him, a fine gentleman. I made him a healthy lunch and a deal with him so you do not have to work tomorrow on your birthday. You just have to stay late tonight."

"I can have off tomorrow?"

"Yes, if you are willing to stay late today."

"Sure, just as long as I don't have to clean anymore glassware."

Gabbie laughed as she started clearing her desk. "Oh I did that as my first assignment when hired as a lab assistant at Oxford University."

"Did you also go to school at Oxford?"

"Yes, I entered Lady Margaret Hall at Oxford University for my undergraduate studies. I then attended medical school after graduation. Anyway, I do not want you to stay late to work. I hope you will stay to join Doctor Mannuso and myself for dinner. Your father will pick you up at eight o'clock. However, before dinner you will have to get your homework done straight away. Afterwards, we will have a lovely meal. Doctor Mannuso is cooking as we speak. He is an excellent cook. Later, I will be making scones and of course we will have a birthday cake for you."

"Oh you don't have to do this. I mean this is very nice, but a birthday cake is completely unnecessary."

"Oh fiddlesticks, how often do you become eighteen and get your senior driver's license. Hot dog! Maybe you can pick me up so we can paint the town red?"

Addie taken aback by the words and Gabbie's mannerisms exclaimed, "I don't believe the way you just said... You sound just like my Grandmother."

Gabbie became a little perturbed, but she quickly asked what she knew would receive a positive response. "Well, hearing that line should never be too much of a good thing, right?"

"Oh no, not at all."

"Well, shall we go then. Since I am the boss around here, I say we cut out of work a little early. Any objections?"

"None from me."

As they entered Gabbie's house, the ceiling light came on automatically. Addie started to look around for the light switch while Gabbie took her lab coat off. She wore a black fleece sweater over a white shirt with just the top collar button fastened on the sweater.

"Let me have your lab coat," said Gabbie. "My word what are you looking for?"

"Where's the light switch?"

"Oh, over there. It's an infrared motion switch. Only when it is dark enough in the vestibule, along with motion and body heat, will the light come on. If everyone used these with energy saving bulbs, we would not need to import any oil... George, I am home with the birthday girl!"

"Is that true? How do you know all this?"

"Addie you have to read and not just read. You have to read all the research, collect all the facts, and then evaluate so you can make your own decisions as what is worth teaching to others. Without an understanding of all the research, you are not qualified to lecture on the subject, let alone teach or preach. Remember, knowledge is power."

"Oh, I see the lectures have already commenced and in the vestibule, no less," George said as he came down the hall.

"Oh stop that George. Addie this is my husband, Doctor Mannuso."

"Very nice to meet you Addie. As you can surmise, I have heard more than a great deal about you."

"Nice to meet you Doctor Mannuso," Addie said with a broad smile.

George wore a suit and tie under a white chef's apron. He stood there holding a wooden spoon. "Dinner will be ready at half past five. That is forty-five minutes from now and I trust that will be sufficient time for you two ladies to prepare."

"Yes, let me just show Addie where the wash room is and where she can do her homework. I'll then come to help you in the kitchen."

Just around five-forty, they were dining on the first course and Addie did not take too long to feel equated with George and Gabbie. George had a red and white checker napkin tucked in the collar of his shirt. Addie had hers placed on her lap and so did Gabbie.

"Doctor Mannuso, did you say this was a wheat pasta?"

"Addie in this house, please call me George."

"Okay, I will." Addie could not help noticing the vast smile on Gabbie's face once George asked to drop the formal Doctor title.

"Thank you and yes, I always make whole wheat pasta or spinach pasta, because they are complex carbohydrates. Regular pasta is a carbohydrate that will only make sugar inside your stomach."

"Addie, George is very knowledgeable on the best ways we should eat. However, it is a combination of several things. Eating right is one, exercise is another. Do you exercise Addie?"

"Officially, no. I do get exercise, but not the way I know the two of you would recommend. I always wanted to join my brother's Dojo and try taking Kempo martial arts."

"You should join," said George. "And if money is a problem, you can always ask your old boss here for a raise."

"George, stop kidding," requested Gabbie.

"Addie," continued George. "Whatever exercise you do, the best time to exercise is in the afternoon around one to two hours before dinner. Exercising in the early morning when you just wake up and on an empty stomach is like trying to drive your car across town with an empty gas tank. Your body doesn't need that added stress."

"Also Addie," Gabbie said with affection. "Make sure you drink water before and after you exercise."

"I know, we learned that in Health class. They say we should drink six to eight glasses of water every day."

"And do you Addie?" asked George as he poured himself some more water into a glass next to his wineglass.

Addie hesitated before she admitted the truth, "I probably drink more diet soda than water."

"Oh no. That is the worst thing to do," Gabbie said sitting back in her chair.

George began with a serious, but concerned voice. "My young lady, with your young molecular structure working overtime to clean your systems..."

"And very efficiently working," Gabbie added.

"That is correct for now, but when you get older your body will not be able to work as efficiently and then problems really build up if you keep clogging up your molecular works."

"Wait, excuse me for a second. Believe me, I am working overtime to learn and absorb as much knowledge as I can from the two of you tonight. But, I have to tell you that has not been easy. I have to interpret words such as vestibule, washroom, and half past five. Who talks that way anymore? Now please, don't get me wrong. I greatly appreciate all the information, data and conversation, but you are losing me here with molecular structure and working overtime. Exactly what is working overtime and why?"

"Oh I am so happy you asked," George answered with a grin.

"Oh now you've done it, Addie. George is going to pull out his pride and joy example."

"Is that a bad thing?"

"Maybe."

George went and opened the cabinet under the kitchen sink. He pulled out an old glass jar that had no label and once used many years ago to hold applesauce. He sat back down while keeping the jar on his lap and out of sight. The jar had white grit filled to the top. There were a few other specs of color throughout the mix.

"Addie what type of water do you drink?" asked a determined George.

"Is this a trick question? Because I drink the same water as everyone else."

"No, you don't," insisted George. "Have you tasted the water in your glass tonight?"

"No, not yet."

"Go ahead," coached George. "Take a sip and tell me what you taste."

Addie slowly took a drink of water while observing Gabbie's casual smile glancing back at her. She put the glass down and started seriously thinking about how the water tasted.

"Well, what do you think?" Gabbie impatiently inquired.

"I have to admit, that I don't taste anything."

"Exactly!" George proclaimed as his long arms went up into the air. "That is correct and water should never have a taste. What you are drinking is Distilled water."

"Distilled water?" a surprised Addie questioned with a wrinkled nose. "That is what my grandfather used to put into his car battery. That is what we use in lab for experiments. Why would you drink distilled water?"

"Here it comes," Gabbie said with a tone of voice that represented her feelings about hearing this dissertation for the one-hundredth time.

"Because I don't want to drink this!" George slammed the glass jar onto the kitchen table and pointed at the jar repeatedly with both hands.

Addie's eyes went back and forth between George, Gabbie, and the jar. When no explanation followed, she cautiously pursued one for herself. "Okay...and what is that?"

"This is a sample of what is in water when it is not purified. One gallon of water is poured into our water distiller that boils the water at two-hundred and twelve degrees Fahrenheit, thus killing all bacteria, cysts and viruses." George did a slashing cut with his finger across his neck. George then immediately raised both arms slowly upward as he wiggled his fingers. "Steam rises leaving behind all the metals, dissolved inorganic solids, minerals, radionuclides, particulates and the dead bacteria organisms. And that is what I collected in this jar." Again, repeated pointing to the jar commenced. "You see, after the steam rises it is cooled and condensed by a small fan. Pure drinking water slowly drips out and into my one-gallon jug. A plastic jug, that is PCB free. You do know what PCB stands for?" George finally sat back in his chair and all of his movements came to a pause.

"Yeah, a toxin called polychlorinated biphenyls."

"Very good Addie, you see George, I only hire the best."

"That's a wonderful thing Gabbie," George said with no concern and carried through with his interest. "So! For several months I collected everything that was left at the bottom of my distiller until I filled this jar." This time several different fingers from both hands took turns pointing to the jar. When both middle fingers took a turn, Addie giggled just a little. "Flying crab crap, what is so funny?"

"Oh nothing at all," Addie immediately and seriously concluded as she reflected on the memory of Jake saying crab crap on her bus. "Hey... Do you know anything about a Hitler rumor saying he was going to..." Addie froze upon noticing the two petrified faces staring at her as if she became some evil entity. "Ah forget it, its just crazy. I don't believe any of it." Addie concluded uncomfortably.

"Okay good... So now listen to this," George announced after a fast recovery. "This is serious stuff. Over an average life, a person will consume over four hundred seventy-five pounds of this stuff. This *gook* goes inside you and your body has to get rid of it! That is what I mean by working overtime. When young, your body can handle this. However, things start to slow once you hit your twenties. Why put this crap into your body when you don't have to?" George concluded with his arms in the air again. His checker pattern napkin fell from his collar as he glanced over toward Gabbie with a concerned look on his face.

"I don't really think I put that into my body," challenged Addie.

"Drinking soda and tap water will put this in you," George insisted with his arms still in the air.

"But, I mostly drink bottled water," Addie defended.

"Bottled water at best is just filtered, which is not as good as distilled!" George fixed his napkin back in his shirt collar, and leaned forward toward Addie. "For all practical purposes, distilled water is the closest definition to pure drinking water that you can get. Also there is the fact that it is much cheaper to make your own distilled water than to buy water. Approximately 65 percent less per gallon of water."

"So you are saying that over my life I will put approximately five hundred pounds of that...that stuff inside of me?"

"Yes, I am afraid so," Gabbie confirmed.

"But, what about water filters?" asked Addie.

"Much better than non-filtered," George answered with authority. "However, filters don't kill bacteria or viruses and just boiling water leaves you consuming the dead bacteria."

"This is starting to gross me out," Addie said as she sat back in her chair.

"You may enjoy your glass of water here, because there isn't any of this stuff in that water." George said as he pointed to the old glass jar and then at Addie's glass of water.

"Wait a second, what about all the people who buy mineral water just to enhance their daily allowance of minerals?" asked Addie with a tone of inevitability in her voice.

"Completely unnecessary!" George professed as he waved his left hand across the table and up into the air.

"All of our minerals are derived from the foods we eat," Gabbie started to say in a calmer voice as compared to George. "Fresh fruits, vegetables, grains, and nuts all supply us with minerals. The minerals in water are not sufficient to enhance your RDA."

"Aspetta un momento," George avowed. Gabbie is being nonchalant about this Recommended Daily Allowance of minerals. Let us look at the facts. On average, to get your RDA of calcium you would have to drink six hundred glasses of water." George pretended to drink water with both hands moving up and down to his face four times. "To get your RDA of iron, about eight hundred glasses of water!" Again, George pretended to be drinking glass after glass of water and he tilted back in his chair. Then with his cheeks and stomach puffed out, causing Addie to laugh, he yelled, "But, wait! We must have our daily allowance of phosphorus!"

"Oh no, yes!" Addie joked fearing the worst.

"Oh yes!" George shouted as he pointed his pinky toward the ceiling. He then started with rapid hand movement from the table to his mouth, acting out drinking until he tilted back more in his chair still with his cheeks puffing out. "You would need to drink about one hundred and sixty-thousand glasses of water to get your RDAAAYYY!"

Gabbie let out a surprised scream. George's chair fell completely over, sending him crashing to the floor. Both ladies ran over to help him and started laughing. George stayed perched in his fallen chair, eyes crossed, cheeks bloated, and both hands over his pushed out stomach.

A short time later the two scientists and their young apprentice retired to the parlor. They were sitting on the sofa with a sterling silver English serving tray on the table before the couch. Tea and scones were for dessert.

"Gabbie, what are Scones exactly?"

"Why of course my dear. A scone is barley flour rolled and baked on a griddle. I do not fry them in oil. After they cool, I cut them in quarters to serve."

"These are very good."

"Thank you Addie, I will give you the rest to take home tonight."

"Oh thank you very much."

"I'm sure your mother will like to try them and I know your gran..."

George started coughing and tried to cleared his throat as he sat forward on the couch.

"Are you all right George?" asked Addie as Gabbie looked at him.

"Yes, yes. A sip of tea and I will be better. How about you Gabbie, I thought I heard something stuck in your throat too?"

"No, I'm fine. I was..." Gabbie paused because she just realized why George said that. "Yes, I was just getting ready to bring out the Birthday cake!"

"Oh no you didn't?" Addie protested. Gabbie had already dashed off toward the kitchen as George took a sip of tea.

"Ah, but she did," George said with a matter of fact tone. He sat back and wiped his mouth with the napkin that remained tucked into his shirt collar. George turned and spoke softly across the sofa toward Addie on the other side. “Addie, Gabbie cares a great deal about you, more than you know. I am afraid you are becoming a long lost daughter to her. Now I am not saying there is anything wrong with that. I just thought things would be best if they stayed on a working relationship between the two of you. However, Gabbie’s little subplot this evening worked very well. She wanted us to get together because she believed that to meet you, is to like you. So I met you and she was right, I like you. You are not the average teenager that will express one’s self with rebellious behavior. You express yourself very well with a diversified attitude that has intelligence as well as honesty, and you laughed at my silliness. Therefore, I just ask one favor of you. If you and Gabbie become friends and I see that the two of you already are, please be that. A good friend. God knows she needs a good girlfriend.”

“Here it comes!” Gabbie called out from the kitchen and swiftly walked into the parlor with a small cake covered with chocolate. Her hand protected the candle from going out until she placed the cake on the table next to the serving tray. “Happy Birthday Addie, blow out the one candle and make a wish!”

Addie did just that and as she sat back, she winked at George to assure him that she would be a good friend. George smiled back and then took a coupon out of his shirt pocket for her.

“What’s this?” Addie asked as she looked at the coupon.

“A birthday gift from me to you, you get ten percent off from Sears. Maybe you can go with your parents to buy your own water distiller. When scaling builds up at the bottom, just pour in two inches of white vinegar and soak for several hours. Some other places sell cleaning agents, don’t buy them, that stuff is poison.”

“Thank you George, I will tell my dad.”

“Very good, now if you ladies will excuse me, I have some reports to read. Addie this was a pleasure, I am sure I will see you again.” They shook hands and before George left the room, he whispered in Gabbie’s ear. “Please be mindful of what you say and God, what does she know of that rumor?”

"Yes, I will and I don't know," a slightly embarrassed Gabbie said in a normal speaking voice as she saw Addie looking on and wondering about all the secret whispering.

"George isn't going to have any chocolate cake?" Addie inquired.

"No Addie, George does not eat cake. Therefore, that only means more cake for us! However, before we indulge ourselves I must ask you something. Would you rather wash the dinner glasses in the kitchen sink or receive a small birthday gift from me?"

"Oh no, this invite was more than enough. You didn't have to get me a gift..." Addie saw Gabbie's face waiting for an answer. "Yes, yes I would rather receive your gift than wash anymore glassware."

They both chuckled and Gabbie reached behind the chocolate cake for a small and very old brooch. Gabbie wore a much larger brooch on the day they met. After handing this real brooch to Addie, they had simultaneous reactions. The response of relief came from Gabbie and one of shock from Addie.

"This is beautiful! I am... This is so kind of you, I thank you so much, but I can't accept this gift. This must be very valuable to you."

"Yes, and that is one reason why I want you to have this."

"No, I can't...and my parents would be very upset if I accepted this."

"Please welcome this, just to make an old person happy."

"Oh I don't know, and I can't believe you would call yourself old. You are far from old Gabbie. I really shouldn't." Addie handed the brooch back to Gabbie.

Gabbie thought for a while as she looked at the brooch. "I will make a deal with you," Gabbie said as she pushed the brooch back to Addie.

"Tomorrow you are off for your birthday. On Friday take the school bus home and since you are eighteen, drive back here for work."

"Gabbie I won't have a car. Both my parents will still be at work."

"Not your dad. When I spoke with him, this came up in conversation and he is taking half a day off from work. He will be decorating the house and getting things ready for the holiday sleepover guests."

"Really! You mean I'll have a car to drive?"

"Yes, so the deal is that after work on Friday, you take me to the mall with you for some holiday shopping. I am tired of shopping through a Purchasing Agent or on-line. This birthday gift helps pay you for driving me around. Deal?"

"Oh, sounds good. I think I can."

"Sure you can. Oh and another thing you can also do."

"What?"

"Since you will be off on Christmas Eve and you have no school Christmas week, I expect you here working the full eight hour day on Wednesday the twenty-sixth, as well as Thursday and Friday."

"Not to scrupulously clean glassware, please Gabbie, no not that!"

"No, no," Gabbie started to laugh. "I promise you will be more involved with our work here."

THE BOND, Chapter Six

The Mall's entrance simulated a vortex to Gabbie. The Christmas music, the lights, the decorations, the people, all seemed to pull Gabbie into a world vaguely familiar to her. To Addie, everything registered normal and her walking pace had been well timed to maneuver around the crowd.

"This is so cool! Right Gabbie?"

Gabbie tried to take in all the sights and sounds. Her eyes were going up, left, right, left, and she lost her equilibrium. She then bumped into a shopper throwing her into a full spin.

"Gabbie, where do you want to go first?"

"Oh my, what?"

"What store do you want to go to first?"

"Oh dear, Addie, I feel lightheaded, I need to sit down for a second."

"Really, oh yeah, sure. Let's go over here." Addie took her by the arm and walked her over to some benches in the center. "Excuse me, may we sit down here, she's not feeling too well." A father and his teenage son immediately stood up and removed their shopping bags.

"No problem, will she be all right?" asked the father.

"Yes, thank you. She's just a little dizzy. Gabbie you *are* going to be all right, right?" Addie whispered in Gabbie's ear for confirmation.

"Yes, I'm terribly sorry. I just became muzzy trying to see everything so fast. Too much eye movement and sounds and people, oh my so many people." Gabbie began to sit back as she opened her eyes.

"Feeling better Gabbie?"

"Yes, thank you. However, I am a bit warm."

"Let's check our coats in a locker so we won't be hot and have less to carry."

"They have lockers here?"

"Sure."

"Very logical thinking Addie. Lead the way, but not too fast this time."

"Gabbie, when was the last time you were here at the mall?"

"The last time? Addie, this is the very first time for me."

Addie immediately had a surprised look on her face, but Gabbie did not notice. Addie realized that this shopping trip would definitely not be what she thought.

"Oh my word. That store is displaying all different women's unmentionables in their front window!" Gabbie exclaimed.

"Yeah, and you should see what they have inside. Let's go! You can get something sexy to wear on a romantic night with George." Addie literally dragged Gabbie, who had her mouth hanging open, into the store.

"Addie I don't believe your mother would approve of this store. This is preposterous!"

"No, it's not. Lighten up Gabbie, it's just women's underwear."

Gabbie turned ever so slowly touching a few items for a feel of the material. Subsequently she started looking at all the styles, designs, colors, sizes and after making a full three hundred and sixty degree turn she faced Addie again. However this time, instead of a smile on Gabbie, Addie saw a tear rolling down the side of her face.

"Gabbie what's wrong?"

"If you ask me how many pairs of chromosomes there are, I would say twenty-three. If you asked me to discuss with you my thoughts on Quantum physics and the Zero-Point Field, I would be happy to. However, I had no idea how many choices there could be in just women's underwear. I am sorry, let's just go to the next store. Hopefully, they sell tissues to help me get past this."

"Hey Gabbie this is no biggie. Here, I have a tissue," Addie said as she walked after Gabbie who headed out of the store.

"Thank you, what do you mean, no biggie?"

"No big deal, no sweat, nothing to worry about...it doesn't matter! We can't know everything about everything. Now I know that wasn't worded very intellectually, but you know what I mean, right?"

"Yes, I do. I thank you. But, my life has been sheltered far too much."

"Crab crap Gabbie, sometimes I think you were born yesterday."

"Oh you do, do you," Gabbie smiled, as did Addie.

They went through store after store, checking or trying things out. After a purchase of a few items each, they stopped for some pretzels. Gabbie insisted on paying although she became more than a little surprised at the price.

"I will have to say," Gabbie announced with a bite of her pretzel. "If they had just one more type of pretzel to choose from, I believe my ancestral beaker would have fallen off the old Bunsen burner."

"Excuse me?" Addie inquired with a face ready to burst out laughing. "What in the world does that mean?"

"That my cheese would have slipped off the cracker."

"What?"

"Oh my, that I would have gone nuts, deranged, insane, demented, cracked up!"

"Okay, okay! I get it," Addie repeated while laughing.

"My Addie, sometimes I think you were born yesterday. Oh, and do you know what? You just about were!" Gabbie said with a teasing smile.

"Oh no, I am eighteen now, you can't say yesterday anymore."

"Fair enough," Gabbie agreed and enjoyed another bite of her pretzel. "Amazing how many types of pretzels they sell... So many choices. I feel like Raisa Gorbachev."

"Gabbie, you lost me on that last line," Addie stated with cheeks filled with pretzel and a face begging for a break on the one line intellectual statements.

"You know Mikhail Gorbachev helped to end the Cold War, bring down the Berlin Wall and start the Information Age. He was even awarded the Nobel Peace Prize in nineteen ninety for that and rightfully so."

"Okay, I know who he is," Addie confidently mentioned.

"Yes, you heard about him, but many believe it was his wife who made him come to realize that their collective system was fundamentally flawed in more than one way. Raisa Titarenko who married Gorbachev was a philosophy student and the story I heard is that she was more than instrumental in making this world a better place."

"How did she do that?"

"Well, in the early eighties when they were in America to meet with then President Reagan, Raisa Gorbachev felt that the tours and roads she traveled were intentionally arranged by our government. Arranged so she would only see a *staged* version of America's best. Raisa ordered a change in their agenda when her husband was with her. Their driver took them into a neighborhood that was not on the schedule and they stopped at a corner food store. There, standing in the middle of the small store filled with different cuts of meats, breads, milk, eggs and so many flavors of ice cream, she started to cry. Supposedly, she told her husband that she would no longer accept the excuses as why there was so little food in the Soviet Union and that he must make the changes to feed his people. Gorbachev, who wanted to make changes because he was an idealist, was not hungry for power nor did he want to rule for the rest of his life. Thus, because of so many choices, the rest is history or should I say *her-story*?"

Addie ignored the question on gender credit and asked what she needed for verification. "Gabbie how do you know about this?"

"I was fortunate enough to meet Mrs. Gorbachev and Mrs. Reagan at the White House one year. Two gracious women, both with a great deal of courage."

"You have been to the White House?"

"In reality, I have been there several times...but enough about that. Where shall we go next?" They both stood up and Gabbie allowed Addie to lead the way as they spoke.

"I was thinking, since I'm off this weekend and Monday, Christmas Eve, I won't see you again until Wednesday after Christmas Day at work. So I want to buy you a Christmas gift and give it to you tonight."

"Oh no Addie, that is very thoughtful of you, but not necessary. I don't want you spending your money on me."

"Next week I'm off from school, so I'll be making extra money by doing eight hour days. And I want to get you a Christmas gift. In fact, I already bought it and they have your gift on hold for me. We just have to pick it up."

"Oh if you did do that, then you have to allow me to buy you a gift."

"Okay, sounds good to me."

"So you did?"

"I did, and here we are," Addie said with a smile and a wave of her hand pointing toward the store's entrance.

"Crochet Barn? Addie I think you just gave away my gift."

"That's okay. Just wait here Gabbie, I'll be right back."

Gabbie began to think about what she might buy Addie, as she stood alone outside the entrance to the crochet store. Viewing some of the different items in the store window, she noticed a reflection of people kicking and moving. However, Gabbie did not notice the reflection of a man wearing a hooded coat and sunglasses watching her from the mall's second level. Unaware that she had a stalker, Gabbie turned to see a Dojo behind her with windows from floor to ceiling. The view of a class going on inside made Gabbie realize that this would be a great gift for Addie. Immediately she went inside to the front desk to get some details.

"Excuse me, does Phillip Erickson attend this school?" asked Gabbie.

"He just left with his father." The woman behind the desk said.

"Perfect," replied Gabbie.

A short time later Gabbie sat on a bench between the Dojo and the Crochet Barn. Addie came out and quickly blended into the crowd so she could circumvent Gabbie sitting on the bench.

"Close your eyes Gabbie!" came Addie's excited voice from behind. Gabbie did just that and turned around. "Okay open them."

"Oh, that is beautiful. You certainly surprised me with this presentation." Addie held a large basket filled with several skeins of yarn, in various colors. Different sized crochet needles and a leather storage case sat together under clear plastic topped with a green bow. Gabbie reached over the bench and took the gift from Addie.

"So do you think you can use these things?" Addie asked as she came around and sat next to Gabbie on the bench.

"Why yes, thank you very much Addie, I love this. This is a most perfect gift. Thank you."

"You're welcome, and I have to say thank you to you. For offering me an opportunity to work at your lab and to learn from you."

"You realize of course that I am learning from you too. Now follow me because I have your gift right across from here." Addie followed Gabbie as she headed toward the Dojo.

"My brother's Dojo?"

“That is correct. I ordered six months of lessons for you. They are writing up the paper work now.”

“Oh no! Gabbie please. I mean thank you, but I cannot accept that.”

Gabbie did not pay any attention to Addie. She already walked up to the front desk where the receptionist had all the paperwork.

“Hi again,” the receptionist said when she looked up to see Gabbie. “All right I have all the papers completed for you. That will be three hundred and sixty dollars. We will need two months deposit of one hundred and twenty dollars now and the rest will be invoiced to the Post Office box you provided.”

“Oh no Gabbie that is way too much money,” protested Addie with a private voice.

“That is correct and here is the deposit,” Gabbie said as she paid in cash.

“Gabbie, please no.”

“Thank you very much,” said the receptionist. Gabbie took the papers, turned, and started walking out with Addie following her.

“Gabbie, I am so embarrassed.”

“Nonsense! Why so much ado about nothing? Here is your paperwork, you start classes on January Second.”

“Nothing? This is something and I don’t want to take these classes.”

“Now please,” Gabbie said sincerely. “This is my gift to you and if you want, look at this as your Christmas bonus. Besides, I heard you say that you always wanted to join your brother’s Dojo and take Kempo martial arts.”

“Oh at your house, yes, but I only said that to answer your exercise question. A Christmas bonus stands true only when earned. I haven’t worked at the lab long enough to earn a bonus.”

"My Addie, that is very commendable of you. Just by saying that earns you a bonus."

"Oh Gabbie I can't."

"Now what is done, is done." Gabbie said as she continued walking. "So I am going to check up on you to see if you are learning your lessons well. I want to make sure that we are getting my money's worth."

"Oh Gabbie..."

"What if we now go and have our photograph taken with Santa? My treat!" Off Gabbie went walking toward the line for photos with Santa Claus.

"Oh Gabbie you've got to be kidding," Addie said with a surrendering sigh as she followed behind her now fast-walking employer.

"You know Addie, you just need to say thank you and be happy. Now I am not too sure about two women, such as ourselves, sitting on the lap of Santa that may have been soiled by some poor child unable to hold his or her bodily fluids."

They both started to laugh openly at Gabbie's comment. Once on line, Addie looked at Gabbie and said, "Thank you Gabbie," with much appreciation in her eyes.

Additional laughs followed as they juggled all their purchases while on Santa's lap. Gabbie paid cash for two copies of their Santa photo and as they walked to a coffee shop each one checked the back of the other's pants with Gabbie persisting in jest that Addie's pants were soiled.

"There, I see a table over there," Addie said and they both went to sit down.

"My, the previous occupants didn't have much manners in cleaning off their leftovers," cited Gabbie after looking at a table littered with spilled sugar, used paper napkins, and coffee cup lids.

"Most people don't," Addie concluded and cleaned up the table herself. "What would you like Gabbie?"

"Oh, a spot of tea would be excellent. Let me give you the money." Gabbie started to take out some cash as Addie whipped out a gift certificate card she had for the coffee shop.

"I have this one all covered, Gabbie. Please put your cash away, this is my treat. Just stay here and watch our bags and table. If you get up we may lose the table."

"Understood and thank you," Gabbie said with a smile.

A few minutes later Addie came back with a tray in hand. "Okay, tea for you, coffee for me and a bran muffin to share."

"Thank you Addie. This is just what I need, a spot of tea before you drop me off at home."

"Gabbie, I hope you don't mind me asking, you didn't just bring cash with you tonight?"

"Why yes, is that a serious problem?"

"Not really, don't you have a credit or debit card?"

"No, I am afraid not."

"Gabbie you should look into getting one. Cash makes things easier for thieves."

"I did think of that, nevertheless I didn't have any other choice for tonight. Perhaps for next time."

Addie sat there with a smile and watched Gabbie eating one small piece of the muffin after another. Slowly Gabbie glanced up at Addie.

"A penny for your thoughts?" asked Gabbie.

"Oh nothing, I just can't place where I've seen you before. You also remind me of someone, I can't place that either."

"Well, I hope you don't get stuck thinking about that until next year."

"Me too," Addie agreed before speaking a thought aloud, "Hey

Gabbie, why don't you and George come over my parent's house for New Year's Eve. We are having a buffet dinner for everyone to welcome the New Year. We're not doing any big party with games this year. Nobody is really in the mood for a big party."

"Thank you dear, that is very kind of you to think of us, however neither of us drive and..."

"I can pick you up and drive you home!" Addie proclaimed as she took out her cell phone. "I'm going to make a call. Wait here, I just have to go to a different spot to get better reception."

With their table by a window, Gabbie watched Addie talking on her cell phone just outside the entrance to the coffee shop. Two men looking down from the second level of the Mall were also watching Addie. They wore black hooded coats and sunglasses. Addie completed her call and looked at her telephone when coming back into the coffee shop. Accidentally Addie bumped into a woman standing in the doorway.

"Sorry, sorry," Addie said as she continued walking back to their table. Gabbie took note of the woman Addie bumped into and saw that the she had now leaned against the inside wall of the coffee shop with her head in both hands.

Addie plopped back into her chair with a big smile. "I spoke with my mom and I told her everything you did for me tonight and she insisted that the two of you come over."

"Are you sure dear?" Gabbie asked as she leaned over to get a better view of the woman.

"Definitely, and my mom said it was okay for me to pick you up. However, my dad will come with us when I drive you home after midnight." Addie finally noticed that Gabbie had been watching something or someone else.

"Oh my, she just slid down the wall to the floor." Gabbie quickly went over to the woman who now sat on the baseboard heater by the floor.

"What, who slid down..." a confused Addie said as she turned to watch Gabbie rushing off to the side of this stranger.

"My word are you all right?" Gabbie said as she held the woman's wrist for a reading on her pulse.

"I don't think so," the woman said from the floor. "I have the chills and I'm dizzy."

"Why sure you are... Your pulse is racing and you are burning up. Addie please help me get her to our table."

"Thank you," said the woman. "Maybe I should call my husband to pick me up."

"That will be a splendid idea," emphasized Gabbie. "Here you go, sit here. Addie take a few dollars, here is five, buy this nice lady some hot tea. Oh and let me borrow your cell phone, I want to call her husband."

"No problem, here's my phone and keep the cash Gabbie, I still have credit on my gift card."

As Addie waited for the tea, she turned to see Gabbie the doctor and scientist helping this stranger. All this just solidified Addie's admiration for Gabbie as a person.

* * * * *

The minivan's hatch closed and Addie handed the last shopping bag to Gabbie as they stood in the driveway of Gabbie's house.

"I had the most wonderful time Addie. Thank you so very much, I enjoyed myself thoroughly."

"You're welcome. I had a great time also. Everyone should have a boss like you, Gabbie. Thank you so much for the lessons at my brother's Dojo."

"Thank you for your most perfect gift for me," exclaimed Gabbie.

Addie gave Gabbie an unexpected kiss on the cheek and stepped toward the front of her minivan.

"Well, yes, I..." a pleasantly surprised Gabbie tried to say. "I will see you Wednesday after the holiday."

“Yeah, my first full eight-hour day.” Addie announced as she went to get back into her car. “Have a great Christmas and can you say hello to George for me?” She closed her car’s door and drove toward the security booth by the front gate.

THE ALERTS, Chapter Seven

Morning came too early for Addie, nevertheless she had to get up for work and catch a ride with her father. At eight o'clock sharp, they pulled up to the entrance of the lab.

"You have a good day at work Addie," said Stewart. "I hope you're awake."

Addie tried to cover up a small yawn unsuccessfully as she said, "We should have off the day after Christmas just so we can recuperate."

Stewart enjoyed a quiet laugh, "Welcome to the real world, my darling." He watched his daughter walk to the security booth and waited until he saw a guard come out to meet her before driving off.

"Good morning, Miss Erickson. Did you enjoy your holiday?"

"Yeah, thank you, and you?" Addie placed her right hand on the scanner.

"Enjoyable... Okay Miss Erickson here is your ID badge and work assignment for today. The golf cart on my left is at your disposal for the day. Please report directly to your assigned lab station to initiate work."

"Thank you, ah...should I report to somebody?"

"Someone should be there to help get you started."

* * * * *

Around two forty-five that afternoon, Addie sat at her computer station inputting data one number at a time. A coworker came over and sat down next to her, "Hello, you are Addie Erickson?"

"Yeah, hi."

"I'm Charlotte Binsnou. They told me to take over so you can get a fifteen minute break." In her early forties, Charlotte wore her unwashed blonde hair up in a bun, black men's style glasses, and a gray lab coat. She did not wear any makeup, nor did she seem to take proper care of herself.

"Thank you, I sure can use one," Addie responded as she stood up and stretched her arms over her head. "By the way, can you tell me if Gabbie is available?"

"Gabbie?" Charlotte cringed slightly as she wished to confirm Addie's question.

"Yeah, Gabbie, our Director."

"My...on first name terms, are we?" Minor jealousy echoed in her tone of voice. "I guess you weren't informed, but *Gabbie's* log shows her out sick today. First time I ever heard about her being sick in the fifteen years that I worked here."

"Do you know if she is all right?"

"All I know is that she was well enough to work yesterday."

"She wouldn't have worked yesterday, it was Christmas Day."

"She did. She works every Christmas. However, this Christmas she did log out early reporting that she wasn't feeling well since last Sunday. It seems that she became very sick after lunchtime. Now, are you going to spend your whole break talking about this?"

"I just don't get her working yesterday," wondered Addie.

"Look, she did," continued Charlotte with a cynical voice. "I check the printouts everyday to see who's ID badge was used to access what lab and when. Your *Gabbie* was in and out of several labs yesterday morning until she logged out sick after lunch. I'm not making this up!"

"Okay, I'm sorry I asked." Addie headed out of the lab as fast as she could walk.

* * * * *

The next morning Addie's assignment sent her to Doctor Janet Barkly's office. As the Assistant Director, she met Addie the first Saturday morning for the tour. Her open office door allowed her to see Addie from her desk, "Good morning Addie, good to see you again. Come in for a minute and sit down."

Doctor Barkly's office had a similar size as Gabbie's, however, the room could not be more organized. Bookshelves stood along one wall and none of the books were piled up on the floor. The walls had several diplomas, awards, and certificates. Also there were two real windows behind Doctor Barkly's swivel leather chair.

"Thank you Doctor Barkly," Addie said as she walked in and sat down on the couch across from the Doctor's desk. "Did you have a nice Christmas?"

"Yes, I did enjoy the holiday. Did you?"

"We did have a very blessed Christmas...holiday." Addie then whispered to herself, "We don't *celebrate* holiday."

"Good, happy to hear. Now in a minute I will bring you over to the lab for your assignment that will last today, Thursday the twenty-seventh of December and tomorrow, Friday the twenty-eighth." The Doctor multitasked by writing while she spoke those words.

"Excuse me Doctor Barkly, do you know if Gabbie will be in today?"

Doctor Barkly put her pen down and looked up at Addie, "I thought you knew. She has a very bad case of Influenza."

"Ooh no, I didn't know."

"Doctor Mannuso is taking good care of her. So hopefully she will be in the lab tomorrow."

* * * * *

The three days Addie worked that week were direly long, especially since this had been the first time she worked eight hours per day. She had worked isolated; identifying and titling glass slides. By four o'clock Friday afternoon, Addie stood intensely tired. She also had not seen Gabbie at all.

The double doors opened to the lab where Addie worked alone. As she looked over the computer printing out the titles for slides she identified, a smile came across her face.

"Doctor Mannuso, how are you? Is Gabbie better?"

"Hello Addie, no I am afraid Gabbie is still sick in bed. Her fever is finally down, so I hope she will be up and around in a few more days."

"Do you think she'll be well enough so the two of you can come over for New Year's Eve?"

"That is why I stopped by. After a long debate with Gabbie, a debate that I believe I won, Gabbie sent me here and told me what to say."

"That doesn't sound much like a victory to me."

"Tell me about it. If I didn't come, Gabbie would give me a swift kick in the bone. That's her favorite coercion."

"I figured that," Addie responded. "I've already heard her say that a few times."

"I can imagine. Anyway, Gabbie said that if she is not at work on Monday that means we are not going to make the dinner. However, if you want, here is our number at the house. Call us before you leave work... Are you working New Year's Eve until five or are you leaving at noon?"

"Doctor Barkly has me scheduled to work until five and my dad is off from work so I'll have the car."

"That is...oh so nice. As you may tell from my poor candor tone, I am not in favor of us attending this invite, no offense to you or your family. I say this especially because of Gabbie being in her present condition.

"Anyway, Gabbie accepted your invitation and she wants to go. So, please call us before you leave Monday. We will see how Gabbie is doing and let you know if we shall accompany you...in your car...to your house." Those last few words seemed to drag out of George's mouth.

"No problem, thank you George and hopefully Gabbie will be well enough to come in on Monday for work," stated a hopeful Addie.

"Yes, hopefully. I will talk to you Monday, have a nice weekend." With that George left the lab and went back to his house.

* * * * *

George slowly closed the bedroom door and walked over to the side of the bed. "Are you awake?" he gently whispered.

"Yes, George, I am awake," a hoarse and scratchy voice came from under a pile of blankets. "I trust you were civil about the matter with Addie?"

"Yes, I was polite as possible."

"Ooh no."

"Gabbie... Yes, I left off that she should call us before leaving work on Monday."

"Thank you Love."

"I just don't know what you could have been thinking that you would accept this invite to her house. You know what problems this may cause." George started to pace back and forth alongside the bed.

"I am sorry, I wasn't thinking. I do not even know if I officially accepted Addie's invitation. I was preoccupied with the woman that took ill in the coffee shop. How many times do I have to repeat myself?"

"That individual made you ill!"

"Obviously!" Gabbie shouted as best as she could in conjunction with slamming her arm down on the bed, thus removing part of the blanket covering her face. "But I didn't wash my hands before rubbing my eye, thus all my fault."

"All I am saying Gabbie is that you can't go running around a mall filled with people. People carrying bacteria and viruses." George had his two hands opened and facing Gabbie as if to plea with her. "Your immune system probably has not seen Influenza since you were eighteen and what are you doing? Running around as if you were eighteen! Well, you certainly are not." George went down on his knees next to Gabbie on the bed. Slowly he put his arm around her. "Gabbie you could have died from this...don't you realize that. After all we have been through, all the work you have done. I could never accept losing you to a bug."

"No bug is going to do us in. I'll be well in a few days."

"Yes, you getting well I do need from you," George lowered his head to the corner of Gabbie's pillow.

"And I need a cup of hot tea from you, please."

* * * * *

Addie closed her bedroom door so she could have privacy while talking to her boyfriend. She hopped up onto her bed, folded her feet under her and flipped open her cell phone.

"Hi Chris! I'm home now."

"God Addie, it's after ten. Saturday is over and I didn't get to see you for a minute."

"Maybe we can still catch a late movie."

"No, it's too late," Chris said with a disappointed voice.

"I'm sorry, I really had no idea the day was going to be this involved. Between the errands, picking up my Grandmother at the nursing home, who by the way will be sleeping with me in my room for the next four nights, and helping my mother get ready for the New Year's dinner Monday night, I had no time for myself."

"Do you think we can go out to eat together tomorrow night?"

"I don't know... I mean I have to work Monday."

"We'll just do dinner, no movie, and you'll be home earlier than you were tonight."

"Okay deal... Oh I hear my Grandmother knocking at my door. See you tomorrow. Pick me up at five. Bye."

* * * * *

Addie drove Chris' car down Main Street in Cold Creek Harbor. About eight o'clock Sunday night all the shops were already closed. The Christmas lights were still on adding a decorative flavor to the store windows, street posts, and the overall atmosphere of the evening. All the gift shops were on the north side of Main Street. Across the street, an empty public parking lot went back about sixty feet into the tree filled hillside.

"Chris the car really does handle great. Thanks for letting me drive."

"No problem Addie."

"Dinner was great Chris, we didn't have to go to such a fancy restaurant."

"It wasn't that fancy."

"So am I driving myself home or do you want to go somewhere else?"

"Do you want to find a quiet place to park?" Chris asked cautiously.

"Okay, but not the parking lot."

"I think I know a spot that is private enough. Head through town and go past your lab."

Addie now drove past the lab's security booth and up the hill on route 5A. At the top of the hill, Chris told her to make the first right turn onto Harbor View Road. They passed a few houses on the left and on the right were trees with a hurricane fence hidden within. Soon the trees on the right ended and only a guardrail with the hurricane fence remained. The road became the leading edge to a bluff overlooking the harbor. Upon a break in the guard railing, the hurricane fence ended and a dirt road ran parallel with the paved road until descending halfway toward sea level.

"Chris are you sure it's safe to drive down here?"

"Yeah, people fish off the end of this road when it's warm out. Just go slow."

The dirt road continued for about fifty yards before coming to a Dead End sign and railing blocking almost a ten-foot drop to the water below. Addie put the car into Park and placed the emergency brake on.

"Wow, beautiful view," admired Addie.

"It sure is. Hey look over there, those three stars in a row are Orion's Belt." Chris abruptly turned in his seat to look behind the car and to the right.

"Too bad we can't see the rest of Mister Orion," joked Addie.

"Addie, isn't that... I'm going to take a look. Shut the engine and come on." Chris stepped out of his car, closed the passenger's door, and started walking back up the dirt road.

Addie closed her eyes and shook her head as if to shake off a ridiculous assumption. "Silly, I thought he wanted to park here so he could kiss me," she mumbled to herself before getting out of the car.

Chris had walked back almost all the way on the dirt road and now looked about twenty feet down to a skinny strip of land ending at the base of the bluff. Shadows danced about as Chris waited for his eyes to get accustomed to the dark. Just off the end of the land and to Chris' left stood an old wooden pier jutting out into the water about ten feet. Also a large wooden deck went from the pier to the right of Chris for about twenty-five feet or so. Toward the back of the deck, a small dilapidated shack stood. At the water's edge, a section of sand went back about a tenth of a mile and ended before a small incline littered with large boulders. Tiny dried up brush covered the slope with trees at the top. Beyond this, the land widened into the larger property of the lab.

Addie came up along side of Chris and took his arm to hug. "You know it's warmer in the car."

"Look over there, that's where your lab buildings start. Do you see some of the roof tops beyond that fence in the woods?"

"Not really, it's too dark. Besides, it's warmer in the car."

"Okay, I just wanted to check this out. What do you think those shadows are on next to the side of that old shack?" Chris pointed down to some shapes that seemed to be half covered with tarp.

"Chris I have no idea," Addie said with a non-caring voice.

"Let's go down and check it out. We can take this dirt path over here."

"Oh no, let's not. That's lab property down there."

"I doubt it. Their property ends by those trees and that fence. This looks like some abandoned fisherman's shack. Come on Addie, it'll be a fun adventure."

* * * * *

A fire roared in the Marble fireplace at Gabbie's house. The parlor room reflected a yellow glow with George and Gabbie sitting in their chairs facing the fireplace. They had their feet up on the ottomans. George had open back slippers on and Gabbie wore white fuzzy rabbit shaped ones. Sitting warm under a blanket, Gabbie slowly sipped some hot soup from a mug that had the following words printed on the front: **Only Tea Please**! George wore a Cardigan and peacefully read his newspaper. However, their composed comfort concluded with a beeping sound emitting from the pocket of George's sweater.

"Is that your beeper, Love?"

"Yes, I can't imagine why."

George could not read the printout on top of his beeper until he moved the beeper further away from his eyes for a second look. "Oh dear," George said as he looked toward Gabbie. "The lab is under Yellow alert."

* * * * *

Chris cautiously moved down the dirt slope toward the old shack. He held Addie's hand to help guide her.

"I just hope we can get back up Chris."

"We will, that wasn't so bad coming down. Hey look at this." Chris moved part of the torn tarpaulin off the objects.

"Just looks like a bunch of old rotten wooden barrels to me."

"Not too exciting is it?" a disappointed Chris said.

"What did you expect to find?" Addie asked pretentiously.

"A treasure chest would have been outstanding."

"Let's go back to the car Chris," a slightly annoyed Addie commented. "I'm getting cold."

Chris really did not hear Addie because he went over to the shack and pushed the door open. "Nobody is home. Shall we?" With that, Chris went inside this one room shanty.

By the time Addie followed Chris inside, he started tinkering with something on the floor. "What are you messing with?"

"It's a portable Kerosene heater. I just turned it on for some light and heat."

"Chris this is not yours, stop messing around."

Some old fishing nets, a wooden bench, and one very dirty window gradually came into view. Chris put his arms around Addie and deliberately began a very long kiss. They hugged each other tight when the kiss leisurely finished. Looking over Addie's shoulder, Chris noticed something carved in one wooden panel of the wall. The word **TELOMERE** over a heart holding the letters **G + G** within, had been chiseled and below the heart, Chris read **4-EVER**.

"Look here," Chris requested as he pointed to the wall. "We aren't the first ones to kiss in this shack."

Addie stared at the carving and slowly moved Chris to the side for a better look. "That is the strangest... What does telomere forever mean?"

"That's their name," Chris said with a matter of fact tone.

"G and G are their names," Addie corrected. "Nobody puts last names on these things."

Chris turned Addie around and back into his arms. "Who cares," Chris declared and started another long kiss.

* * * * *

George came back into the parlor with a cordless telephone. "Yes, she is right here, hold on."

"Hello this is Doctor Maida... Yes, I understand... Fine, contact me when you know more. Bye."

"What did they say?" George inquired.

"They have reason to believe that intruders are on the property. They are staying at Yellow alert. If they go to Red alert all residents will be directed to stay inside for protection."

"Okay so we sit and wait."

"The waiting is what I hate the most. Every time we have one of these alerts I go back to that awful New Year morn in forty-two."

"Everyone since then has been a false alarm or just some kids," George assured.

"I know, but nevertheless, this is still frightening."

* * * * *

The inside of the shack now warmed up. The dungy window fogged as the span of their kiss became undersized by a flash of light going across the glass with increasing condensation.

"Chris I just saw a light."

"Really? Are you sure?"

"Yeah, there it is again."

"All right, you stay here while I check it out."

Chris cracked opened the door to glance around outside. He stepped out to investigate behind one section of tarp covered barrels. As he tediously stepped around, he felt someone lurking in the darkness behind him. Thinking that Addie had followed, Chris turned insouciantly.

"Addie please stay..." Chris initiated and then froze.

Two men with night vision goggles strapped just above their eyes were standing in the shadows. "You are under arrest for trespassing. Who is with you in the shed?"

"My girlfriend," Chris answered.

The second guard banged on the wall of the shack. "Please make sure you are dressed and exit the shed. You are under arrest for trespassing."

Immediately the door of the shed swung open all the way and Addie stepped out. "I don't have to make sure I am dressed, because I am dressed. You assumed wrong."

Chris heard the anger in Addie's voice and by the maniacal look she sent his way, he knew the embarrassment this incident would cause, had her very concerned.

* * * * *

The telephone rang and Gabbie immediately answered, "This is Doctor Maida."

"Doctor, this is Security. We are removing the Yellow alert. We apprehended two teenagers at Land's End."

"Thank you, excellent work. Do you know why they were on the property?"

"They were using the shed by the end of our property. Infrared heat sensors indicated that they were engaging in serious osculation."

"All right, follow normal procedures. Notify the police and their parents."

"I normally would, however the young woman claims she works here and she has asked for you by name."

Gabbie's eyes widened and her mouth hung open. George saw this and instantaneously became concerned.

"What, Gabbie what is wrong?" George asked in vain.

After tediously closing her eyes, Gabbie quietly said into the phone, "Escort them both here."

* * * * *

From across the harbor and through another pair of night vision goggles, five figures standing on the road were in view. Two of the figures moved toward the front gate as three walked up to Gabbie's front porch. The dirty old blinds, covering the trailer's window, snapped closed as the night vision goggles retracted.

* * * * *

Addie's voice sounded outside the front door as Gabbie turned on the porch light. "I greatly appreciate this," Addie said to the guard, only to turn and see Gabbie opening her door wearing a white and blue bathrobe.

"Gabbie I am so sorry. I am so sorry. The last thing I want to do is disturb you as you are getting better from the flu. You look okay, are you feeling better... I am so sorry."

George came up from behind Gabbie and placed a long black coat over her shoulders. "Please come in before we all get sick," he said with some urgency.

"Thank you for your service, I will take care of things from here," Gabbie said to the guard and pointed to the parlor for the two teenagers to enter.

The guard handed a sealed nine by twelve brown catalog envelope to Gabbie. "We also have the young man's car by the front gate."

"Very good, thank you again."

George took the coat off Gabbie and closed the front door. "I shall wait in the kitchen if you need me."

"Thank you George. The two of you shall sit on the sofa..." Gabbie said followed by several coughs as the two teenagers went into the parlor.

"One more thing Gabbie," George continued. "I believe that you will go inside and have a reaction that, psychologically speaking, will be an effort to make up for everything you lost. Gabbie, please realize you cannot do that in one night."

"Well, I am certainly going to try." With that retort, Gabbie marched into the parlor.

"Oh Gabbie I am so sorry," Addie repeated again.

"I do not believe we have been properly introduced young man," Gabbie said firmly as Chris sat down on the sofa next to Addie. Upon hearing Gabbie's statement, and since she remained standing, Chris instantly stood back up.

"Sorry, yes I'm Chris Wilkins, Addie and I have been dating for almost one year now and I am to blame for this evening's mix up. This is my fault, because I didn't think the shack stood on your property. We just went into the shack to warm up for a minute. I figured it to be an abandoned fisherman's shack and I..."

"Well, you figured wrong young man. Now sit down, you are rambling." Gabbie looked at Addie whose face showed the epitome of quandary. "What am I to do about this, what will your parents say Addie?"

"Oh my God, please Gabbie my parents don't need to know about this."

"No? The two of you in a secluded area, and as a young lady you left yourself vulnerable perhaps from your date..."

“Oh no, please I assure you, Addie is never in any danger from me.”

“Young man I was still talking.”

“Sorry.”

“Here is another alternative you didn’t care to think about. What if the guards were muggers with guns? How would you protect your girlfriend?”

“I am not saying this to brag or to prove that I could have stopped muggers with guns, but I do have...” Chris paused as he absorbed a stern look from Gabbie. “I do have a Black belt,” he said delicately.

“Oh dear, another Dojo student. I just don’t know. You leave your car on an isolated road, climb down a cliff in the dark and all for what. Do you think that is a romantic place?”

“Oh no, I assure you that nothing happened. We just went inside for a minute to warm up.”

“Again with the, ‘I assure you’ bit?” Gabby started to open the envelope that the guard handed to her.

“I think they have my wallet and car keys in there,” Chris also said delicately.

“Why yes they...” Gabbie interrupted herself by coughing into her shoulder. “Yes, they do Mister Wilkins. Here you are.”

As Chris put his wallet and keys back in his pockets, Gabbie analyzed three images printed by computer on four by five paper. “Well, young man according to these infrared images, the body heat from the two of you takes a much different shape. And if I am not mistaken, the times shown at the bottom state that the two of you were inside that shack for more than a minute or two.”

Gabbie passed the photos to Chris who started sweating profusely. Addie, clearly nervous, slowly inched closer to Chris on the sofa.

Soon as Addie caught a look at the heat image of their bodies that outlined them French kissing, she put both hands over her face and announced, “Oh my God! I am so mortified!”

"Addie I'm truly sorry," Chris said. He slowly stood up to hand the photos back to Gabbie who began coughing again. Chris patiently waited for Gabbie to regain her composure from coughing.

"Do you have something to say to me?" asked Gabbie.

"Yes," Chris said sincerely and nervously swallowed. "Those outline images of our body heat show us kissing and yes, it was more than a minute or two. However, this fact remains. Your guards could have come by twenty minutes later and the pictures would show us doing exactly the same thing. Kissing, hugging, no more, and no less. I do know the definition to words such as respect, honor, and virtue."

"So you expect me to believe that you would never ask Addie to do it?"

"Excuse me?" a shocked Chris, asked.

"Come on Mister Wilkins, I can talk in today's terms. You wouldn't insist on Addie going 'all the way' with you?"

"As I just said, I know the meanings to respect, honor, and virtue. Whoever I marry, that is when I would...no, we would romantically plan 'doing it and going all the way' for our wedding night. Period."

Gabbie cut a look at Chris from the corner of her eyes and saw that he was truly sincere and resolved. Gabbie also noticed that Addie, who remained sitting on the sofa, had reached up to hold Chris' hand. Addie finally looked up at Gabbie after wiping some tears away.

"Thank you Mister Wilkins, that is how I wanted to hear you explain this. Now would the two of you like to have some tea?"

* * * * *

The next day, New Year's Eve, had Addie very apprehensive about going into work that Monday morning, especially after all that had occurred. This trepidation lingered even with Gabbie's understanding actions toward her and Chris. She checked in at the security booth like always, but this time Addie felt very uncomfortable. She let assumptions get the best of her.

"Here is your ID for today," the security guard said. "After you park your car on the side you may use that golf cart."

Addie believed that the guard's look toward her reflected his briefing about the events from the previous night. Uncomfortably, she looked squarely at the guard, "Listen, about what happened with me last night..."

"Pardon me?" replied the guard.

"I know you weren't here last night, but what you were told is going to be blown out of proportion and I..."

"Pardon me Miss Erickson, the fact of the matter is that I don't know what you are talking about. I am unapprised of any prior events concerning you. We work on a need to know basis here. Therefore, you should not feel a need to tell me."

"Oh, thank you..." Addie said with relief. "I'm sorry I don't know your name."

"Charlie," the guard systematically answered before repeating with empathy in his voice, "I'm Charlie, Miss Erickson."

"Thank you Charlie, please call me Addie."

"Sorry Miss Erickson, there are rules I have to obey. Referring to Doctors who work at this lab by their first name is not allowed."

"Charlie..." Addie spoke as if to say don't you realize, "I'm not a Doctor. I'm a senior in high school, I don't have a doctorate in anything as of yet."

"All the same Miss Erickson, no can do. Sorry."

"Okay Charlie, I understand. Listen, I won't see you on the way out, I know your shift ends at four, so have a happy New Year."

"Thank you, and you do the same."

Once Addie arrived at her workstation she became greatly disappointed upon hearing that Gabbie had not come in to work as of yet.

Addie started to believe that last night had given Gabbie a relapse and that she wouldn't feel well enough to attend dinner at her parent's house.

When lunchtime arrived, she joined several other lab workers in the kitchen and dinette area just off to the right side of the lab's lobby. Conversations were dry and all about work, so sitting alone was not at all unappealing to Addie, particularly when Charlotte Binsnou came into the room.

Addie sat at a small table with only two seats, so she felt safe from Charlotte sitting down with her. Addie assumed wrong. Charlotte first stopped at a few tables and spoke briefly with some people, but she never joined any group of workers for lunch. Until she came directly over to Addie's table and sat down with her little brown lunch bag, neglected appearance and black glasses on the edge of her nose.

"So did you hear what happened here last night?" she said with a thrill.

Addie swallowed hard and her eyes felt like they were bulging out of her head. However, she managed to speak just a few words in hopes that her worst fear would not come true.

"No, what?" Addie vocalized irregularly.

"There was a Yellow alert and security caught two teenagers making out on the property."

Addie struggled to keep her cool, because she had a Red alert going on in her brain at that moment.

"Oh, so no biggie," Addie calmly said.

"Yeah, no biggie, if all proper procedures where followed. But, for some reason, last night they weren't."

"What are you talking about?" Addie said with some difficulty due to swallowing at the same time.

"Normally the police and parents of the teenagers are supposed to be notified. This time they weren't."

"Okay so?" Addie wanted to disappear because she feared that Charlotte had discovered the identity of the teenagers.

"So, I am going to find out who screwed up and inform Doctor Ma... No, I'm sorry. I'm going to inform *Gabbie*, proving to our *Director* that I am on top of everything."

Addie took another bite of her tuna on whole wheat roll and looked down at the table to move her eyes back and forth in relief.

"These two teenagers are not going to get away with trespassing either. The nerve to use our lab as a make-out spot." Charlotte opened her lunch bag and took out two candy bars and a sandwich.

Surprised by Charlotte's remark and that she now stood up to leave, Addie blurted out, "Aren't you having lunch?"

"Yes, I am... Oh, but not here with you." Charlotte said as she took a bite of her jelly sandwich.

Addie now felt a little insulted and had not one thing to lose by asking a personal question. "Charlotte you're not married or dating anyone are you?"

"No, haven't found Mister *Right* yet," Charlotte declared and strutted away to sit by herself at another table.

"Yeah, especially if you are always *Miss Wrong*," Addie added slightly under her breath.

At ten to five, Addie still did not see or hear from Gabbie. Disappointment set in about the very real possibility of Gabbie not feeling up to going out tonight. Addie took out her cell phone only to see her power level at maximum and reception at zero. She shut off her cell phone and decided to conclude the workday by cleaning up her workspace. Afterwards she started the lengthy walk toward the oval shaped lobby at the other end of the corridor.

The double smoked glass doors opened and Jim the elderly gentleman, who happened to be on duty this New Year's Eve, sat by his peanut shell-shaped desk.

"Goodnight Miss Erickson, have a happy New Year."

"Thank you Jim, and the same to you," Addie replied as she turned her cell phone back on.

Jim noticed Addie with her cell phone and provided the explanatory data she needed. "Those things don't work in here. The entire place is mostly underground and we are behind twelve inch thick cement walls that are lead lined."

"That is unbelievable. What in the world for?" inquired Addie.

"Way before you were born this lab extension was built. During the time construction was heavily influenced by the Cold War going on."

"Oh I see. Thanks Jim, I guess I'll make the call from outside."

Jim reached over to his left and took a folder from the top of a large pile. Next he swung his chair around to face his computer on the right where Addie stood. "That is the only way you will get any reception."

Addie shook her head in agreement while observing Jim at work behind his odd-shaped desk. "Jim this desk design is very efficient. Narrow at the center where you sit and wider at both ends for telephones, computers, and anything else. All conveniently within arm's reach. I like it."

"I thank you very much, because I take that as a personal compliment," Jim said.

"Really? Did you design this yourself or something?"

"Yep, I did. Designed and made by yours truly. And because the shape is symmetrical I can move my chair to the center of either side and work."

"Cool Jim, that's impressive. Perhaps when I have an office you can make me one."

"I will be happy to."

"Thanks... All right don't work too late and have a happy New Year."

"Same to you."

Addie drove her golf cart out of the underground garage and stopped under the first large tree. This time her cell phone had full reception for her to call Gabbie's house. After several rings, Gabbie finally answered.

"Hello, we are not available at this time."

Disappointment traveled across Addie's face upon hearing the recording. She could not understand why Gabbie didn't answer her phone. Once Addie hung up, her phone rang.

"Hello," Addie rushed saying.

"Hello, Addie?"

"Gabbie is that you?"

"Yes, George and I are at the front in the security booth. We are all dressed up and waiting for you."

"Great Gabbie, I'm so happy to hear that you are better. I'll be right there."

Addie had a beautiful smile as she parked the golf cart and saw Gabbie coming out of the security booth. Gabbie walked straight over to where Addie parked the golf cart and George soon followed wearing a long black coat. He carried Champagne in a wrapped box.

"I am so glad to see you're feeling better," Addie said as she gave Gabbie a kiss on the cheek. "Thank you so much for last night and keeping the event between us," Addie whispered into Gabbie's ear.

"You are welcome."

"Hi George, how are you doing."

"Very well, thank you."

"All right let's get going. Does one of you wish to sit in the front with me?"

"Yes, I'll take shotgun!" Gabbie called out to the sheer amusement of Addie.

* * * * *

Addie's father who wore a jacket, tie and casual slacks, opened the door before Addie could put her key in the lock. "Welcome. Hi sweetie, how was work?" Addie's father asked.

"It went very well," said Addie.

"Good...come in, come in."

"Hello Mr. Erickson, happy to see you again. This is my husband George."

"George, how are you? Thank you for coming, just call me Stu for short."

"Thank you very much for having us," said George as the two men shook hands. "This is a little something from us both." George handed the wrapped box to Stewart.

"Thank you George, but you didn't have to bring anything. Here let me take your coats."

"Dad I'm going to change before helping out," Addie said as she closed the front door. "Is that okay or should I introduce Gabbie and George to everyone first?"

"Go ahead Addie, everyone isn't here yet and I'll show our guests around."

"Thanks Dad," Addie reached up on her toes to kiss her father on the cheek. The loving kiss she gave her father translated into a simple delight for Gabbie to watch. "Okay Gabbie, George, I'll see you in a few minutes."

"That's fine dear," Gabbie said as Addie flew up the stairs. "You have a wonderful daughter," Gabbie said as she turned toward Stewart and adjusted her velvet shawl over her green off-the-shoulder evening dress.

"She is also a very brilliant young lady. I have seen the results of her work at the lab," George added as they all stood in the foyer of the house. George then adjusted his large out of style bow tie and his navy blue jacket.

"Thank you very much, that means a great deal coming from two established scientists such as yourselves."

"Stu, was that Addie I heard running... Oh hello. I am so happy that you were able to join us." Addie's mother came walking down the hallway from the kitchen. Her pearl necklace stood out against her black evening dress.

"George, Gabbie, this is my Wife; who by the way is named Gabrielle."

"Oh yes, yes, I am so happy to meet...finally meet you." Gabbie seemed a little nervous and her breathing increased as she took Gabrielle's hand. Gabbie held on tight as if to calm herself down.

Immediately seeing this handhold, George also noticed that Gabbie's eyes had started a fixation. Fearing that Gabbie would start to react in an odd way, he stopped the action by placing his hands on top of their hands. "I must say that this is such a pleasure to meet another beautiful woman named Gabrielle," George said rapidly.

Addie's mother did a double take toward George, breaking the eye contact she had with Gabbie. She finally acknowledged George's comment by shaking his hand. "Why thank you very much George. I am happy the two of you joined us this evening. I know Addie would have been very depressed if you were still ill and couldn't make it."

"That's true," Stewart continued. "Especially since she had to get over her boyfriend not making it tonight."

"Ooh, her boyfriend," Gabbie gradually said as she raised her head up at a leisurely pace to look at George with a nodding grin.

"Hun," said Stewart. "Take our guests into the family room to meet your mother. I'll hang up the coats and then bring in some wine and cheese."

"Sure, just follow me."

"So Gabrielle..." Gabbie started to ask.

"Please call me Brielle, I always used Brielle for Gabrielle."

They entered a country style family room, where an elderly woman sat in an armchair watching a special television show on football. She wore glasses and her hair had a style sporting a gold hairpin on one side. After standing up, she carried her cane halfway across the room to meet them.

"Mom this is George and Gabbie. Two scientists from the lab where Addie works part time."

"Happy to meet both of you. Thank you for giving my granddaughter such a wonderful opportunity."

"My pleasure, and most exciting to meet you Brenda." Gabbie's smile washed away once she saw the concerned face on Addie's grandmother. Gabbie turned back to see George with his eyes wide opened and just as concerned.

"How did you know my mother's name?" Brielle asked most curiously as George took a step backwards.

Instantaneously Gabbie came out with the answer to the ample relief of George. "Addie told me during the ride over. Oh my, look at the size of that telly. Have you ever seen one that big, George?"

"Never," came the short and unconcerned answer from George about the television's size.

"Come on you two, sit down on the sofa and tell me how my granddaughter is doing at her first real job."

"Please make yourself at home," said Brielle. "I hope you don't mind football shows?"

"Oh there isn't anything wrong with football," Brenda defended.

"Okay mom, I'm just checking with our guests. So while you guys are talking, I'll be in the kitchen." Brielle left the family room with a smile.

"That's fine, I promise we will not just talk about football," Brenda said as she waved her arms at her daughter's back as if to say go already. "My late husband, God rest his soul, played football both in college and professionally. I have followed the sport ever since I met him."

"That is if you want to believe in that soul nonsense," Gabbie muttered.

Brenda did not hear Gabbie as she turned her attention to the television. However, George heard the comment and that infuriated him.

"What are you doing?" George forcefully demanded to know with his lowest possible tone of anger. "Don't start that debate here!"

With an equally tempered tone of anger, Gabbie shot back at George. "I damn bloody well will express what I believe and don't believe. She is my..."

"Can you imagine! Do not dare say that! Don't even think that, not while we are in this house!"

"Will you two stop gritting your teeth at each other and talk to me," Brenda reprimanded. "I have the TV loud for a reason and it's not because I'm going deaf!"

Stewart looked at his wife as they put the finishing touches on a cheese tray. "So is your mother talking to George and Gabbie or is she just watching her football special?"

"A little bit of both," Brielle said.

"I better get in there then. In the meantime, tell our son Phillip to stop playing video games for a minute and come upstairs with his cousin to say hello."

"Fat chance, Stu, your video crazed brother and his wife are down there playing with them."

"All right, forget it. I'll get them later."

Stewart came into the family room with a cheese tray and an open bottle of white wine. The television commercial playing inundated the room with sound.

"This is a lovely house your family has," shouted George to Brenda once he eyed Stewart coming into the room. Brenda lowered the volume on the television with the remote control, which she operated without any uncertainty.

"I'll just leave this here and I'll be back with some napkins and wine glasses. Unless you would like some freshly made distilled water?"

"Aah wonderful! You purchased one?" an amazed George asked.

"Okay, talking about water is not my cup of tea... Time for a little exercise," Brenda claimed as she stood up from her chair. "Come on Gabbie; let's go see what my granddaughter is up to."

"Okay, that sounds refreshing."

As the two women walked up the stairs, Brenda, who carried her cane to the stairs, now began using her cane to assist herself. Gabbie stayed close behind Brenda and observed her progress.

"How is walking upstairs?" Gabbie asked with a true concern in her voice.

"Better... Getting better. I'm still a spunky old lady."

When they came to the first closed door at the top of the stairs, Brenda went to knock, but stopped. "I should knock, but since we are sharing rooms I don't have to knock."

"Oh no, please..." Gabbie protested too late.

"Hi ya Roomie!" Brenda shouted as she opened the door and walked in.

"Grandma..." Addie quickly said as she sat in the center of her bed talking on her cell phone. "And Gabbie! Oh my God, Chris I'll call you back." Addie's cell phone disappeared faster than any magician could have done. Addie's bedroom still had the air of youth with white walls and a pink ceiling. Her white furniture had pink trim.

"Hey young lady, this is also my room for a few days and besides the men are talking boring stuff about water downstairs so I invited your boss up for a tour."

"Addie I'm sorry, I didn't mean to intrude, but your grandmother..."

"Don't worry." Brenda said and continued with a sarcastic voice. "She is already dressed and look how beautiful her clothes are. A lovely dinner occasion and she is wearing jeans with a tee shirt."

"I will change into something dressy before we eat dinner, don't worry. Anyway, anyway... You know," Addie said shaking her head up and down. "Seeing the two of you together, I now know where I've seen Gabbie before."

"Really," Gabbie said with a forced smile.

"Yep, at my Grandmother's adult home."

"Oh, I did not know. So Brenda you must be at the one I do some volunteer work for."

"See I knew it, but Gabbie, why my grandmother wants to live at this adult home is beyond me. We told her she could live here with us." The downstairs doorbell rang and Addie took advantage of the situation. "Grandma, could you and Gabbie get the door so I can get dressed for dinner, now that everyone will be arriving?"

"Very well, let's go, Gabbie. I can take a hint." Once Brenda closed the bedroom door behind her, she spun toward Gabbie like an old friend. "You know she's calling her boyfriend back."

"Oh yes, I know about him," Gabbie said as she rolled her eyes. "I must meet Phillip now."

About one hour later everyone gathered around the dining room table. Most children were standing in the entrance of the dining room. Some of the younger children were standing next to or held by their seated parent. Stewart and his wife sat at the head of the table by the windows. Down Brielle Erickson's side of the table were her Mother Brenda, Addie, Gabbie, George, and so on. Down the side of Stewart Erickson were his elderly parents, followed by his two brothers and their wives. With folding chairs between the padded dining room chairs, fourteen adults sat at a table made for ten.

"Before we partake of our dinner tonight," announced Stewart.

"I would like to say Grace. Will everyone please bow their heads."

Addie lowered her head and quickly looked back up for a second to take a sneak peak at her youngest cousin of twenty-three months across the table. The child's head rested on her mother's chest and offered a beautiful image. As Addie slowly lowered her head she noticed that Gabbie, who sat next to her, had a blank stare on her face.

"Dear Lord, all of us gathered around this table give You thanks for our food in which we are about to enjoy. Deep in our hearts we thank You for our safety this year, we pray for those who lost loved ones and our neighbor who was one of the so many rescue heroes that lost their lives. This New Year's Eve we will not wait for the coming of the New Year by playing silly games and contests. Instead, we will enjoy everyone's presence and their company through conversation and hugs. God bless us all, God bless America and may the coming New Year bring us world peace. Amen."

"Amen," resounded upward from the table. Even Addie's youngest cousin reacted positively. After hearing everyone else say Amen, she raised her head from her mother's chest and shouted out the cutest belated Amen that made everyone chuckle. However, Addie took note that Gabbie never bowed her head, did not say Amen, and did not laugh with everyone else.

Time went by and rapidly concluded the last hour of the year. As Stewart cleaned up in the kitchen with his wife, he viewed his mother-in-law again talking with Gabbie and George. They were standing down the hall by the base of the stairs.

"Your mother has definitely made two new friends," Stewart commented as he started to take out plastic Champagne glasses and set them up on assorted styles of serving trays.

"Who's that?" Brielle asked without much concern as she loaded the dishwasher.

"George and Gabbie. They are talking up a storm in the hallway."

"Really? Hand me that gravy boat. Is that the right time?"

"Yeah it is," Stewart answered as he handed his wife the dirty gravy boat.

“Twenty after eleven already?” Brielle said as she placed the gravy boat in a fully stacked dishwasher. “I don’t believe how fast this eve... What’s that beeping sound?”

“I know that isn’t our smoke alarms. Could it be the CO detector?” Stewart asked aloud.

Addie came down the stairs still dressed up from dinner with her high heel shoes and a purple evening dress. At the base of the staircase she saw Gabbie looking at her beeper. Just as Gabbie shut off her beeper, George’s beeper went off.

“Oh my God, it sounds like the house is burning down,” Phillip shouted from the top step. Next came the sounds of yells and barreling feet running down the steps. Phillip and his two cousins, who were shouting fire warnings for all to hear, pushed past everyone at the bottom step and into the family room.

Gabbie slowly looked up from her beeper toward George, who just shut his beeper off. Addie’s Grandmother Brenda, waited for an explanation as Stewart and Brielle came walking down the hall.

“Is everything all right?” Brielle asked as she wiped her hands on a dishtowel.

“We don’t really know,” Gabbie answered. “It’s Security at the lab. I’m sure this isn’t anything major. Addie may I use your computer to go online and check in?”

“Sure, my computer is already on. Let’s go up to my room.”

All the track lights were on in Addie’s room, as well as her new white iMac computer with the flat-panel swivel display screen. A custom made photo collage of current singing artists illuminated the monitor as a screen saver.

“Very nice,” Gabbie said as she sat down in front of the computer. “May I?”

“Yeah, please look up what you have to.”

With that permission, Gabbie went straight to work. Apple’s web site came up as the default Home page, but before the page could fully load Gabbie had already typed in the web address she wanted: Triple "w" dot cchlabmail dot gov.

The web page came up on the computer screen and simply requested a password. As Gabbie typed in the password, only asterisks appeared in the white text box. Just as Addie counted and noted fourteen asterisks, her father came to the door taking her attention away from the computer screen.

"Addie, is everything all right?"

"Oh Dad," Addie said as she turned and walked toward her father. "I don't really know, Gabbie is checking out her mail site now."

Gabbie had typed some more things on the keypad and read for a second before clicking the window closed.

"I'm afraid George and I will have to leave," Gabbie mentioned. "Security stopped someone from robbing our house."

Addie's eyebrows went up and her father immediately responded, "I'll get my coat and drive you home right now."

"I will never allow that. We shall call a taxi. Addie may I borrow your cell phone?"

"Sure Gabbie here, but I can drive you home. Dad tell her that I can drive her and George home. You stay here with everyone, otherwise you'll miss twelve o'clock."

Addie's dad led her into the hallway before whispering to his daughter, "Let them take a cab home Addie. It's going to be twelve o'clock in thirty minutes, I have a full house here, and I don't want you driving after midnight. I'm fearful about possible drunk drivers."

"Dad I'll be back by twelve fifteen. You wouldn't even know that I left."

"I will know because when I go to hug my daughter at one minute after twelve, you will not be here."

"Ooh Dad thank you, but I'll be back a few minutes later to mingle in with everyone's good wishes and hugs."

"I'm sure Gabbie already has a cab coming. Oh she may need to give them directions to our house." Stewart went back into Addie's room, but Gabbie already concluded the phone call.

"Oh dear, I am so sorry to wreck your party. We had a wonderful time...seeing everyone. However, we do need a ride. I have to get back now and after calling two local taxi companies, the earliest a taxi can get here is one fifteen. It seems people have already reserved rides home after the twelve get blasted drunk hour. I'm sorry, I don't mean to get testy."

"That's all right, Gabbie," said Addie. "I would be upset if someone tried to break into my house. I'll drive you home right now."

"Is this all right with you Stewart?" asked Gabbie.

"Alright, only if you leave right now and she gets back home no more than ten minutes after twelve."

"Thanks Dad, come on Gabbie I'll get your coats, you get George."

They arrived at the security gate about ten minutes to twelve. Before Addie even stopped her parent's minivan, Gabbie jumped out of the car and ran over to the guard in the security booth. George, who sat in the back, opened the sliding door on the van and hopped out once Addie came to a full stop. She rolled down her window to hear the conversation.

"The entire lab is on Red Alert and is in a lockdown. I suggest that Miss Erickson drive the two of you up to the entrance doors of the lab. The graveyard shift was called in early for this and one guard is waiting to brief you there."

"Okay, thank you. Now open the gate! Back in the car George. Addie please drive us up to the lab's entrance."

"Gabbie I thought you said that your house was being robbed?"

"Yes, I know. Go ahead, you can drive fast Addie. Go faster.

Apparently, I was wrong, they targeted the lab. There, there is the guard. Go up that way, very good." They drove up the hillside toward the entrance of the building that looked like a small auditorium. "Okay, park in front of the steps," continued Gabbie with directions. "Don't go toward the guard by the garage. Stop, stop!" Gabbie impatiently ordered.

All three of them jumped out of the car and jogged toward the guard.

"Do you have a briefing for me?" Gabbie called out in the cold night air.

"I do, Doctors," answered the one guard under a poorly lit entrance to the underground parking garage. "At twenty-three hundred hours the perpetrators broke the lower glass on the first door of the lab's main entrance."

"But, nobody ever uses those doors, how can this be a main entrance?"

"Addie please don't interrupt," Gabbie said. "Go ahead."

"Soon after notification went out to you we chased two men in dark overalls and ski masks down into the garage. They are handcuffed and being held in the garage now."

"Have you called the police?"

"Yes, they are on the way. Follow me."

"Addie, please stay here by your car," Gabbie ordered. "We will return shortly. Best call your parents and tell them you are stuck here for a while because the lab is in a lockdown. We'll let you out once this is over."

Gabbie, George, and the security guard ran down into the underground parking garage between the bushes. Addie found herself standing alone in high heel shoes among Oak and Maple trees that were at least two hundred years old. In the distance she saw the faint light of the security booth next to a deserted Route 5A. Not a single porch light for any of the Victorian houses could be found on and the wind coming off the harbor turned bitter cold.

Slowly Addie walked back toward her car with folded arms that held her black raincoat closed. Carefully she looked around before getting back in her car. She started the engine, turned on the heat and locked her door. The clock in the minivan showed two minutes after twelve. Using her cell phone, she called her parents.

"Happy New Year!" shouted Phillip over the celebratory noise in the house.

"Phillip, it's Addie. Listen tell Dad I'm stuck at the lab and not to worry."

"What?"

"I said that I'm stuck at the lab..."

"What?"

"Oh brother! Put Dad on! Put Dad on!"

Addie waited in the dark car as some leaves swirled with abbreviated scratching noises upon random contact over the hood. Her mind fixated on the creepy sounds and found relief only when she heard her father's voice on the phone.

"Addie are you all right?"

"Yeah Dad, I'm fine." A false security emerged since she failed to realize that Gabbie and George didn't lock their doors.

"What is going on over there?"

"It's just security will not let me out until they solve this. I'm stuck here at the lab for a while, so don't worry."

"All right, but you call me once you're leaving there."

"Okay, Bye..."

"Wait Addie!"

"What?"

"Happy New Year Sweetie, I love you."

"I love you too Dad. Happy New Year and save some champagne for me."

"Okay, be careful. Bye."

Addie shut off the cell phone and leaned forward to put the radio on. However, a slight peer out the front of the car stopped her. Addie thought she saw a cat moving inside the entrance through the broken glass panel. She turned on the car's headlights, but that didn't do much. After turning on the car's high beams, Addie stepped out of the car and put on a black beret. With her car still running, the door open, and the headlights on, she went up the four steps to a cement apron sixteen feet wide in front of all the doors. A raw wind blew and some leaves started to rustle about. As she slowly approached the broken door, the shattered glass on the cement cracked under her purple shoes. Only the bottom half of the glass panel had been broken, so Addie squatted down to look inside.

"Here kitty, kitty," she called out.

Not seeing or hearing anything, she moved closer to look within. There in the car headlights just three feet inside the door stood a cement wall. The wind continued to blow and leaves danced in the shadows.

"What in the world is this?" Addie asked herself. "This is all fake," Addie said to answer her own question. Without thinking she foolishly stuck her head between the broken glass for a better look. "Shit, this isn't used, because it isn't real!"

She now turned her head to look down the deceptive empty space behind the rest of the bogus doors. "This is all... AAAAAH!" Addie screamed, as she never did before. In the dark shadows just inches from her, moved a much darker sable. A movement, done by something much larger than any cat.

She grunted as she pulled her head out and caught a jagged edge of glass. The bottom of her chin slashed open before she fell back onto the cement within her car's headlights. With fear and shock she cried out, "Help! Help me!"

The glass door next to the broken door, slammed open with such hard force that once the door banged to a stop in its fully open position, both the upper and lower glass panels exploded into a thousand pieces. The sound resonated as glass rained upon Addie causing her to scream again. A man dressed all in black fell to the ground next to her. He had kicked the bar to open the door and now through a black wool ski mask he looked into Addie's eyes. He turned and stood to run, but after two steps, he saw Addie's car running with the door open. Frantically he rotated and ran back to grab Addie by the arm.

"We're leaving now and you're driving!" A hoarse voice uttered through the mask.

"No!" Addie protested and tried to reach for the handle on the open door to abate being dragged away. Her fingers missed catching the handle by an inch and thus, the dragging toward her car began.

"You're driving, got it!"

"Oh my God no, no. No!"

Going down the steps Addie lost her footing. She lunged forward toward her assailant and car. Amazingly, just six feet from her open car door, Addie put the brakes on by planting her heels into the dirt at the edge of the pathway. Leaning her body weight back toward the steps, her three inch heels sunk into the ground helping to hold her position.

"I said move it, you lab nerd bitch!"

Addie saw no help coming, she had to do something herself and amidst fear her mind scrambled. No time for frantic action, she had to use her God given intelligence. She released all resisting action against her towing direction and push this man right into the car door that slammed shut. They both fell to the ground with Addie losing her shoes and her captor's grip. A new objective developed for the assailant, because a beam of light now shined upon them. Driven by fear, he just started running toward the harbor. The security guard from the entrance gate went in pursuit. The beam of light grew in size on Addie as Gabbie, George, and the security guard that had been with them, came up to Addie's side.

"Addie are you all right," Gabbie asked nervously as she kneeled and saw blood coming from under Addie's chin.

"My God, how can this happen?" George inquired of the security guard next to him. "Gabbie here is my handkerchief, use this to apply pressure to her chin. Don't worry Addie, you are safe now."

"Looks like we had a third suspect hiding out in the false entrance," said the guard with Gabbie and George. "Don't worry, he didn't get far. I just saw Steve from the front gate do a flying tackle off that rock near water's edge. I'm going down there to help him out."

"Yes, please do," said George. "We'll help the young lady to our house." Gabbie help me get her in the car. I'll drive."

"Oh no George," Addie started to say with some difficulty. Gabbie continued applying pressure to the bottom of Addie's chin, thus making talking and moving her jaw difficult. "You said you don't drive."

"I know how to drive, I just don't have a license. I assure you that it is perfectly legal for me to drive to my house from here."

"Yes, however the real question is, how safe is your driving?" Gabbie cracked her remark while smiling at Addie. "Come on, give me a little smile."

Down by the water the two security guards walked the thief back up the hill toward the front security booth. Unknown to them, three pairs of Night Vision goggles were watching them from the other side of the harbor. One pair of goggles turned from the window and viewed a box filled with ski masks on a fold-down table inside the dark trailer.

Inside Gabbie's parlor, they sat Addie down on the sofa. George put on the lights and took Gabbie's coat. Gabbie slowly removed Addie's coat and hat before handing them to George.

"Let me take a look," Gabbie requested. "Oh a bit deep. We are going to need a suture or two, but I promise not to charge a penny. George please go downstairs and get everything I will need to close this up for her."

"Will I have a scar?" Addie feared.

"I doubt it, and being located directly under your chin where nobody ever looks...except maybe your boyfriend Chris. Only kidding...there isn't anything to worry about."

A brief time later, Addie had a small bandage under her chin. George came back into the room and placed Addie's coat on the sofa next to her.

"I believe that I was successful in removing all the glass from your coat. I even found glass in your coat pockets. I am happy that you had a hat on or we would be removing a window load of glass from your hair. Feeling better?"

"Thank you George for cleaning my coat. I'm much better now, but my chin still stings a bit."

"Well, that sting will be with you for a few days," Gabbie confirmed. "George, Addie told me what happened while I was closing her laceration. She did some smart thinking, I will tell you later. Love, get the blanket off the top shelf in the closet for Addie."

George went over to the closet door in the parlor and reached to get a blanket on the top shelf. First he grabbed and then dropped the blanket, because he paid more attention to Addie's questions than his task at hand.

"What I don't get is why those entrance doors are dummies?"

"Well, they were real many years ago," Gabbie began to answer.

George picked up the blanket as he listened. He didn't notice that the blanket caught on some of the picture frames in the box Gabbie placed on the closet floor the other week. When George turned away with the blanket, the box pulled out of the closet slightly before coming free. This box, scarcely sticking out of the closet now, prevented the door from closing all the way.

"They decided to close them up when the lab was remodeled. Probably the cheapest way to go," Gabbie assumed.

"Here you are Addie," said George. "This will keep you warm. Should I start a fire?"

"No Love, please put all the medical supplies away. I am going to call Addie's parents before they start to worry. I will be right back Addie.

I need to wash up and I will explain everything to your parents. You just rest here for a while."

"Thanks Gabbie," Addie said as she sat back on the sofa and watched George leave with Gabbie and the medical supplies.

Addie settled down on the sofa and gazed at the box protruding from the closet. Curiosity had her stand up and wrap the blanket around her shoulders so she could walk over for a gape. She crouched down to find picture frame after picture frame together with doilies. There were black and white photographs of babies and young girls. One old wedding photograph had a woman that seemed to look like a younger Gabbie with a man in uniform standing next to her.

"These aren't on the mantel?" Addie said to herself as she flipped through the photographs. "I tell you...lab is loaded with brains, but all are slightly fried. Except Charlotte...her cerebrum is burnt... Keep talking to myself I'll start to fry... Whoa, crab crap? Looks like my grandmother when young? Nahhh, no way."

"Addie would you like some tea?" Gabbie called out from the kitchen at the same time the telephone started to ring. "George has already boiled some water."

"Oh shit," Addie said to herself and placed the frames down into the box and hurried back to the sofa. "Ah, yes please Gabbie. Thank you!" Addie said as she sat down.

"All right here is some hot tea," Gabbie called out as she came into the parlor. She carried the same silver tray from the other week. As she placed the serving tray down, the telephone stopped ringing.

"Thank you Gabbie, I didn't get any Champagne tonight so tea will have to do."

"Oh I am so sorry, this wasn't such a happy New Year's Eve."

George walked by the entrance to the parlor with his coat on. "Security called, the police are at the booth. I will head down to answer questions and I will call when Addie's father arrives. In the meantime, someone from security will be here in a minute to get a statement from Addie for their report."

"Thank you, Love."

"Gabbie, my father is coming here?"

"Yes, I spoke with your parents and I explained everything that happened. I immediately informed them that we were all well, however you received a cut under your chin. The details followed. Now since the time is so late, your father is coming here so you can follow him home."

"He didn't have to..."

"Your parents love you, let them have this. You know...it's no biggie."

Addie smiled at Gabbie and they shared their first tea of the New Year.

Twenty minutes later the police left with the three accused men. As the police cars pulled away, Addie drove to the security booth in the minivan with Gabbie. The security guard that took the statement from Addie followed in a golf cart. George came walking over as they stopped at the gate. Addie's father had parked on the other side of the gate and they all went over to meet him.

"Oh Addie, you okay? Let me see." Stewart hugged his daughter.

"I'm fine Dad, Gabbie fixed me up."

"Thank you for taking care of her."

"I am sorry this happened. I should have never left Addie by the car. I would never forgive myself if she had been seriously injured. Unfortunately, security was duped into believing only two thieves were on the property. We had a false sense of security not realizing there were three perpetrators. Errors were obviously made and I promise you they won't be made again." Gabbie showed signs of definitively being upset and her voice echoed that emotion.

"That's okay, the important thing...everyone is safe," Stewart said with one arm still around Addie. "Something to be most thankful to God for at Mass tomorrow. Gabbie, George, please join us tomorrow at the twelve o'clock Mass being held at Saint Peter's Church. With so many people sleeping over our house, going to Mass together has become a tradition."

"Thank you, but no. We will not be able to make that." Gabbie's irritated tone of voice carried in this answer.

"What were they trying to steal?" Stewart inquired.

"Lab equipment, microscopes, anything that they could resell," George answered. "The police said that these guys work for outfits that resell stolen merchandise to pawn shops."

"I see, kind of like the car Chop Shops I guess," Stewart imagined verbally. "All right let's get going. Are you up to driving?"

"Yeees, Dad. Goodnight Gabbie, George."

"Goodnight, thank you."

* * * * *

Following several hugs and kisses in the hallway from her mother. Addie's father handed a glass of Champagne to his daughter.

"I saved you one. Happy New Year sweetie."

"Thanks Dad, Mom. Happy New Year," Addie said as she took a sip from the plastic Champagne glass.

"Listen Addie, your father and I didn't tell anyone else the details of what happened tonight. We didn't want everyone to worry. So in the morning get ready for a barrage of questions about your chin."

"No problem... Hey the Champagne tastes okay, but that's enough for me tonight. My head is pounding, I'm going to bed." Addie handed the glass to her father and started to climb the stairs in her mud covered shoes.

"Okay, good night and remember Grandma is sleeping in your room."

"Okay mom, good night."

Addie quietly entered her room lit only by a nightlight. She saw her Grandmother sleeping in the bed and a sleeping bag set up on the floor. Her computer remained on, but in Sleep Mode. Tilting over her desk to shut the computer Addie suddenly changed her mind. Quickly she sat down and brought the computer out of Sleep. Addie moved the mouse and clicked on Window in the Menu Bar. She dragged down to History and a window opened showing the web addresses of all the previous pages visited by date order. Under December 31, 2001, the last web page visited listed as cchlabmail dot gov; the web page Gabbie visited.

"That's it!" Addie whispered with some excitement.

The web page came up on the computer screen and requested entry of the password into the text field box.

"Okay Gabbie what is your password...what password would you use?" Addie mumbled to herself. "It had fourteen asterisks. So let's see... *Granny Squares*?"

The computer showed a new window with a loud beep sound. Addie quickly lowered the volume with three more beeps and the computer spoke. "Alert! Password is incorrect. Do you wish to try again?"

"Damn, Granny Squares was only thirteen spaces. I need fourteen. Microscopes, no that's only eleven. What, what would...that's it. Oh I know that's it."

Addie typed in **flyingcrabcrap**. "Yeah!" I knew it!" Addie's grandmother began to turn in the bed provoking a concerned glance from Addie.

A new window opened on the computer screen that read:

Welcome Doctor Gabrielle Maida.

"Who is Maida," Addie wondered to herself. "She's married to Doctor Mannuso."

The computer began talking and reading the remainder of the web page. "Alert! Please enter security password to avoid automatic virus. Fifteen seconds."

"Oh crap! What? What! Oh no, I didn't see this part. What to do? Shit, Escape button. Again, again. Shit nothing."

A new window opened on the computer monitor, "Alert! Excuse me, virus protection program has detected a virus downloading on hard drive. Attempt to delete in progress."

"Oh thank you, yes delete that bug."

Another new window popped open. "Alert! Alert! Virus activity could not be deleted."

"God, what's gonna happen?"

Again a new window opened and the computer started talking. "Excuse me, virus protection program has activated Quarantine System. Virus has been successfully Quarantined."

"Thank you, thank you!" Addie said in relief as she dropped her head to the desk.

Then unseen to her another new window opened. Addie's head shot up in fear as she heard the computer one last time. "Alert! Alert! Quarantine has failed."

All the windows that were open on the computer started to close, one after another. Then programs started to shut down and delete. Utter shock fell upon Addie's face as she watched her computer memory being erased one item after another. Only a black and white drawing of a square computer remained on the screen with a sad face.

"Oh my God!" Addie screamed and fell back to the floor. "Aah, all gone. Oh no. My English report, no backup, all fifteen pages gone. Happy flying crab crap New Year to you Addie Erickson."

Addie's grandmother moved in the bed to see her granddaughter lying on top of an unopened sleeping bag. Addie returned the look with tears in her eyes.

"Addie it must be two in the morning. If that damn computer of yours goes 'Alert, Alert' one more time I will drop kick it out the window." Her grandmother reached for her glasses on the night table and took a better look at Addie after putting them on. "What happened to your chin?"

THE SUSPICIONS, Chapter Eight

Three months later the nourishing weather of April settled upon the town of Cold Creek Harbor. Springtime had an early start from a compassionate winter.

Addie had excelled with the work assigned to her at the lab over the past few months and her relationship with Gabbie grew more valuable as both of them welcomed open conversations on just about anything. Anything except God, that topic Gabbie never wished to indulge. Nevertheless, Addie shared her excitement with Gabbie about working at the lab, graduating from High School, starting college, and continuing her relationship with Chris. Life started going very well for Addie; things were better than average.

Addie knocked on Gabbie's office door. "Come in Addie, come in," Addie heard Gabbie call out as the buzzer allowed the office door to be open.

"Hi Gabbie. You wanted to see me?"

"Yes, sit down," Gabbie spoke as she sat behind her desk and opened a brand new folder. "How was school today?"

"Ridiculous... April fools jokes don't go well with a Monday morning," an exasperated Addie answered as she sat down in one of the armchairs.

"My... I guess I can relate to that."

"Really?" Addie reacted with some surprise; she did not expect practical jokes to have a place in a scientific lab.

"No...not really," a serious Gabbie stated. "I guess I just did my first April fools on you," Gabbie said with a proud smile. Then she became serious again. "However, your first impression was correct Addie. We don't fool around here."

Addie leaned forward in her chair upon Gabbie's initial response, but now she slumped back after fooled by a person who never commemorated April Fools in her life.

"Addie I know you have heard about the Modified Magnetic Resonance Imaging study over the past several weeks, otherwise known as the Double MRI study. Doctor Barkly will be directing the program with several other top scientists assisting her. The study had a Monitoring staff assigned. However, I need to select one more person."

Addie sat up straight in the chair and gave Gabbie her undivided attention. If Addie surmised correctly, Gabbie will offer her an assignment on this newest study.

"Would you be able to..." Addie cut Gabbie short with her premature answer.

"Yes, I would love to! Thank you so much. I will need to be briefed and..." Gabbie now cut Addie off.

"Addie, Addie, excuse me. I was about to ask if you would be able to work an extra hour each day. I need you to pick up on Charlotte Binsnou's work, so she can have the time to monitor the Double MRI study."

Addie sat back into her chair and struggled to maintain eye contact with Gabbie as she contained her disappointment. "Yes, I can work the extra hour to help out." Addie then thought some more on the question. What possible insufficiencies did she have that prevented her from participating in the study? "But, it will be hard for me to continue that work schedule when final exams come around. I don't think I'll have enough time to do both."

"Understandable," Gabbie replied with doubt that the real reason involved exams. "I know you are doing a great deal more now such as your Karate lessons, by the way I heard you are already a Blue belt. Congratulations."

"Thank you," answered a disillusioned Addie.

"You are also spending a great deal of time with your boyfriend Christopher Wilkins." Gabbie stated and proposed as what she believed to be the real reason for Addie's lack of time.

"He has helped me study the forms. That's probably the main reason why I already have a Blue belt and I'm being tested for Blue Stripe in a few weeks."

"Well, I have noticed that you are talking a great deal more about Chris than your work or studies."

"Things have gone well between the two of us. He is in most of my classes and he never acts like all the immature guys."

"You know Addie, when I was your age I had to deal with a male oriented world of education, business and social contacts. I did not have boys on my mind for several years later. You should concentrate more on your education, not boys. You are young and I didn't get married until I was much older."

"But, different things work for different people."

"You are not very different from me Addie. We have a great deal more in common than you realize. We have the same blood in our veins."

"You say that as if you mean it literally?"

Gabbie paused and looked at Addie affectionately. "What I mean is that if you had some more time I would pick you instead of Charlotte to help with monitoring the Double MRI study."

"I can work Saturdays as well as the extra hour each weekday." A hopeful young lady expressed jubilantly. "Also I don't want to sound like I'm bragging or anything, but I have my final exams well under control. I can work the extra hour during final week, no problem."

"Then this is settled. I will be briefing you instead of Charlotte this afternoon. Get your notepads and meet me in the briefing room ten minutes from now."

"Thank you Gabbie, I will do the best job!"

"I know you will, go ahead go. I'll be there in ten minutes."

In only five minutes, Addie had a seat at the center desk in the front row of the briefing room. A podium stood front and center. Two screens were on each side of the wall mounted blackboard and projection equipment hung from the ceiling. About twenty additional desks filled the room without windows, but all of them were empty.

The door slammed wide open and the person who entered had a red face from embarrassment and anger. The loud bang from the door startled Addie, but she managed to compose herself.

"What did you think? That I was just going to let you steal my job from me. I have been struggling to move up the ladder in this lab and then you come along without even a high school degree and take my assignments. This is the last one you'll steal from me. Do you understand Erickson?" Desperation carried in her voice and her stare meant to intimidate.

"I wasn't trying to do..." Addie attempted to speak in her own defense, but Charlotte didn't give her a chance to say a word more.

"Stay away from me, you little lab nerd bitch!" Charlotte placed her hands on each of Addie's shoulders and held her down in the seat. "Ah, now I know your pretty little brain is working. What I just said you heard before on that terrible first night of this year. Could I be involved with those thieves? That's what you are thinking, aren't you? You are not that lucky. I'm far worse than some drug addict thieves. I have my ways to read the security report about what transpired that night."

Charlotte's glaring stare had penetrated into Addie's exuberance and her spoken words shredded Addie's energy apart. Now completely lost of all excitement for receiving this assignment, Addie only had anger and a basic Kempo White belt move as her answer. Sending her arms up through the center of Charlotte's arms and directly between their faces. Addie split her arms asunder, causing Charlotte's hands to come off her shoulders.

"What's with you, Charlotte?" Addie spoke firmly as she stood up straddling the chair.

"Watch where you drink Erickson. Around here your coffee can easily be contaminated accidentally with cyanide." With that threat, Charlotte turned and marched out of the briefing room.

Addie sat back down, took in a nervous gulp of air, and dropped her head into her folded arms. "Crab crap, she is whacked."

The door opened again and Addie immediately popped her head up to see Gabbie walking over to the podium.

"Did I wake you up Addie? I can't have a person low on sleep monitoring the Double MRI study."

"No! No, not at all. I am just shifting gears from dealing with a social issue on the low end of the spectrum to now learning from you on the opposite end."

"And what spectrum are you referring to Addie?" Chalk started clicking when Gabbie turned to write on the blackboard.

"The spectrum scale of human intelligence."

Gabbie stopped writing and turned back toward Addie with concern. "Why? What happened, Addie? You have a perturbed look about you."

"Nothing. I'll be able to deal with it. No biggie."

"All right if you say so." Gabbie picked up some notes and continued writing on the board. "All right let's get started. The Double MRI study is a farfetched study if you ask me. Since nobody did, I now have the research grant monies specifically allocated to this study to spend appropriately. The main objective is to determine Values, however the research over all is on aging. Are you ready Addie?"

"Yes, as ready as anyone could be."

"Excellent, now Albert Einstein presented us with the theory that stated the faster we go the less we age. We all know the story of the two brothers. The older brother gets on a space ship and travels at the speed of light, while the younger brother stays on Earth. Now because the older brother traveled at a speed of one hundred eighty-six thousand miles per second, when he returned to Earth he was now the younger brother. The brother who stayed behind was an old man.

"With that, we should look at the following,"

Under the study's title and Mister Einstein's name, Gabbie wrote the following on the blackboard:

The faster we travel, the less we age.
or
The faster state of motion places us in a slower state of aging.

"Thus, our motion or speed is in direct correlation with how fast we get old. The less we are in motion the faster we age. The faster we are in motion the less we age. That is the theory here.

"Now separating oneself from the motion of our current state, our present dimension, as I like to say. We may be able to place oneself at a rate of motion where we do not age. Or at least slow aging down considerably."

Gabbie started pounding the blackboard with her chalk again.

Type of Motion + Speed of Motion = Rate of Aging

"Our research here is to give a numeric value to each type of motion. We will work backwards with the belief that the following values are correct." Gabbie added the following directly under what she just wrote on the board:

Speed of Light (value=0) + 186,000 (value=0) = zero aging

"These are the obvious values when traveling through space at the speed of light. Therefore, we shall say, the faster your rate of motion, the less you age. Why? Because if you go the speed of light, time stops! You cannot go faster than the speed of light, Einstein said. Therefore, if time stops, then time does not exist. Alpha Centauri is our closest star system, so if a person were to travel at the speed of light, she would be there instantly. No time would have passed for the traveler, while four and one half years would have gone by for us here on earth. Those of us at a different rate of motion."

Addie raised her hand and waited for Gabbie to acknowledge her. "As far as space travelers moving at the speed of light with no time passing for them and arriving instantly at their destination, doesn't that mean it's completely unnecessary to place astronauts into frozen animation for long trips?"

"That's correct. Being on a ship traveling to Alpha Centauri at the speed of light does not give you four and one half years to do things while you don't age. You are there instantly and continue to age from then on."

"So what you are suggesting is that time is something man made up to measure the coming and passing of things here on earth."

"Very interesting Addie, yes, I never thought of wording this premise that way."

"One more question," Addie said. "If the space travelers were moving at the speed of light and arrived instantly at their destination, would the distance traveled through space even exist?"

"Oh you are getting ahead of me and I am not even going to go there. That is the other half of this topic of Time and Space. We are just working on Time. NASA is conducting research on the Zero-Point Field in order to develop a space drive to get us across the galaxy. If you have not read a summary about this topic, then that is your homework for this week. You can find the topic on the web."

Addie took notes as Gabbie spoke. From the corner of her eye, Addie noticed an image in the door's small window. By the time Addie looked at the door, Charlotte's choleric face disappeared.

"Now back to our task at hand," Gabbie continued. "We have adopted two male lab mice to live with us at our facility. They were born just a minute or two apart. The older mouse we named Spring and the younger one is named Autumn. The older mouse will have modified MRI machines over his sleeping, eating, and play areas. Thus, the older mouse will have its molecular structure in a different state of motion all the time. End result, the study will show if the older mouse aged slower and became the younger mouse. Our objective during the study is to determine if molecular motion created by a MRI is valid to fit into the *type of motion*," Gabbie pointed to those words in the formula on the blackboard. “And if so, what value do we give this. Now, you’ll be recording data during the time you observe the two mice. Here is a printout of what we are looking for and blank data sheets that you’ll use to record information.”

Addie took a binder from Gabbie that had two hundred plus pages. After one look at the binder’s size, Addie spoke with apprehension, “Are we going to review this binder now?”

“We have to do everything now,” Gabbie stated with some authority and cited the reasoning for her answer. “I leave at six tonight for Plum Island. I will be consulting with scientists there for the week on various topics. I will be back Friday night around eight, so I will see you on Saturday when you come in to work at three. You did say you will be able to work Saturdays?”

* * * * *

At the end of the workday for Addie, she found herself trying to start her golf cart inside the parking garage with little success. Only a click sounded each time she turned the key. As Addie sat there thinking of what to do, she saw Charlotte exit the elevator and walk over to her car, an old Oldsmobile Delta 88. A stifled snickering sound seemed to echo through the garage just before she closed her car door.

About fifteen minutes later, a security guard rubbing dirt off his hand came along side Addie, who sat in her golf cart.

“Try starting up now, Miss Erickson,” spoke the security guard. The motor started on the point of Addie turning the key. “There you go. Good as new Miss Erickson.”

“Thank you so very much, Tommy. Was the cable loose like you thought?”

“More like disconnected, if you ask me,” the guard said with a quizzical look. “I doubt this, but since today is April Fools, I’m going to have the surveillance tapes of the garage checked. If somebody did this to play a joke on you, we’ll know who did this soon enough.”

“I do appreciate your help. Where did you learn how motors work and everything?”

"Before my father came to the United States he worked for a British car manufacturer in Hong Kong. When I was born here, the first thing my father handed me was a spark plug wrench. I was working on cars before getting out of diapers."

Addie finally cracked a smiled. The situation had caused her concern, especially when she suspected Charlotte. A second or two later a crackle of static came over Tommy's radio.

"Front gate to mobile. I have Miss Erickson's father here to pick her up."

"Roger that, she's on her way. A good night Miss Erickson."

"Thank you." With that, Addie drove toward the exit of the garage.

A few minutes later Stewart and his daughter pulled out from the entrance of the lab in their minivan. Addie sat in the passenger seat discontented and this very noticeable feature about her broadcasted loud and clear to her father.

"So did you have a good day at school and work?" asked Stewart.

Halfway up the hill, a black SUV pulled out from the side of Route 5A. The vehicle rapidly increased its speed to close the distance between the cars.

"Dad, both were awful."

"Why, what happened?" Stewart asked with a concerned look at his daughter, followed by a routine check of the rearview mirror that showed the vehicle about twenty yards back. All the windows of the SUV were shaded and no license plate hung in the front. Unfortunately, Stewart concerned with his daughter, had not noticed these details.

"With today being a Monday and April Fool's Day, it was a no win situation."

"You know, I didn't even realize today was April Fools' Day. We've been swamped at work and I... I'm sorry go ahead, I interrupted."

"No, not much more."

Stewart curved to the right, as Route 5A became Main Street. After winter ended, Main Street did pick up some more color. The town installed American flags on ten feet high aluminum poles along the edge of the sidewalk. Old Glory flew on both sides of the street approximately every thirty feet. Additionally, American flags flown one way or another at each gift shop, and restaurant. The public parking lot on the south side of Main Street also acquired a new entrance sign in red, white and blue colors.

"What happened Addie?" Stewart sincerely wanted to know of his daughter as he saw the same black SUV behind him, but did not give that a second thought.

"Just the same jealous, ill educated people playing jokes on everyone at school. Work did have an exciting element though," Addie continued.

The shaded passenger side window of the black SUV behind them steadily opened all the way. The remains of a pear's core flew out the SUV's window, striking one of the American flags that gently moved with the breeze on its new pole by the parking lot entrance. Temporary protuberance occurred in the midsection of the flag until the pear's core fell to the curb below and down into the obscure dirty depths of a sewer. The dark SUV window slowly went back up.

"And what was that?" Stewart urged of his daughter.

"I was assigned to be on the monitoring staff of a new project called the Double MRI study. Doctor Barkly will be directing the program to see if motion or speed is in direct correlation with how fast we age." Addie's excitement about the assignment started to return and all the ado about this, faded away in her voice.

"Ookay," Stewart said as he continued to listen, but had no idea what double M and RI meant.

"To be assigned to this I had to promise that I could work to six o'clock each weekday, instead of just five. Also I have to work three to six on Saturdays."

"Sweetie, Saturday isn't a problem, but by six I'm already home, we're just finishing dinner and errands start. Like food shopping, driving your brother to the Dojo for a lesson, doing laundry, or visiting your grandmother. Also what about your homework and studies?"

"I have my studies under control, really. As for working to six, I was thinking I'd ask Chris to pick me up and save you or mom the trip."

"Only if this is okay with your mother, Chris and his parents."

"It is!"

"How do you know?" Stewart saw Addie's big beautiful smile and realized, "You called them already."

The minivan turned onto their street and so did those followitng them. Pulling into their driveway Stewart did not see the SUV behind him or when passing by his house. Nevertheless, they definitely acquired a tail. Behind the shaded windows of the SUV, a gloved hand recorded their house address in a small book with a pencil.

* * * * *

Upon arrival at school Wednesday morning, Addie and her friends were getting off their school bus only to see several police cars up on the sidewalk in front of the main doors.

"Looks like Hump day is going to be a big bump day for somebody," Jake said regarding the police cars.

"I guess so. See you later, Jake," Addie responded.

"What do you think happened?" Jannelle asked of Addie as they came off the bus.

"I have no idea, Jannelle. There's Chris, maybe he knows." The two young women walked toward Chris who met them halfway toward the front doors of the school.

"Hi Addie, hi Jannelle." Chris and Addie kissed before holding hands. "What's going on here?" Chris inquired.

"We were just about to ask you the same thing," Jannelle expressed.

About ten minutes later in Addie's Homeroom class everyone gathered their books, finished homework or spoke with friends sitting next to them. The bell sounded over the Public Address speakers and morning announcements began.

"Good morning," a woman's voice came over the public address speaker. "Before we begin with announcements, would Addie Erickson report to the Front Office immediately."

The entire Homeroom erupted with very audible 'Oooohs' and comments started as a surprised Addie gathered her books.

"What did you do Addie?"

"I bet that's why the cops are here!"

"She's off to the slammer I tell ya!"

"All right, settle down!" the elderly Homeroom instructor shouted as she slapped her hands together. "Be quiet and listen to the rest of the morning announcements. Addie you best be on your way. I am sure that you do not have anything to do with the police visit."

Addie grabbed her backpack and headed for the door without saying a word. Upon entering the Front Office, Addie broke into a cold sweat, for she knew instantly that she was the reason behind all the commotion. Principal Browne, two policemen, and one policewoman were around the desks behind the front counter. Two other men in suits were sitting at the desk with the computer while dusting for fingerprints. Most of the file cabinet drawers were open. Papers, folders, and glass were all over the floor. The center window behind everyone had been completely smashed open and showed obvious evidence of previous dusting for fingerprints. School maintenance personnel were cleaning up the glass and cutting wood to secure the window temporarily.

"Oh, here she is now," one of the three secretaries in the room announced once the noise of the circular saw had paused. Everyone gaped at Addie.

"Addie," Principal Browne repeated. "Thank you for coming down. Let's go into my office where we can talk."

One of the detectives and the police woman followed Addie into her Principal's office. As Addie glanced back over her shoulder at the two law enforcers following her, Kathryn Browne sat behind her desk.

"Addie please have a seat," Kathryn said as she gestured toward one of the two uncomfortable cafeteria-style seats in front of her desk.

The policewoman sat in the second seat, while the detective closed the office door suppressing the noise of the circular saw. He remained standing behind Addie and the police officer. Addie became very concerned and her eyes dotted everyone's face several times while she waited for the reasons behind all this.

"Addie as you can see, somebody broke into our office around four this morning. This is Detective Rodriguez and Officer Rampey." Rodriguez acknowledged Addie with a nod and Rampey smiled. "We called you down to see if you can help with the investigation."

"Me?" a puzzled Addie quietly impressed. "I can't image how I could help."

"We just have a few questions," a thin voice came from behind. Addie turned to look at the detective standing with a notepad in his hand. His unshaven face and loosely hanging tie around his neck, didn't shine professionalism.

Seeing the amount of torment on Addie's face, the woman police officer contributed to the conversation. "Perhaps your answers may shed some light on the clues. This won't take long, I promise. You see, we woke Detective Rodriguez up this morning and he hasn't had breakfast yet." Officer Rampey wanted to maintain a sense of calm for Addie.

"Addie, there isn't anything here to implicate you with committing this crime," Kathryn Browne reassured.

"Okay, but there is something implicating my involvement, otherwise you would not have called me down."

"Smart kid," Detective Rodriguez stated, and without a pause he began the line of questioning. "A silent alarm was triggered at ten after four this morning. Donna Rampey here was the first officer on the scene. At four seventeen, she proceeded through the south entrance toward the front of the school. Halfway across the parking lot she observed a black SUV racing out the north entrance gate. Do you know anyone who owns a black SUV?"

"You're kidding right? That has to be the most popular color of the most popular car on the road today. My cousin has one, a few seniors have one, and my neighbor has one."

"I think it was a Mercedes SUV," Officer Rampey added. "However, I cannot be sure. Half the parking lot lighting was not on at the time."

Addie slowly shook her head, "I'm pretty sure everybody I know with a black SUV doesn't have a Mercedes."

With a long exhale, Detective Rodriguez went over and dropped his card on Principal Browne's desk. "We'll need that list of everyone who is attending school and who works here. Please call me at this number when you've compiled the names and addresses. I'm sorry to give you the extra work, but we'll have to run a check on everyone with the DMV to see who owns a black SUV. Mercedes or no Mercedes." Detective Rodriguez turned back to face Addie and asked, "Miss Erickson, do you know any student who might have a reason to break into the school's office and files?"

"No, not one person," she answered without any hesitation.

"Do you know anyone who has something against you and who'd want to get detailed information about you?"

"What do you mean? Now you're scaring me." Addie's appearance had dismay written all over her face.

"That's just a possibility we have to look into," said the detective. "No cause for alarm."

Detective Rodriguez began to stroll toward the office door with his hands behind his back. Upon reaching the door he turned around, flipped open his notebook, read briefly and looked up at Addie for an answer.

"No, no I don't have enemies that would go to this extreme," Addie finally answered.

"But, you do have enemies?" the detective snapped back to clarify.

"Just one scientist at the lab where I work. She's jealous that I received an assignment over her. No way she would do this, really."

“ ‘Really,’ you say. Are you asking me if she would do this or are you just trying to convince yourself that she wouldn’t do this?” asked the detective trying to clarify again.

“I guess to convince myself that she wouldn’t,” a reserved Addie spoke slowly.

“I’ll need her name.”

“But, why? What makes you think this break in is about me?”

“Our investigation saw that the copy machine was the only office equipment on and under the cover was the last page to Addie Erickson’s file. We first checked to see if anyone in the office was working with your file at the end of the previous day and forgot the paper under the cover. That wasn’t the case. Additionally, Principal Browne has informed me that even if somebody left the copy machine on, a timer would shut it off at ten in the evening. Somebody pulled the plug out of the timer and plugged the machine back into the outlet to make copies. In their rush to leave, they forgot to put the last page of your file back into your folder, because everything else was in your folder nice and neat. Although, despite your folder being on the floor with other folders, each having at least one or two pages tossed about. Your folder wasn’t tossed, it was placed.”

Addie slowly dragged her left hand down the side of her face. The buzzer ending Homeroom went off as a muffled sound from the outer office. The words the detective spoke were concerning, very concerning. “Her name is Binsnou, Charlotte Binsnou. I am not sure on the spelling of her last name. I believe it ends with a U.”

Addie came out into the hallway filled with students and Christopher stood there waiting for her by the door. “I heard your name called to the office, first thing over the PA. Everything okay?”

“I don’t know Chris, I’ll tell you on the way to class.” She swung her backpack over her shoulder and took Chris’ arm as they walked down the hall.

Shortly after six that evening Addie parked her golf cart at the lab’s front gate. Chris had already parked on the other side of the gate with his Mazda’s top down.

"Good night, Tommy!" Addie called out as she hurried by the security booth and handed in her ID pass.

"A good evening to you, Miss Erickson." Replied the security guard.

Addie tossed her backpack behind the two seats and hopped into Chris' car. Happy and relieved that the long day finally ended, she had a big smile for her boyfriend.

"Cool. Top down drive," Addie said as she threw her lab coat to the back and let her hair down.

"Yeah, it's a beautiful evening for sure. Seat belt on?"

"Yeah...you know I've been thinking of you all afternoon. That was really sweet of you to meet me outside Principal Browne's office this morning." Addie leaned over and gave Chris a kiss on his right cheek.

Chris smiled and looked toward Addie a few times while driving with the wind in their hair. "Do you feel up to going to class at the Dojo tonight?"

"Yeah, of course. Pick me up at fifteen to eight."

"No problem. And speaking of problems, did you see Charlotte at work today?"

"No not at all. I don't know where she was. The less I run into her the better."

"Hey, I'll buy you an ice cream in town here. What do you say?"

Addie pushed her hair back, "No thanks Chris, I'm going to eat dinner once you drop me off at home."

Chris pulled into Addie's driveway as she reached back for her belongings. She took the seat belt off and placed her stuff on her lap. With a smile she leaned toward Chris and they met in the middle for a prolong kiss. Thus, even with the top down, neither of them noticed a black SUV slowly go by on the street.

"Oh my God!" Addie said while inhaling, sitting back, and suddenly opening her eyes. "I completely didn't realize the top was down and everyone can see us."

"That's okay, I'll take full responsibility," Chris mentioned, as he admired the way Addie looked in the setting sunlight.

"What are you looking at?" Addie asked with a smile.

"The most beautiful girl I ever saw."

Addie quickly leaned over and kissed Chris again. She turned with her stuff and stepped out of the car. "I will see you later Mister Christopher Wilkins."

"Yes, you will. Bye." Chris put his right arm across the top of the passenger's seat and began to back out of the driveway. After seeing Addie go in the front door, he pulled out to drive home.

Chris went the opposite way the previously unseen SUV went just a minute ago. However, once Chris turned the corner the SUV went by Addie's house again and sped up to follow a temporarily unsuspecting Chris.

Chris happened to be looking in his rearview mirror to see the black SUV turn out from Addie's block. Immediately he correlated Addie's Street with what she told him in the morning about the black SUV seen by Officer Rampey. Chris recognized the front of the car behind him and knew a Mercedes when he saw one. All this caused Chris to develop high anxiety.

"Shit. This is freaking me out," Chris said under his breath.

First reaction for Chris had him speed up; then he took hold of his senses and maintained his speed. "Don't jump to conclusions," Chris mumbled to himself. "Let's see if they follow me all the way back to the lab."

Down through Main Street and along the water of the harbor, the SUV followed Chris at a safe distance. Before passing the gravel entrance to the parcel selling used RV units and Trailers, Chris saw the SUV in his mirrors. Before turning right at the light onto Route 5A that ran along the end of the harbor, Chris checked his mirrors and the SUV had disappeared.

That night around ten minutes to ten, Chris and Addie were leaving the mall's Dojo with some classmates. They each carried their own duffel bag that held their uniforms and sparring equipment. A husband and wife in their early fifties were with Chris, Addie, and another young man in his twenties.

Stopping to talk at the edge of the sidewalk, a warm evening breeze blew through their wet hair. Chris had obviously been sweating the most and perspired still.

"Sensei didn't let up on you for a moment tonight," the older gentleman said.

"Tell me about it. I'm exhausted," Chris claimed as he swung his duffel bag over his right shoulder.

"Sensei is coming down hard on you so that you'll be ready for your Black Belt Second Degree test next month," concluded Addie.

"I'll say this, I'm not looking forward to my Black Belt test in August." The other young classmate declared.

"All right, everyone have a good night," the older gentleman's wife said. "Jeff do you have a ride home?"

"Oh no, I told my folks I'll walk home since it's a warm night," Jeff, the other classmate, said.

"We'll give you a ride."

"Yeah, come on Jeff. We're parked over on the right," the husband said.

"Okay, thanks. See ya Chris, Addie."

"Goodnight," Addie replied as she went to the left with Chris.

Cars sparsely filled the parking lot, stores in the mall closed a half hour ago at half past nine. Chris and Addie's friends were parked two rows over to the right and five spaces down. They arrived at their car first and the wife opened the hatch before going around to the driver's side. As she started the green SUV, her husband put all the duffel bags in the back with Jeff.

Meanwhile, Chris opened his trunk and tossed his black duffel bag in. Wheels of a car screeching sounded in the background. Addie handed Chris her white duffel bag as the sound of a roaring engine came to a skidding stop behind them. Addie turned, Chris swung around with the duffel bag still in hand, doors of a black SUV flew open, Jeff and the woman's husband looked over and watched in shock as two men in ski masks jumped out.

Immediately a backhand punch from one of the assailants hit the left side of Chris' face. Addie watched in horror as Chris fell to one knee. The other aggressor then tore Addie's duffel bag from Chris' hand.

The husband's wife, who sat in her SUV with the engine running, screamed, "Go help them!"

"Key-ah!" Addie yelled as she sent a kick to the now fleeing masked man with her duffel bag. The ball of her foot hit the man's hand causing the bag to go flying a few feet past Chris.

Jeff and the husband were now running between cars to get two rows over. The wife drove around to the scene with the hatch door still open.

Chris now back on his feet, saw the guy who punched him turned back to get the duffel bag. Chris wasted no time in grabbing the back of the man's head as he went by and pushed the assailant's head downward so the man's nose could be introduced to Chris' rising right knee. As the attacker reeled back with blood already oozing through the ski mask, Addie blocked a backhand punch from the other attacker.

The wife pulled out her cell phone as she drove down her parking lane to go around the parked cars and dialed 911. "We need police assistance immediately!"

A car blocked the woman's husband and Jeff when the driver stopped to watch the fight. Annoyed by the fact of being blocked just one parking aisle away, the two men continued running right over the hood of the car. The bellowing sound of the hood buckling under two pairs of feet scared some bodily fluids out of the two women in the stopped car.

Addie now blocked another backhand punch as Chris slammed his attacker into the black SUV with a two handed push. He immediately turned and threw a strong chokehold on the guy fighting with Addie.

The horn sounded from the SUV and the guy with the broken nose struggled back into the vehicle. Addie laid a kick right into the groin of the guy Chris had in a chokehold. Chris let him loose as he doubled over in pain. Jeff then flew over the roof of the last parked car in his way and fell behind Addie pushing her into Chris' arms. The husband came running between the cars and yelled a lie, "Here comes mall security!" Next he added, "Don't let them get away!"

Unfortunately, the guy with the bloody nose already grabbed his partner in crime by the collar and hauled him back into the SUV as Chris helped Jeff to his feet. The car started to peel out with doors still open.

"Get the plate number!" Addie yelled.

"The numbers are covered!" Chris shouted as he saw black electric tape over the departing license plate.

"Oh my God, that's my wife coming around! They're going to crash!" The doors on the fleeing SUV slammed shut and both vehicles swerved just enough to miss a head-on crash. As the black SUV accelerated out of the mall parking lot, the husband went running toward his wife who had stopped just inches from a parked car.

"Shit, first time I ever used this stuff in real life," a shaking Chris realized.

"You guys were great," Jeff declared. "I'm going to flag down mall security. I'll be right back."

"You okay, Addie?"

Addie put her arms around Chris. "I am now, I am now." Both of them were staring at her white duffel bag laying on the parking lot blacktop.

Fifteen minutes later the lights of two mall security cars and two police cars were still blinking when an unmarked car pulled up. Detective

Rodriguez stepped out and went over to talk with the police officers. Everyone still stood around talking when one of the security cars from the mall drove away and Detective Rodriguez walked up to Addie.

"Twice in one day, Miss Erickson. Please let's not make this a habit."

"No sir, I don't want to," Addie said as she still had one arm around Chris' waist.

"So we definitely have a black Mercedes SUV this time and blocked out license plates. I know that this was not the work of an irate coworker at the lab because I interviewed Miss Binsnou this evening just ten minutes before all this started to happen. I also seriously doubt she has the money to hire three people just to steal your duffel bag. Why are masked men after you Miss Erickson?"

"I don't know, believe me I don't know what all this could mean."

"Along with your gym equipment, did you have anything else in your bag?"

"Just my pocketbook. If they wanted to steal money then..."

"They were not after your money, Miss Erickson. They are after your identification. At least that's what the school break-in was about."

"There's something else that happened this afternoon to me," Chris injected. "I wrote it off as a coincidence, but now I know different."
"What happened son?" Detective Rodriguez asked as he scratched his chin.

"I'd picked Addie up at work today and after I left her house I saw a black Mercedes SUV turn out from Addie's neighborhood. It followed me through town as I headed back toward the lab where Addie works. But, just before getting to the lab it turned off somewhere. So I wrote it off."

"What street did the SUV turn on, son?"

"I don't know, it kind of disappeared."

"Let me have your name."

"Christopher Wilkins."

"Chris why didn't you tell me about this?" Addie asked as the detective wrote Chris' name in his notepad.

"I didn't want to worry you any more than you already were. And as I said, I saw this as a coincidence. Sorry, I didn't know."

"All right, I think this is going to lead me to the lab you work at. Not that Charlotte Binsnou has anything to do with this. This may be associated to your work at the lab. Perhaps you have keys to storage space of some expensive equipment."

"No, I really don't have any keys," Addie set out to prove.

"Well, I won't know what all this is about until I talk to someone. Who should I speak with over there?"

"Oh brother," Chris muttered.

"The director of the lab is Gabrielle Ma..." Addie paused in thought for a second or two, but the pause was not to remember her last name. The delay happened so she could think about which last name. "Mannuso, but she may also go by Maida. That might be her maiden name. I really don't know."

"All right, good enough, thank you for your help. The two of you should get home. And put some ice on that face kid."

Addie finally tossed her duffel bag into Chris' trunk. "God am I going to hear a crap load at work tomorrow from Miss Psycho Charlotte."

"What about your Director? She's going to drill you on this," Chris added as he closed the trunk of his car.

"At least she's out of town until the end of the week. I won't see her until Saturday afternoon. I hope that by then all this is solved. Now to face my parents, they are going to freak out more than us."

The next day Chris drove Addie to work from school. With everything going on, he needed to make sure she stayed safe. His car's top couldn't be down today because rain started falling intermittently and the temperature had cooled down a bit. The side of Chris' face remained swollen from the confrontation at the mall.

"Thanks for the ride, Chris," Addie gratefully acknowledged. They kissed before she stepped out of the car with her lab coat folded in her arms.

"Listen," Chris requested. "If you run into you know who, don't take any crap from her."

"I won't. See you around six. Bye."

Half past four Addie took a break in the kitchen and dinette area on the right of the lab's lobby. Addie sat alone in the empty room and she hoped to prevent Charlotte from finding her. Tired from not sleeping well last night, Addie closed her eyes to take the edge off. Just thirty seconds after doing so, Charlotte banged her way into the room. Her lab coat flew open, emphasizing her pear-shaped body. She walked straight toward Addie.

"Oh God, here we go," Addie told herself as she stood up. "Good afternoon Charlotte. You look cheerful today."

"Oh, yes I am. At first when that cop showed up at my mother's front door last night I was ready to ream you." Charlotte started to walk in a circle around Addie. Once behind Addie, Charlotte pushed the chair Addie sat in out of the way to continue walking.

"Your mother's house?"

"Yes, my mother's house. I live with my mother. Do you have a problem with that?" Charlotte bellowed as she continued to walk another circle around Addie.

"No, not at all. I live with my mother too," Addie expressed with a sympathetic face and a sincerely understanding voice.

Charlotte stopped walking in a circle, only to start again after changing direction. "I calmed down after I heard the whole story about your school's break-in and you as the possible reason. Oh happy day. You thought I did this to get you. How rich! Well, I don't own a black SUV, nor did I break into your school. You white trash. I can get all the dirt I want on you, right here at the lab."

"How convenient," a stern Addie replied.

"Yes, it is, isn't it? Don't worry Addie, I'll help you turn in your lab coat and ID after you get canned. And the best part about this, I may not have to do a thing." Charlotte now began to walk toward the door. With her back facing Addie she concluded, "You'll get yourself fired! Oh how rich is that!"

Addie sat back down after Charlotte left. Slowly she shook her head as she removed a small tape recorder from her lab coat pocket. Addie pressed the rewind button and after a whirl of sound stopped, she pushed play.

"...Afternoon Charlotte. You look cheerful today."

"Oh yes I am. At first when that cop showed up at my mother's front door last night I was ready to ream you."

Addie clicked the tape off and went back to work.

Time slipped by and before Addie realized, the evening's time of six twenty surprised her. Upon leaving, she first called the lab's security booth with the land line telephone just inside the door of the lobby's kitchen and dinette area. After several rings security picked up.

"Security, Tommy speaking. How may I help you?"

"Hi Tommy, this is Addie. I'm running late, is my boyfriend Chris waiting for me?"

"Yes, he is right here with me."

"Please tell him that I'll be right there."

"No problem, Miss Erickson. This is going to be a late night for everyone."

"Thanks, bye." Addie hung up and developed a confused gaze on her face. Why did Tommy say that this would be a late night for everyone?

Instantaneously upon exiting the parking garage, Addie saw the blinking lights of patrol cars in the distance. They were next to the security booth by the entrance gate.

"Oh my God, now what happened?" Addie said as she pushed the power pedal of the golf cart all the way down.

As she came closer to the front gate, Addie saw police cars, security, a rescue fire truck, and ambulance at the entrance on Route 5A. She became seriously concerned and frantically looked for Chris. Several men were walking into the security booth one at a time. She then saw Chris' car parked on the inside of the gate. That definitely went against SOP, Standard Operating Procedures. Once she pulled into her golf cart's parking space by the security booth, Chris and Tommy came out. The night air stood still and a cold drizzle began. Wipers on the fire truck and ambulance started going back and forth. The darkening overcast triggered the Low Pressure Sodium streetlights to come on in the early dusk. Their amber color light made everything vibrantly visible, yet distorted the true color of all objects below.

Tommy wore the standard navy blue security uniform and for the first time, Addie saw a security officer wearing a hat. The navy blue baseball cap had some lame lightning bolt icon on the front. Chris who wore a leather jacket saw that Addie's lab coat could not keep her warm.

"Addie, where is your jacket?" Chris asked as he placed his arm around Addie's shoulder and rubbed his hand up and down her arm in hopes to warm her up.

"I left it in your car this afternoon with my backpack," Addie answered and folded her arms across her chest. "Tommy what happened here?"

"You're cold, let's go inside the security booth," Tommy suggested.

"I'll get your jacket from the car," Chris stated.

Tommy led the way and once inside they could hear voices of several people at the bottom of the stairs that went below ground.

"Who and what is down there?" Addie asked.

"Some detectives, our security personnel, and Doctor Barkly. The rooms are everything from equipment storage to living quarters. They are going into the briefing room down there."

Sure enough, right after Tommy said that, the voices below subsided and a door closed. The wind picked up and the drizzle turned into a downpour. Chris ran into the booth with Addie's jacket and put the small garment over her lab coat. Tommy pushed a button and a sliding glass door automatically slid closed, protecting them from the elements outside. Addie looked back down the empty staircase before searching for a place to sit.

"I'm sorry Miss Erickson, no chairs up here. Nobody may sit when operating the booth. I can offer you a cup of hot coffee. Would you like one?"

"Yes, please...just some milk, no sugar," Addie requested as she folded her arms across her chest again.

"Would you like one?" Tommy asked of Chris while pouring a cup for Addie.

"No, thank you," Chris replied.

"Miss Erickson did you know Sal?" Tommy asked as he handed her the cup of hot coffee.

"Thank you Tommy. No, I don't think so. What project was he working on?"

"Sal Kayaian wasn't a scientist here. He managed maintenance's graveyard shift."

"You are using past tense Tommy. What happened?"

"We are not one hundred percent sure, but we believe he was hit by a car walking home this morning."

"Oh my God," a stunned Addie responded.

"He has been with us since he came to this country in nineteen-seventy eight. A year or two later Doctor Maida helped him get U.S. citizenship. She is going to be..."

Addie stopped drinking her coffee and stopped Tommy from talking. "Wait, wait. When you say Doctor Maida, do you mean Doctor Mannuso the Director of this lab?"

"Aah, I'm not sure that I am following you Miss Erickson, but Doctor Mannuso has never been, nor is he now the Director of this lab."

"He? Wait, no... Doctor Mannuso is a she. I mean Gabbie, who hired me. She is the Director of the lab. Yes, Gabbie is married to Doctor Mannuso, but I don't mean him, I mean her."

"I think we need a score card for that," Chris chuckled.

"Chris please," Addie begged as she became earnestly upset about this.

"I think you pre-concluded the wrong last name for the lab's director," Tommy deduced in hopes to unscramble this question. "Yes, Doctor Maida is married to Doctor Mannuso, but she never took his name. She kept the name of her first husband."

"That seems to explain it Addie," Chris said in hopes that she would settle on that being an adequate answer.

"No, no there is something about this and I can't put my finger on it."

"Why is this so important to you Addie?"

"Because... Chris you don't understand." Addie paused to think. "Because there is something very familiar about the name Maida."

Just then, they heard a pair of footsteps coming up the stairs. They belonged to Detective Rodriguez. He stopped at the top step and looked seriously at Addie and Chris as he exhaled a deep amount of air.

"Do me a favor Miss Erickson. You and your boyfriend, please be careful. Watch over your shoulders until we solve this case. I don't want to see you kids get hurt. I can't do anything else. This case is now in the hands of the FBI. They'll want to interview you here at work tomorrow. So, please be careful until then. Come on, I'll follow both of you safely home."

THE INTERROGATIONS, Chapter Nine

Silence arranged itself inside the silver minivan so acutely that this became the very first time Stewart felt uncomfortable with his daughter. Had he lost control? On the other hand, did he start to realize that a parent never really has any complete authority over all the things involving their children? Addie had become a grown woman, working, ready to graduate with honors. Regardless, he could not help worrying about the fact that the FBI needed to interview his daughter about a possible hit and run crime. Picking Addie up at school and driving her to the lab, seemed to be the only way Stewart could help his daughter at this time, nevertheless the discomfiting silence lingered.

After turning onto Route 5A and slowly driving down toward the entrance of the lab, Addie broke the absolute quiet.

"Dad...thanks for coming with me. I'm pretty nervous about all this."

"I wouldn't be anywhere else in the world right now. And for what it's worth, I'm nervous too."

Charlie stood on duty when they pulled up to the entrance of the lab. He immediately stepped out of the booth and held up his right hand singling them to stop.

"Afternoon Miss Erickson, Mister Erickson," welcomed Charlie's by-the-book voice as he looked in the driver's side window.

"Hi Charlie," Addie answered. "My dad is going to come in with me for the FBI interview. Could you please get him clearance?"

"Actually, that will work out fine Miss Erickson. And Sir, would you please park your minivan over there. I will then need the two of you to exit the vehicle and wait here with me. I just gave the signal for an unmarked car to leave the underground garage and to pick the two of you up. Two agents will be in the car and they will drive you to the FBI's satellite office about fifteen miles from here. A second car will join you en route, just as a precautionary step to make sure no black SUV is following you. At the end of the interview they will return you both here for your car."

"Okay Charlie, I thank you," Stewart said as he continued to mull over all the directions he just heard and gradually drove over to park the car.

As the three of them waited for the approaching car, nobody spoke a word. A green Crown Victoria pulled up with two men inside wearing suits. Both of the Ericksons went to sit in the back seat. Charlie held the door on Addie's side and in doing so, he broke one of the rules at the lab.

"Don't be nervous, Addie, they are here to help," he whispered in her ear.

Addie smiled and whispered back, "That's much better than Miss Erickson. Thanks."

Charlie closed the door for her and stepped back so the car could leave.

"Good afternoon," the driver said without turning around.

The man in the front passenger seat did turn around to make eye contact. "Hello Miss Erickson and Mister Erickson, I presume?"

"Yes, that is correct," Stewart confirmed as he adjusted his tie.

"All right, we will be at the office in twenty minutes or so. Please relax." With that, the agent in the front passenger seat brought his attention back to his notepad.

Addie reached across the car's seat and took her father's hand. Squeezing his daughter's hand gently, Stewart smiled at her without parting his lips.

Almost five minutes into the trip they heard a voice over a radio.

"This is backup. Divert off main road onto side streets and then back on. Wish to confirm a possible tail."

The driver immediately looked in his rearview mirror and picked up a handheld radio. "I see a black vehicle, confirm?"

"Affirmative. Please divert to confirm," a now static-filled voice squawked over the radio.

The agent in the passenger seat looked out the rear window before he addressed the Ericksons. "Do not turn to look out the window. Just slowly slouch down a little and stay that way until we know for sure if we are being followed."

The driver left the main road and went down a side street past an auto repair shop and a carwash. "He is following, we are doing the same," continued the voice over the radio.

Stewart held Addie's hand just a little tighter. The car made two more turns and went back onto the main road with increasing speed. "He is increasing speed also," came the blaring voice over the radio. "You have a tail and we're going to pull him over."

The driver picked up the radio again. "We copy, we'll continue to office."

"Okay, you guys can sit up again," the agent who wasn't driving said.

"What was that all about?" Stewart inquired.

"I'm sure we'll hear soon enough since they pulled him over."

"Was it a black SUV?" Addie wanted to know.

"No SUV, but I saw a black car."

A few minutes later the radio announced, "This is backup. We have a young male driving a nineteen eighty-eight black Mazda convertible who is frantically telling us that Miss Erickson can vouch for him. Can you confirm?"

Addie had both hands over her mouth and her dad just rolled his eyes before asking, "Is his name Christopher Wilkins?"

The driver picked up the radio and asked just that. "Can you give us an ID on the male?"

"Affirmative. A white male, eighteen years of age, his name is Christopher Wilkins."

"Roger. Stand by," said the driver who turned slightly to see the Ericksons. "Who is this Wilkins guy?"

"Oh dad, he wanted to come with me. I told him I would be fine with you going. What is he doing?"

"He's okay," Stewart said. "He's my daughter's boyfriend. He was just looking out for her. That's all."

The driver gave a twisted smile as he kept one eye on the road and one on Stewart in the mirror. Bringing his attention back to the front, he concluded this episode. "Backup, he is clean. Let the boyfriend go home."

Carefully noting the location when they pulled into a large parking lot, Addie also looked ahead at the entrance of a four floor rectangular glass building with both sides angling upward and out. The building resembled the shape of a giant barge out of water. However, that did not concern Addie; the taxi already in front of the entrance did. A woman wearing a raincoat stepped out with a briefcase and file folders under her arm. Painted on the side of the cab's door Addie read:

The Point's Taxi Company
631-555-TAXI

Addie sat back and whispered to her father, "Oh God this is serious, they called Gabbie back from Plum Island. She wasn't due back until eight o'clock tonight."

The driver pulled up behind the cab and turned toward the Ericksons. "Agent Epstein here will escort you both inside. Please follow him. I'll see you both again for the drive back."

When Addie and her dad stepped out of the car, they could hear

Gabbie repeating a question to the cab driver. “Why can’t you drop my suitcase off at the address I gave you? Just leave it with the security guard at the front booth. I will pay you extra for this.”

“Mr. Epstein,” said Addie. “That’s the director in charge of Cold Creek Harbor lab. If you are driving us back to the lab later, can’t you...”

“Enough said, I’ll get the suitcase,” Agent Epstein answered.

“Gabbie!” Addie called out. “We’ll take your suitcase in this car.”

“Oh Love,” Gabbie exclaimed with relief. “Are you all right?”

“Yeah, I’m fine Gabbie. Here let me take those folders. Agent Epstein will put your suitcase in the FBI car. It’ll be safe there until they drive us back to the lab.”

“Oh, thank you sir, the suitcase is in the back seat. Mr. Erickson, I am so happy to see you and I am so sorry about what has happened. The loss of Sal is a tragedy.”

“Let’s hope this afternoon will provide answers so that we can close this case. Here, let me take your briefcase for you,” Stewart suggested as he extended his hand forward.

“Oh thank you, but no. This has to stay with me.”

The trunk of the FBI car slammed shut after Agent Epstein placed Gabbie’s old wicker suitcase inside. After he stepped back onto the sidewalk to join the others, Epstein led the way to the doors of the building’s lobby.

Inside the lobby, a few people went about their business and Agent Epstein waited for an elevator that only they would occupy. After the elevator door closed, he inserted a round key in the control panel. The ride went down to the lower level, which had no identification on the elevator’s controls. Conversation did not occur and the ride went too slow. The doors opened and they stepped into a hall that had a double steel door at the end. Agent Epstein pressed several small numbered buttons on a two by four inch panel just above the doorknob before he opened one of the two doors for everyone else to enter.

"I shall wait out here," Epstein said and closed the door behind them.

All three of them stood inside a large single basement room that operated under the pretense of an office. Pipes ran along the ceiling, the cement walls were painted white, fluorescent shop-light fixtures were hung by chains from the empty squares of framework for ceiling tiles that weren't there. The back of the room stored a wall of unopened boxes. Several desks were set up on both sides. Metal folding chairs were all about. Some chairs had opened boxes on them, while others were substituting for file cabinets. A woman and a man were using two of the chairs at a portable folding table in the middle of the room. Both wore glasses and looked up from the files they were reading to acknowledge the arrival of their three visitors.

Gabbie looked squarely at Addie and after making eye contact, she slowly stated her name. "I am Doctor Mannuso," Gabbie spoke after obvious consideration.

Addie thought to herself about that answer being a direct contradiction to what the security guard, Tommy, told her last night.

"This is Addie Erickson and her father," Gabbie continued. "May we sit down?"

"Yes, of course, please sit down," The woman said as she cleared away some files on the table, stood up, and extended her hand. "I'm Susan Rigano and this is Richard Cooper. I'm sorry that we have to meet for reasons of an investigation and under these conditions."

Richard also stood and shook hands with everyone. The two agents were wearing business suits. They sat back down on one side of the rectangular folding table. The table's opposite side, by the door, had seats for their guests.

"Did you just move in?" Stewart asked after sitting down next to Addie.

"Yes..." An exacerbated Susan answered and added the rhetorical question, "You can tell?"

"Addie, please let me take my folders from you. I'll put them on top of my briefcase," insisted Gabbie.

Addie looked at the overstuffed and worn-out soft leather briefcase. "That's okay, they may slide off," said Addie. I'll put them on the table here."

"Oh no, I need those folders back at the lab. Please I may forget them or mix them up with some of the police folders...all about...here...and everywhere."

Addie noticed Gabbie's high level of tension. The disorganization of the room only added to Gabbie's stress. Then without warning, the second Gabbie removed her folders from the table, a drop of water fell from above hitting the spot where Addie placed the folders a second ago.

"Oh my!" Gabbie spouted as her reflexes sent her back in her seat to avoid the small splash of water expanding outward.

Richard had already reached under the table by his feet and pulled up a toy beach pail. He placed the pail on the table in plenty of time to catch the next two drops of water that came down in tandem.

"The dripping will stop with one or two more drops," Susan reassured.

"I trust that is not dripping from a bacteria-filled sewer pipe above?" Gabbie asked.

"No, not at all. Just some condensation building up," Richard trustfully expressed.

"Gabbie, why don't you take off your raincoat," Addie suggested after noticing that Gabbie started sweating.

"Yes... I will, thank you." Gabbie handed her briefcase and folders to Addie. She stood up, took off her coat, placed it over the back of her chair. She had her lab coat on with a turtleneck underneath. Sitting back down she took her belongings back from Addie, who now took off her denim jacket.

"All right, if everyone is comfortable now, let's get to this." Susan reopened the folder she held. "On January First of this year, three men were arrested on the property of your laboratory's facilities. All three are still in custody. Since then, the police have determined that these three men did not work with a Pawnshop Ring, nor were they trying to steal equipment for drug money. However they all have police records, thus it's only a matter of time before they're convicted. Due to various reasons, the FBI reviewed the case, and ascertained they were doing a job for hire. Interrogation of the three men disclosed that they were given instructions, ski masks, and payment by men in a black SUV."

"Oh my God," commented Addie.

"The same SUV used when my daughter was attacked this week?" an anxious Stewart demanded.

"We believe so," answered Richard. "Doctor, you received my fax briefing you on all the events that occurred this week?"

"Yes, I did."

"Let's review the facts so if there are any errors the Doctor can correct me," Susan proceeded in a rather rapid pace. "Mister Sal J. Kayaian was fifty-nine and worked over twenty years at the lab. He enjoyed working the graveyard shift and was the manager of Housekeeping for the lab. He lived at the end of Harbor View Road, house number one fifteen, which is located just about one mile away from the lab. He always walked to work in good weather and drives... I'm sorry." Susan paused for a second before continuing, "He drove to work, only when the weather was bad. Doctor is that pretty much correct about Mister Kayaian?"

"Yes," Gabbie said with a sad voice.

"On Wednesday evening of this week," Susan continued as she observed another water drop hit the bucket on the table. "Mister Kayaian walked to work since the evening was unseasonably warm. He left his house approximately eleven fifteen in the evening according to his wife. Upon arrival at work he reported an incident to security at eleven fifty." Susan picked up another piece of paper that obviously came from a fax machine. "This is the report security at your lab wrote up. Okay, here... 'Approximately thirty minutes after twenty-three hundred hours, Mister Kayaian was approach by a black Mercedes SUV. The vehicle stopped next to him as he was walking down the normally tranquil Harbor View Road toward Route 5A. The passenger side window went down only one-third of the way. The window was shaded and he could not see any details about the person talking to him. He knew additional people were in the car besides the driver because he heard them whispering in another language,' you have a question?"

"Yes, all this happened right after my daughter was attacked at the mall?"

"Most definitely," Susan said after looking over the top of her glasses. "And according to this copy of the police report, Addie and her friends were a great deal more fortunate than Mister Kayaian. To continue with the report from security, 'He was casually questioned on directions to the lab and then he was asked if he worked at the lab. Upon them asking him what his job was at the lab, he became suspicious. Next he received an offer of fifty-thousand dollars in cash to make a copy of anyone's ID at the lab. When he refused, they handed him the cash to prove they were serious. He refused a second time and pushed the money back into the partially opened window. As he walked away, the vehicle backed up to keep pace with him. They then made him another offer just to think about. Provide them with a copy of his ID and in return, they would set up a new life for him in another country. A bank account would also be set up for him and his family with a million U.S. dollars. The vehicle then made a U-turn and drove out to Route 5A. He was unable to obtain license plate numbers.'

"The next morning, security said that Mister Kayaian refused an escort home." Susan took her glasses off after all that reading.

"Walking home... He never made it," Richard added. "His body wasn't found until later that afternoon. An apparent hit and run car accident."

"Oh Sal..." Gabbie said softly.

"So they were trying to steal my daughter's ID to the lab."

"Yes, most definitely," Susan agreed.

"But, we never leave the lab's property with any lab identification or codes. I turn my credentials into security every time I leave," Addie explained.

"Nobody would be allowed to leave until they turned in their ID," Gabbie stated. "They receive their credentials back each time they return only after security clears them with an electronic handprint reader."

"Those lab security procedures are obviously not known by these men," Richard concluded.

"Has the FBI confirmed this apparent hit and run accident?" Stewart inquired.

"This was no hit and run accident, Mister Erickson. Sal Kayaian was murdered."

"Oh God," Addie said softly.

"I helped Sal become a citizen, find a house nearby the lab, went to his son's wedding," Gabbie rambled as she shook her head sluggishly. "I have to visit the family first thing in the morning and offer my condolences and help."

Stewart moved closer to the table. "May I ask how you know he was murdered?"

Susan put her glasses back on to check some papers. "His leg injuries were consistent with trauma from an automobile collision. Now I don't know if you're familiar with Harbor View Road, it overlooks the lab's property and the harbor."

Gabbie and Addie just looked at each other. Ultimately, Gabbie slowly shook her head yes, as she gave Addie a look with the corner of her eyes.

"His body was found off the road and down the slope in some trees up against a hurricane fence. Just before where the road becomes the leading edge to a bluff overlooking the harbor. At this section of the road there are no houses across the street, just large boulders and a sharp incline."

Susan again removed her glasses before talking. "The location of the body was not congruent with a hit and run. The calculations done several ways prove his body could not end up in that final position. The slight curve in the road and the angle all prove that.

"In addition, the forensic report determined the following points." Susan placed her glasses on to read again. "One, the blow to his head did not conform to the rock his head was resting on. Two, the little amount of blood on the rock or ground by the rock did not correspond with the head injury. Three, microscopic fragments of black paint were found in the head wound. Four, blood found on his wallet and house keys that were still in his pockets. Five, too much blood was found on the road for a body that was hit and thrown into the woods. Additional evidence was found, but inconclusive due to the rain affecting the results."

"The body was moved to this spot off the road," Richard presented. "The ugly picture we see is that Mr. Kayaian was approached on the way home by the same individuals who wanted to buy a copy of an ID off of him. After refusing again, he suffered a strike to the head by a narrow round pipe. Perhaps a tire iron, they are usually painted black."

"Oh my God," Addie said softly.

"As he was unconscious they drove over his legs with their vehicle," Richard continued.

"Oh my God," Addie repeated.

"Moving his body off the road caused blood to get on their hands that transferred onto his wallet and car keys when they went through his pockets looking for his ID. An ID he didn't have on him."

"Oh my God," Addie persisted.

"Addie, please," Gabbie exhaled with tears in her eyes. "Constantly calling a god, for what? Sal is dead, he is not coming back."

"I know Gabbie, I know. I just can't understand how one human can do things like this to another."

"What's behind the reason for this crime?" Stewart inquired. "What do they want so badly, that they would pay for a new life abroad with a million dollars?"

"That is why you are here. We don't know. We are hoping that the Doctor or your daughter could tell us. The issue is, what do they want from the lab so badly that they will commit murder?" Susan looked directly at Gabbie.

"I have no idea," Addie innocently confessed.

Gabbie sat quietly as she tightened her grip on her folders and briefcase. She started slowly to shake her head no with an excellent poker face.

"Susan, my issue is my daughter's safety," said Stewart.

"Understandable," said Susan. "That is why we think Addie should take a leave of absence from the lab until we solve this case."

"I agree," Gabbie decided. "I will pick up your duties at the lab Addie, and when this case is solved your job will be waiting for you. By the way, security briefed me on Charlotte. The garage video surveillance showed her disconnecting the battery cable of your golf cart. The incident will go on her record and a letter of reprimand in her file."

"I guess I don't have any other choice," Addie regrettably replied.

"Then that is it for now," Susan expressed. "Agent Epstein will accompany you back to the lab. Thank you for coming."

They all stood and in doing so, the top folder Gabbie held, opened up. A few white business envelopes fell to the floor. As Addie picked up the envelopes for Gabbie, she noticed words written on the top one.

ATTN: Doctor Gabrielle Maida

"Thank you dear," Gabbie acknowledged and put the envelopes back into the folder.

"Doctor, we do need to bring you up to date on some security issues for the lab. Agent Epstein will return to pick you up after dropping off the Ericksons."

"Oh my, will this take that long?"

"I'm afraid so. As director you'll need to know how we will be working with your security."

"All right, Addie please remind them to leave my suitcase with security. Thank you for coming Mister Erickson." Gabbie cautiously sat back down.

“Goodnight Doctor,” Stewart replied as he opened the door to see Agent Epstein step out of the way.

“Don’t worry Gabbie, I’ll remind them about your suitcase. I guess I’ll call you in a few days to see how things are going.”

“All right dear, I’m sure you’ll be back at work before you know. Bye.” Gabbie looked down at the gray cement floor. All this became very troublesome for her.

The door closed and the two Agents sat back down with their glasses off. Richard began staring at Gabbie, thus making her uncomfortable.

“Doctor,” said Susan. “This is far more serious than you think. Earlier you mentioned Charlotte Binsnou, who we know works at the lab and caused Miss Erickson some hurt feelings. Charlotte is the least of Miss Erickson’s problems. That young woman’s life is still in danger. We don’t know what these murderers will do next to get what they want. And there is the question again, what do they want from your lab?”

“Well, we do have a great deal of scientific equipment that would bring a fine dollar on the black market.” This answer from Gabbie sounded like she just pulled the words out of a hat.

“That is not what they are after,” Susan stated firmly and eventually relented. “Let’s just talk about security at your lab for one more minute. We know who your security guards really are. We know who pays them. We know the extent of their facility below the security booth.”

“All right, obviously you know,” a frustrated Gabbie blurted out.

Susan paused to hear Gabbie and then continued. “We worked through the night with them to set up security surveillance on the Ericksons’ home. Some of our agents went out last night as the Phone Company and placed a small camera on the telephone pole across from the Ericksons’ house. The transmission goes to a monitor set up in the downstairs meeting room of your security booth. We feel there is a strong possibility that a move may be made at the Ericksons’ house.”

“Oh my, are you sure. Everything is about the lab. Why would they go to Addie, especially if she doesn’t report to work at the lab anymore?”

"They would go to Addie to get to you."

"Oh this is awful."

"Yes, it is. You see Doctor, I'm with the FBI, and Mister Cooper is with the CIA. We are working together on this. It's a new thing for us. I'm sure you heard about it on the news."

"Why did you lie to us?" Gabbie demanded.

"I'm sorry, we didn't lie. All I did was introduce ourselves by name, not title. However, speaking of lying, I noticed your own introduction to be...let us say...confusing. Why did you introduce yourself as Doctor Mannuso? You don't use your husband's name. You go by Doctor Maida."

"Oh that is just silly. When Addie first met my husband and I, she just assumed I also went by Doctor Mannuso. That was no biggie, as Addie would put it, so I let it go."

"I see," Susan said suspiciously.

Agent Cooper finally broke his stare and silence, "Doctor Maida, please don't mind me saying this, but you look remarkable. You must be well past retirement age and yet you don't look much older than Fifty or fifty-five. What is your secret?"

Gabbie clearly did not like this man or his question. She squirmed in her seat before answering, "Common sense. No indulgent behavior and I avoid carcinogens. I exercise, get eight hours of sleep each night, eat and drink right. Oh yes, and never in the sun without sunscreen."

"I see," Richard Cooper said with a nod or two, of his head. "And that's it?"

"Yes, that is it."

"Gabbie, we don't have much time here," Richard became determined and serious. "The CIA has picked up extra chatter with a few key words being repeated. Those words were 'Matron's secret' and 'CCH chemistry workshop.' Does this mean anything to you?"

"No," Gabbie immediately said and thought again, only to repeat the same answer.

"So you don't think that CCH stands for Cold Creek Harbor?" Richard inquired.

"Oh my, I guess that could. Then again, CCH could also stand for cucumbers, carrots, and humus. A very healthy lunch by the way.

"That is wonderful Doctor, I've cut back on my red meat also," sarcasm sounded in Richard's voice.

"Really, you know there is a new brand of veggie burger on the market that is quite good. I was..."

"Doctor! Please stop the charades," Agent Cooper demanded. "These are terrorists after something in your lab! If you care about that young woman's life you must answer me. Are you known as the Matron of Cold Creek Harbor lab within your circles? And what is your secret?"

"Of course I care about her!" Gabbie said as she choked back tears. "But, I cannot possibly have a secret that terrorists know about."

"Shit, I told you!" Richard shouted to Susan as he jumped up out of his seat in disgust. "My theory is right about her."

"Richard that is so far fetched..." Susan muttered as she ran her hands through her black hair. For a brief moment she held her hair back and released.

"I'm sorry, but my data adds up Susan. Our good doctor here, has a secret and yes, the terrorists know the secret! They not only know, they want it so bad that they will murder for it."

Richard sat back down and looked at Gabbie who had her head in her hands. Her elbows were on top of her folders and briefcase. "Look Doctor, things didn't add up with you. I checked around and I had to do some serious digging. Luckily, the Internet made things easier for me. The people in our Government who knew about you, who helped protect you, are all dead now. I found out when you were born. So did these terrorists and they want your secret. We can't help until you level with us."

Gabbie slowly looked up at him, "Level with you? That is what you want? Who ever leveled with me? My life turned inside out and even with all that bloody protection, I was left hanging out there for the worst of mankind to discover. This is Top Secret! This was supposed to be top secret." Gabbie put her head back into her hands. "The Internet!" She yelled into her hands before looking back up. "You tell me the Internet gave you an important piece of my puzzle. Damn the Internet! Because it obviously gave the same clue to the terrorists! So much for government protection, I can only imagine what was on the Internet to add me up. Now I also put Addie's life in danger." Gabbie dropped her head to her hands again and started to cry.

Susan pushed her chair back and walked around to Gabbie. She put her arm around Gabbie's shoulder. "I'll make you some tea and we'll talk. Your meeting with us in this location was intentional. We knew whatever you have or do at the lab would be top secret. Richard and I have clearance for this."

Gabbie looked up with swelled eyes and a little surprised. "You didn't say coffee."

"I found out that you prefer tea."

"Thank you, some tea will be most helpful right now."

* * * * *

Stewart's minivan gradually rolled by the security booth on the way out.

"Tommy don't forget to give Gabbie her suitcase when she comes back," Addie said after rolling down the van's window on her side facing the security booth.

"I won't, Miss Erickson. I hope to see you again soon."

"So do I, Tommy. Thank you for everything you did for me." Addie looked back with a melancholy face as her father turned left onto Route 5A.

Halfway home, Stewart noticed the long silence in the car. "Do you want to hear the radio?"

"No, that's okay."

"Listen, don't worry about all this. These guys are looking to steal some expensive equipment from the lab and maybe they didn't intend to kill this manager, Sal. Maybe they scrambled to cover up the fact that they did kill him, because they didn't mean to. Don't worry. The FBI will catch them and you'll go back to work."

"I hope so, Dad."

"Right now, I'm relieved that you aren't working there. Okay, so what else is bugging you?"

"Nothing."

"Addie, I know you. There is something else. What?"

"Just... I don't know. When we were leaving the FBI's incredibly organized office, I picked up some letters Gabbie dropped. On the outside of one envelope, somebody wrote attention Doctor Gabrielle Maida on it. I always assumed she was Doctor Mannuso, since she is married to George Mannuso. You know what I mean?"

"Sure, that's no big deal."

"Then, why didn't Gabbie tell me she went by that name? Especially since everyone else referred to her as Doctor Maida."

"I don't know Addie. Call her in a few days, see how everything is going and ask her."

"What am I going to say, 'Gabbie, how come you never told me you don't use Mannuso and that you go by Maida...' Come on Dad."

"Hey, that may work just fine. Look, you're making something out of nothing. Why does this bug you?"

"I don't know. Something about the way everything went. I never saw her last name in writing. No diplomas or certificates on her office walls. No photos hanging on walls around her house. I don't know. It just bugs me."

"Then look her up on the Internet. You'll probably find her full name, where she went to school with all her degrees and awards."

"Yeah, I guess I could do that. Gabbie told me that she went to Oxford."

Stewart turned onto his block and went past the telephone pole with the hidden camera on top. The minute camera lens adjusted to zoom in as the minivan pulled into the driveway.

"Don't forget your backpack, Addie."

"I know, hey Dad... How long are we going to keep the American flag out every day?"

"Until one year has passed Addie. One year."

Addie slid open the middle door on the minivan and took her backpack out as her father walked around from the driver's side.

"Dad, since I'm not working tomorrow, I can go with everyone to visit Grandma."

"Oh, that will be great. Grandma will be happy to see all of us together... By the way, did you know that Grandma's maiden name was Maida?"

Addie stopped and turned to look at her father, "Really?"

"Yeah, I'm pretty sure. Check with Mom."

That night Addie stayed up late searching the Internet. She had several windows open on her computer screen as she probed for information on Gabrielle Maida. The date and time showed in the upper right corner: **Sat 2:10 AM.**

* * * * *

George Mannuso stood in his pajamas by the bedroom window. He pushed the curtains closed after glancing out and looked over at Gabbie sleeping in bed with concern and empathy. He couldn't sleep so he went downstairs to make some warm milk.

Gabbie could not sleep well; images of times gone by were in her head. Addie failed to read well; the bright computer screen in her dark room irritated her eyes. George didn't stir well; causing milk to spill over the pot's rim and onto the gas burner stove. Three people were dealing with turmoil in their own way.

Information came up on the computer for the Oxford University laboratory in England. At the same time, the beginnings of a nightmare were starting for Gabbie. Dreamy images of a middle-aged man and a woman of twenty years were waving goodbye to a middle aged Doctor Maida. Everything appeared in black and white; a dark night revealing only the white steam from an engine of a locomotive. Slowly the images faded into the distance to form a sole figure in a dimly lit window. Nazi World War Two planes dropped bombs on the farmland around the window on the second floor of an old house. Slowly, pure black surrounded and moved closer to the window. Gabbie broke into a cold sweat as the window grew in size and a white figure within remained unrecognizable. Next, there were test tubes filled with blood on the windowsill and finally the figure in the window became visible as she knocked the test tubes away. The image presented a very decrepit old woman staring out the window with one hand pressed against the foggy glass. The woman became Gabbie and written on one of the steam stained windowpanes, read the word Telomere.

"Aah!" Gabbie shouted as she sat up in bed gasping for air. She heard footsteps running up the stairs outside her bedroom. She panicked even more when she could not feel George in the bed next to her. "George! George are you all right?"

"Gabbie, I'm here! What's wrong?" George called out as he came back into the bedroom from the downstairs kitchen.

"Oh Love, a horrible nightmare."

George sat down on the bed next to her and put his arms around her, "Don't worry, I know everything will be all right. We will get through this in the best way. I promise."

* * * * *

Addie appeared in the kitchen doorway yawning and wearing her bathrobe. Her parents and brother had already finished eating breakfast.

"Finally, your scrambled egg is ice cold!" Phillip professed as he cleared his dish off the table.

"I'll warm it up for you," Addie's Mother Brielle offered and went to do so.

Addie sat down at the table and plopped her head down on the placemat. Her father held some papers for proofreading and poked her arm several times with the eraser of his pencil.

"Well, good morning sleepyhead," he joked.

"Dad stop poking me, it's annoying," voiced Addie, muffled from talking into the table.

"Ookay, we have a grumpyhead instead."

"I'll be in the backyard cleaning up my bicycle," Phillip called out as he left the kitchen.

"Put a jacket on! It's chilly out this morning." Brielle shouted after her son as the microwave beeped. Brielle brought the egg over to the table, "Addie please wake up. Here is your breakfast."

Addie sat up in her chair as her mom put the dish down on the table. "Mom, who are you named after?" Addie asked with her eyes closed.

"My Grandmother Gabrielle."

"My Great Grandmother right?"

"Yes, the same one you asked about last night with the last name Maida."

"How did she die?" Addie's eyes were wide open now as she started eating. Her mother cleaned the table off and stopped upon hearing this question. She sat down next to Addie and looked at her.

"What time did you go to bed last night? Were you surfing the web all night? Why are you obsess with this?"

"Geees Mom, this sounds like the Spanish Inquisition. I'm just asking."

Brielle capitulated and started cleaning off the table again. "As far as I know, she was killed during World War Two. To tell you the truth, I don't know that much more. When you see grandma this afternoon, ask her. She's the one that knows the most about her mother."

"Mom, do you know that Great Grandma has the same exact name as my Director Gabbie at the lab?"

Addie's mom looked at her daughter with skepticism as she walked over to the sink. "I thought you said her last name was Manso or something?"

"Mannuso, Mom."

"Okay, Mannuso. How does your Director get Great Grandma's name?"

"Apparently our daughter noticed an envelope that said Doctor Maida instead of Doctor Mannuso," Stewart explained just as he finished correcting his papers and sat back in his chair. "So I told Addie that Maida is her grandmother's maiden name. That's why she checked with you last night about that."

"Yeah and that means Maida was Great Grandma's name," Addie emphasized by waving her fork.

"Wait a second, let me get this straight," Addie's mom walked over to the table and leaned on the back of a chair. Doctor Mannuso does not really go by that name, she legally is Doctor Maida?"

"Yeah! I guess...legally," rethought Addie.

"All right, so she has the same last name, do you know how many people in this world have the same name?"

"Yeah, I know Mom, but she has the same first and last names. Don't you find that odd."

"No, I can't say that I do. Do you know how many people have the same..."

"Okay Mom, I know, I know."

Later that afternoon, the Erickson family sat all together in Brenda's room at the adult home. Phillip, while sitting on the end of the bed, watched the History Channel as everyone else spoke.

"I can't get over how good you are looking, Grandma."

"Thank you sweetheart, but you haven't seen me in over a month. I guess that is why you noticed. I bet I look the same to your parents?"

"No, actually I agree with Addie," said Brielle. "You look, well rested, Mom. So I guess you were right with wanting to come here. This place has worked out well for you."

"But, Mom," Stewart joined in with a reiterated offer. "I want you to know it's still okay for you to live at our house."

"I know, thank you very much, but I can't do that. However, since I have been feeling better, I have been thinking of leaving here and getting my own place again."

"Wait, Mom what?" a bewildered Brielle spoke with a shake of her head and scrunching of her eyes.

"Stu, what's the matter with my daughter? Is her hearing going?"

Addie giggled at what her grandmother Brenda said as she glanced across the room to see her brother watching some news footage from World War II on the television.

"My hearing is fine, Mom. What are you talking about? You cannot move out and live on your own again. Are you crazy? Stu, tell her she's crazy."

"Mom, you're crazy."

"So what else is new?" Addie's grandmother huffed and she directed that toward her daughter, not her son-in-law.

“Seriously, Mom,” Stewart pleaded. “Why would you want to move out on your own, only to do the things that someone does for you here?”

“That’s just it. So I can do things for myself again.” Brenda saw the concerned looks on her daughter and son-in-law’s faces. “I just needed some rest and that is all I have been doing in this place. To tell you the truth, I’m sick of it. I’m tired of resting. I want to live. I want to have my own garden again.”

“And there it is, reason and justification,” said Addie.

“Addie, that is not helping,” Brielle half reprimanded her daughter. “Mom, we will talk about this on Wednesday when I pick you up for your eye doctor’s appointment.”

Addie had strolled over to her grandmother’s bureau. There she took a glimpse at all the photos. The photos were recent ones of all the grandchildren. Once Addie’s mom finished talking she turned to face her Grandmother.

“Grandma, I want to ask you something, but I don’t want to get you upset with old memories.”

“What is it Addie? My old memories will not upset me.”

“Are you sure? Because you never have old photos out, only recent ones.”

“Well, I don’t want to live in the past, so that is why I like looking at current photographs.”

“Do you have old ones?”

“Sure, as far as I know a few albums are in my chest up in your parent’s attic. Was that your question?”

“Actually, I wanted to know more about Great Grandma? How did she die?”

“Oh my, that was so long ago. The family was living in Washington D.C. and my mother was still working with the Army. She was in England and the day before her scheduled trip home one of those...”

Addie's grandmother motioned over to the television and then paused. "One of those V2 rockets your brother is now learning about on that History class channel hit the building she was in."

Phillip turned and with an astonished face stared at his grandmother, "That's what killed her?"

"I'm afraid so."

Phillip shut the television with the remote and put his feet up on the bed before putting his chin into his knees. "I didn't know," he said with a heartbroken voice.

"I wish that I could have known her," said Addie.

* * * * *

Throughout all of next week, Addie spent serious time on the Internet trying to learn more about Doctor Gabrielle Maida. The name in various forms brought up numerous web pages on sites that never gave any details on such a person, but one way or another the Hyper Links brought Addie to information cited from a specific research paper. However, despite all the different quotations and other topics referencing this research paper, Addie failed to obtain the complete version. She also did not have information on the paper's publish date or the author. She only had the fact that this scientific paper titled *Self-Chromosome Growth: Theory, Action and Future Augmentation* had been the first published with these new doctrines. Addie even sent e-mail to the University's Historian at the Oxford University website asking if they had any information on Doctor Gabrielle Maida. Evidently, the Doctor's name was associated to the University's website because her name brought up a web page called:

Renowned Accomplishments of Oxford Graduates

Addie searched the long list of accomplishments and found the title of the scientific paper on *Self-Chromosome Growth* that had been cited on other sites brought up by variations of Gabbie's name. However, no additional information about the scientific paper showed up on the University's site, thus the reason she sent out the e-mail.

Additionally to web surfing, Addie spent the week making calls to the United States Army. A strong desire to learn more about her great grandmother and family had possessed her. However, hours of being on hold, directed to different departments, transferred from one person to another, didn't disclose any records on her great grandmother.

The disappointment became worst when she made a telephone call to Gabbie to see if progress had been made in solving the case and when she could return to work. Addie sat at the end of her bed wearing a pink cap-sleeve tee shirt and black cinch-front leggings.

"I'm so sorry, Addie. Believe me, I am so upset about all of this that I'm having nightmares. I'll call you when things are back to normal."

"Perhaps we can meet at the mall for lunch or you can come to my exam next week at the Dojo?"

"I'm incapable, Addie. They believe I'm being watched. I don't want to drag you into this anymore. Please stay safe and we'll talk again soon. I promise."

"I understand... Gabbie, take care of yourself."

"I will, bye dear."

Addie hung up her telephone and turned to see her mother standing in her bedroom doorway. "That didn't sound too promising," Addie's mom said.

"Wasn't..." a despondent Addie barely mentioned.

"All right, don't worry. You'll be working back at the lab and going out for your dates soon enough."

"Yeah, but Gabbie sounds really down. She sounds like a different person. I know she's my boss, but we were also friends."

"Give this time. Let the FBI do their job. Now come downstairs, dinner is ready and Chris will be here soon."

"Okay, but this is no way to spend a Friday night with your date."

"Addie you know this is for your own safety and only until the case is solved. Dad rented a movie we can all watch together. He said Chris will love it and you'll probably be embarrassed out of your mind."

Addie's mother headed downstairs. Before Addie followed, she mumbled, "You think?" She grabbed her gray ankle-sling wedge shoes and carried them down.

A little after eleven that night, Chris and Addie went into her bedroom. Chris took his denim jacket from Addie's bed and headed for the door. Addie turned on her computer and walked over toward Chris.

"Goodnight Addie, I really did have a good time tonight. Your parents are cool, don't sweat this so much. The FBI will crack the case soon enough, and besides your dad was funny tonight."

"Thanks, I know. I had a good time also." They kissed in the doorway, once, twice and a third time. "I'll walk you down," Addie said with her eyes still closed.

Chris watched her slowly open her eyes and he pointed to her computer with an inquiry, "You're not going to do work on your computer now?"

"No, I just want to check e-mail."

Addie, you checked e-mail when I got here. It's after eleven on a Friday night, who is going to send you e-mail now? God help us if we get that addicted to electronics."

"I guess you're right..." The e-mail program on her iMac set off a pre-program alert signaling that she had received mail. "But, I guess you're wrong."

Both of them walked across her bedroom to the computer. Addie squinted as she approached the monitor to see who sent the e-mail.

"Oh my God, she answered me already?" Addie joyfully spoke when she saw Doctor Gabrielle Maida in the subject box and the sending e-mail address coming from the Oxford Historian. "I have been trying to learn more about my Director Gabbie at the lab. Also my Great Grandmother, who just happens to have the same name."

"Really?"

"Yeah, isn't that whacked?" Addie opened the e-mail and anxiously started to read. Chris scanned from over her shoulder.

Dear Miss Erickson,

Thank you for your e-mail. I must say I am quite amazed about all the recent interest in Doctor Gabrielle Maida who attended our University. In fact, you are the second request this month after several requests made over a year ago.

I was very impressed to hear that you work at the lab in America that once concentrated on Doctor Maida's research.

Concerning your questions, yes she did attend Oxford University and she did write the paper Self-Chromosome Growth: Theory, Action, and Future Augmentation. The paper was published in 1938 and received...

"Wait, what year?" Addie commented to Chris.

"Is that right Addie? She wrote a paper sixty-four years ago?"

"Oh no, that has to be wrong. Gabbie had to be twenty or thirty when she wrote the paper and no way Gabbie is in her eighties. That's a mistake." They both continued reading more closely now.

...and received considerable attention not only from the Scientific Community, but also from zealots of the cause for Hitler to control the world.

To help protect her and her family from Hitler and the Nazi party, the Americans contributed to a plan the British Government had. Unfortunately she was killed by a V2 rocket the day before she was supposed to leave for America.

Addie slowly sat back in her chair as the light from her monitor reflected off her confused face. "Holy flying crab crap!"

"What? What did you read?" Chris demanded.

"No way! Here she is implying that Gabbie is dead and that she was killed by a V2 Rocket in England. Chris...just last week my Grandmother told me that my Great Grandmother died during the second World War by a V2 Rocket."

"Whoa. Addie that is more than whacked, that's scary."

"Maybe they mixed up names and events with my Great Grandmother." Despite her bewilderment Addie kept reading.

Her mortality was a great loss for the world of science and great irony was found in her death, since her paper was on research that may someday help people live longer and perhaps live indefinitely. You may wish to print copies of articles from British newspapers about her death. You can find them at our University website. Just follow the links to the Library, then to the Historian department, then to the Citation section. There you will find a link to Doctor Maida and every publication that cited her.

"Crap, I would have never found those links!" Addie emphasized as she continued reading. In the background and from downstairs, Addie's house phone started ringing.

I will forward you the link that has her complete research paper next week when I return to England. You see; I am actually on holiday this week visiting your country's Hollywood Studios. It is lucky for you that I am accustomed to checking my e-mail, even when on holiday.

I trust this information is of some help. Best wishes and thank you for writing.

Sincerely Yours,
Ashley Maloney
Head Historian, Oxford University

"Chris your father is on the phone," Addie's mother called out from the bottom of the stairs. "They want to know what time you are leaving here so they don't worry."

Chris went over to the open bedroom door and called out his answer, "Please tell them that I'm leaving now."

"All right."

"Thanks, Mrs. Erickson." Chris turned and Addie stood next to him now. "All right, I'm going to go. My parents don't want any black SUVs following me around in the middle of the night."

They kissed each other with a tight hug. "I'll call you tomorrow," Addie said as she moved back toward her computer while still holding Chris' hand. "Bye," she said when they finally let go of each other's fingers.

"Let me know what you find out about all of this name mix up... Bye." Chris left her room and Addie went back to comprehending what could possibly be going on with the e-mail she received.

Two hours later Addie continued going over several articles that she printed out on Doctor Maida's death. One particular newspaper article had very fine print; and Addie read the article for a second time.

Hitler and his Nazi party had made several attempts to kidnap Doctor Maida shortly after her paper was published. Hitler clearly understood the potential of her research and he was determined to be the only human to benefit from her work. Upon learning that Doctor Maida was going to a safe location in America, Hitler made sure that nobody else would gain from her work. At the age of sixty, Doctor Maida was shot by one of Hitler's assassins.

Addie highlighted the last sentence in yellow and rubbed her eyes. "This is not Gabbie at the lab...could this be my Great Grandmother?" An addled Addie mumbled as she slid off her chair without standing and slid onto her bed with her eyes already closed.

Addie did not sleep well that night. She never dressed for bed and tossed about on top of the bed's covers. Around five ten in the morning the e-mail program brought her iMac out of the sleep mode with the preprogram alert signaling that she had received mail. The sound startled her and she jumped over to the computer still half-asleep. The subject box said:

Digital Camera Sale, Prices Are Only...

Just junk mail. Addie quit the program and shut down her computer. As the screen went black, she dropped her head into her folded arms on top of her desk. She started to dream various memories. First, her father taking pictures with his camera, next the pictures on the dresser at her Grandmother's room in the Nursing Home. Her dream concluded with an old photo album in Addie's own hands. Her head shot up! Immediately she ran into the hallway to where a cord hung from a rectangular door in the ceiling. Addie pulled down the cord and unfolded the attic ladder. At the top of the ladder, she fumbled around for the pull cord to the light. Finally she felt the string and turned on the light.

She initiated a rapid search for her grandmother's belongings. There were several boxes marked **Christmas Décor** and one box marked **Easter**. Carefully she walked down the middle of the attic so not to bang her head on the crossbeams. Beyond some old toys in open boxes at the edge of the light's reach, stood a black chest with a curved lid. Addie swung the top open and struggled to see the contents inside the dark cavity. First, she took out a stack of hand crocheted doilies, followed by a handmade throw pillow wrapped in light blue tissue paper.

Several hardcover books were inside the chest, along with a store bought photo album. Addie turned page after page recognizing photographs of her grandparents and mother when they were young. All the clear plastic covers to each album page lost their hold, causing photograph after photograph to come loose or fall out. Addie spent just as much time fixing the photographs as she did looking at them. Finally Addie took out a large heavy album with a cover made of dark brown wood. The words **Family Album** were carved into the wood on the cover.

For some reason, Addie became very nervous as she turned the first black page in the dim light. Each black and white photograph had four white corners holding them in place, a few of which were coming loose. The first page had two photographs of a man in a First World War U.S. Army uniform. Addie turned the page and...

"Ooh holy flying crab crap!" Addie screamed and fell with the album toward the light to get a better view. "Oh shit. Oh no!" She nervously cried and moved closer to the light only to bang her head on one of the crossbeams. The album fell to the attic floor, Addie crumbled into a ball holding her head and crying, "Oh that hurts, oh that hurts."

Addie flashed back to Gabbie's closet door when she stole a look at Gabbie's photographs in the box. Still holding her head, Addie crawled to the album now laying under the light and reopened the cover with a few pages.

The page showed the exact wedding photograph with the woman that looked like a younger Gabbie. However, again Addie could not place the man in uniform that stood in the wedding photo. Addie began shaking like a leaf as she crouched over the album. Page after page, had a photo or two that flashed her back to Gabbie's closet. Then, right there in front of her, the same photograph that Addie recognized as her grandmother when young.

"Oh my God. What is going on here? Gabbie's life is in my attic!" Addie cried as she slammed the album shut and raced down the attic ladder nearly dropping the album to the floor below. Running into her room she tossed the album on her bed and grabbed her cell phone.

"Come on, answer, don't sleep through the rings. Answer the..."

"Hi, what's up?"

"Noo!"

"...This is Chris. Leave a message after the beep and I will call you back ASAP."

"Chris it's me, you'll never believe this. I was just in my attic and I found my Grandmother's old album. Never mind the fact that the bride in one of the photos looks like a younger Gabbie and never mind that I don't recognize the groom. The question is why does my Grandmother have the same exact wedding photograph that Gabbie has? My God, I think... I don't know what to think. Then...then I see in my Grandmother's album a photo of a younger her around thirty. At least I believed it was a younger Grandma when I first saw the same photo at Gabbie's house. Now I know it is a younger Grandma and the thing is... Gabbie has the same photo! What the hell is going on here with these families? I'm going to the Nursing Home now with the album. I have to talk with my Grandmother. Bye."

Addie scribbled a note for her parents at her desk telling them she took the minivan and went to visit Grandma for breakfast. She grabbed her backpack, the album and a gray fleece sweat jacket from her closet. On the way down, she realized the attic stairs were still open. She ran back up and closed the stairs slowly so not to make a loud bang that might wake everyone up.

With the bulky album still under her arm, she ran into the kitchen and slammed her note down on the kitchen table. After grabbing the car keys that were hanging on a decorative shelf above the school calendar next to the refrigerator, she ran out the back door. Five seconds later she ran back into the house. She grabbed an icepack out of the freezer for her head and went back out.

At five fifty in the morning, the Nursing Home did not allow visitors at that time. Addie had to wait until the buzzer went off to get in. She had put on her cropped sweat jacket and pushed the sleeves up to her elbows.

"Hi, good morning," Addie rushed saying to the sixty-something security guard at the front counter. "I'm signing in to see my Grandmother."

The counter had several items on top, such as a large hardcover book for all visitors to sign in and a stack of flyers stating events for the month at the Nursing Home in one corner. There were some extra pencils, a tray with paperclips, a stapler, and small signs telling visitors the basic rules, such as no smoking in the building.

"I'm sorry ah..." the out of shape guard looked upside down at the name Addie wrote in the book after putting glasses on. "I'm sorry Addie Erickson, visiting hours have not started yet."

"Oh, this is an emergency, a few minutes early won't hurt. I'll be extra quiet."

"A few minutes? No, you don't understand. That's an hour and a half from now. I'm sorry I cannot let you go upstairs yet. Please wait here in the lobby."

The guard sounded very serious and Addie knew if she made a big deal she would not get to see her grandmother any sooner. Therefore, she went to sit down on the sofa in the empty waiting area. The large clock on the wall showed two minutes to six. For Addie, waiting ninety minutes before going upstairs fell into the category of torture. She had to find another way.

Addie tried to be casual and opened the album. Upon seeing the same wedding picture, she freaked out and closed the cover. Looking around the room, she saw the guard looking at her and the elevator next to the guard's counter. Next to where Addie sat, she had a door to the Lady's Bathroom and another door to the fire stairwell. Addie looked at her backpack and acted as if this was a matter of circumstance, she started going through her backpack feverishly. Upon finding a rubber band she swung the backpack over her shoulder and picked up the album.

Slowly she walked toward the guard who sat behind the counter. When she arrived, she rested her hands on the counter with one next to the paperclips.

"I have to go the Lady's Room, so I'll look at the album in there," she whispered.

The guard made a face suggesting he did not like the image Addie just conveyed to him. As she left, she swiped a paperclip. Approaching the bathroom door Addie loaded her rubber band. She stopped after pushing the door to the Lady's Room halfway open. While holding the door open with her foot she peered back at the guard whose head continued to look down at a book. She could not abort now. The rubber band came across her pointer and middle fingers, just like a slingshot. With one end of the paper clip wedged into the rubber band, Addie stretched her hands as far apart as she could while holding the heavy album under her right arm. Carefully she aimed the rubber band and sent both of them flying. The paper clip hit the wall behind the counter with a clinging noise and the rubber band fell to the floor halfway across the room. Following the first strike of the paperclip were two subtle clangs as the clip hit the floor on the side of the guard.

The guard put his book down and curiously looked to the side to see what made the noise. Once his head went down and out of sight, Addie broke from her position and let the bathroom door slowly close on its own. She spun around and lowered herself as she pulled the fire stairwell door open so she could enter. Quickly and quietly, she closed the stairwell door. The guard stood up to see the bathroom door slowly shut. Not thinking anything more, he dropped the paperclip he picked up into the tray on the counter and went back to reading his book.

Addie ran up the stairs to her Grandmother's floor. She slowly opened the stairwell door to make sure the nurse on the floor would not see her. Like a bullet, Addie ran down the hallway to her grandmother's room. Again, she slowly opened the door.

"Grandma, are you awake?" She whispered.

As Addie entered the private room she saw the night table light on and the bed already made. Addie closed the door behind her and heard her grandmother gargling in the bathroom. She went over to the bed and placed the album by the pillow. Addie sat in the chair by the night table, placed her backpack on the floor, and patiently waited.

Soon as the bathroom door started to open, Addie called out in hopes that her grandmother would not jump out of her skin.

"Good morning, Grandma."

"Oh my gosh! Oh Addie, you gave me such a fright. What are you doing here?" Then she saw the album on the bed and slowly walked over pretending she didn't. "A penny for your thoughts?"

When Addie did not say a word, Brenda, Addie's grandmother, made sure to notice the album before sitting down on the bed. "Oh my, you found my old album. Oh, did you bring the other one also?"

"No, that was falling apart. I'll have to fix up the pages or put the photos into a new album. Besides, those pictures are not as intriguing as these."

Brenda slowly opened the album, "Ooh it has been so long since I have seen these."

"Who is he, Grandma?"

"That's my father, your Great Grandfather. He was an officer in the United States Army during World War One."

Addie stood and turned the page, "And this is Great Grandma and Great Grandpa's wedding picture?"

"Oh yes. Oh how handsome and beautiful."

"So Grandma, both Great Grandpa and Great Grandma were in the U.S. army?"

"Hmm... Oh look dear," Brenda said as she paid more attention to the photos in the album than to Addie's question.

"How was it that Great Grandma was killed in England during World War Two, if both of them were in the army during World War One?"

"Ooh I know, isn't that something. Oh look! Such a young me with my Mother. Oh I love this photograph."

"Grandma! You didn't hear a word I said."

Brenda looked up and could clearly see that Addie was upset, "Addie, what didn't I hear you say?"

"Grandma, who else comes to visit you here?"

"What do you mean?"

"Does Gabbie from the lab where I work come to visit you? Is she doing tests on you? Because you are not getting older anymore, you are looking... You are scaring me. God, most of your skin spots are gone!"

"Oh, for Pete's sake," Brenda said nervously. "That's the light in this room and the new cream I'm using."

"No it's not, Grandma. What is Gabbie doing when she visits you?"

"Now you are starting to scare me. Nobody visits me except family. What is happening with the FBI case? Your mother told me all about..."

"Oh my God, Grandma! Look at those pictures. Doesn't Great Grandma look like a younger Gabbie? You met her during the New Year's Eve party. They both also have the same full names!" Addie now became very nervous and started breathing irregularly.

"No, no I don't think so. My eyes are not what they use to be. I can't tell. Why is this so important?"

"Because...because Gabbie has the same exact photographs in her house! How does she have my Great Grandparent's wedding picture? How?"

Not a word came from Addie's grandmother, because a thought process failure started in her head. A major factor contributing to the progress of that failure came from her own granddaughter Addie, who conducted this interrogation on her own.

"Grandma, I researched Great Grandma's name on the web. If I didn't know better, she was a brilliant scientist in England and I don't know how Gabbie here at the lab fits into all this, but I think we have three women with the same bloody name! The worst part about all this, is that at least two were killed by a V2 rocket!"

"Oh no the Nazi..." Addie's grandmother mumbled with her eyes closed.

"Grandma don't lie to me, I know that... Oh my God." Addie went into a moment of shock and realization. "You are not lying when you say only family visits you here. Gabbie is family! Grandma! Is Gabbie at the lab somehow related to us because she is Great Grandma's clone?"

"Oh my God, nooo! No child! Don't go crazy, it is because the Nazis were after us. They are after us again!"

"Grandma calm down. The Nazi party is long gone."

"Nooo! They are still around. They destroyed my family. Now they are after you. Hide... You must get to America to hide!"

"Oh shit! Grandma don't do this to me!" Addie immediately hugged her. "All right Grandma, please stop talking. Stop and please realize we are in America. Don't lose it Grandma, please." They both were sobbing in each other's arms.

About a minute passed and the crying settled down, "I'm sorry Addie. I am sorry. Get us some tissues."

"I'm sorry Grandma, I just don't know what's going on here." Addie handed the box of tissues to her grandmother after taking two for herself.

"Go talk to Gabbie at the lab. Bring the album and tell her that I said it has been long enough. Well, go! Just don't stand there or I'll give you a swift kick in the bone."

Addie's eyes and her mouth opened wide once she heard her grandmother say that.

"Yes," Brenda said and started to laugh happily. "Yes, now go! Go!"

Addie grabbed the album and her backpack. She gave her grandmother a kiss and with, “I love you Grandma!” Addie ran out the door.

Downstairs in the lobby the guard looked up to see the elevator doors open with Addie inside. He watched Addie run through the lobby and out the front entrance with his mouth hanging open. The guard looked over to the bathroom door with a confused face, only to look back towards the empty elevator.

Daylight now enhanced the Saturday morning with each passing minute. Addie drove by Cold Creek Harbor and saw several boats already in the water for the upcoming season. Many boat owners were taking advantage of this beautiful day by getting an early morning start. Addie finally pulled up to the security booth at the lab and noticed the car’s digital clock showing seven minutes after seven.

“Miss Erickson, is that you?” the guard requested as he held his hand up.

“Yes,” Addie answered after rolling down her window.

“Oh, good morning Miss Erickson. You may not remember me. The last time I saw you, was New Year’s Eve. I’m Steve... I tackled the guy who ran to the harbor after he attacked you.”

“Ooh, I’ll never forget that night. Do you always work the graveyard shift?”

“Most of the time. We do rotate, however I prefer working at night. So what brings you here so early in the morning?”

“I really need to meet with Gabbie. This is very important. Can you see if she is awake?”

“Oh I know the Doc well enough to say she is awake. Last one to sleep and first one up. I can get away with calling her Doc, because we share many cups of tea together after she takes a late evening stroll and stops off here at the booth. Actually, she would have the tea and I would have coffee. She talks a lot about getting eight hours of sleep every night, but she hardly ever does. I’ll call up to her house because I’ll need her approval to allow you in. I don’t have anything on the docket today for your visit.”

"I understand," Addie capitulated, since she knew there would be no way for her to sneak into this place like she did at the adult home.

A minute later the guard came back out of the booth, "I'm sorry Miss Erickson. The Doc said for safety reasons, it is best that the two of you just talk on the phone. She said call her once you get home."

"Oh no, Steve, please ring her back and tell her my Grandmother told me to come and that I have the family album. Please!" implored Addie.

"All right, Miss Erickson," Steve said with a perplexed face. "I'll tell her what you just said, but you lost me on all this."

A minute later Steve came out of the booth again. "That sure hit a nerve with the old Doc. She told me to send you to her house."

Addie rang the doorbell and waited on the porch with album in hand and backpack across her shoulder. The front door opened and in the doorframe stood Gabbie looking a little more like a middle-aged woman. She had her faded lab coat on, but her skin remained smooth and radiant. She took off her glasses and her blue eyes looked seriously concerned. She seemed to have some more gray strands amongst her shiny chestnut color hair. Her ears were still slightly disproportionate to her face due to their ample appearance. The morning sunlight emphasized her cheek-bones and her nervous smile. Under the long lab coat, she wore blue jeans; a hand crocheted blue turtleneck sweater, and the same human heart deprived of so much joy.

"Good morning Gabbie," Addie said cautiously. "I hope this will be a beautiful day for us." Thoughts of the first day they met went through Addie's head. She remembered when they finally shook hands, much to the relief of Addie, because she thought Gabbie just wanted to hug her on that day of the tour. All Addie wanted now was that hug, but a security barrier built over so many years still stood around Gabbie.

"I hope so too, Addie," a sober Gabbie said. "But, I have terrible mixed feelings about today. I am sorry, I do not know why. Please come in."

They went into the parlor and George, who still had his bathrobe and slippers on, sat on the sofa. "Pardon me Addie," a disquieted George said. “Such an early and unannounced visit finds me in unpresentable attire.”

“I’m sorry George, but this is very important to me.” Addie placed the album on the table in front of the sofa. George sat forward and Gabbie stood in front of the coffee table. They both stared at the album as if some ancient top secret formula hide inside.

“So you brought your family album,” Gabbie started a process of exegesis although she had no idea where this would go. “I’ve wanted to see this since New Year’s Eve. Your grandmother told me about some photos where the resemblance between me and her mother were uncanny. I assume after seeing them you felt the same way?”

George looked at Gabbie partly in shock, because he bought into what she just said. Gabbie felt Addie did too and smiled first at George and then Addie.

Addie looked down at the floor in disappointment. She had hoped Gabbie would open-up and tell her the truth. Now Addie had to force the issue. She looked at Gabbie and as she spoke, Gabbie’s smile slowly faded away.

“That’s not going to work. I saw the same photographs hidden in your closet on New Year’s Eve. Why would you have a copy of my Great Grandparent’s wedding photo? The pieces slowly came together and I still don’t believe what I believe. But... My Grandmother implied that what I realized is true.” Addie’s voice started to crack. “Despite my Grandmother’s reassurance, I still need you...to tell me that what I believe is true. I need you to say, that this far-fetched puzzle I just put together is real.”

A tear started to roll down Gabbie’s cheek as she stood there staring at Addie whose eyes filled with tears.

“Are you really Gabbie?” asked Addie. “Right this second, I don’t care about how, I just want you to confirm the truth.” Tears were now coming down the sides of Addie’s cheeks. “I feel you have been watching over my family and me all this time. You did this because I’m your great granddaughter and whatever that may entail... I still came here to hug you...as I only can hug my Great Grandmother.”

The interrogations were over. Almost a century of family heartache ended and Gabbie broke down as she hugged Addie.

"Oh my baby," Gabbie moaned as she hugged Addie. "Oh my baby Great Granddaughter."

Addie's watery eyes opened upon hearing Gabbie say those words. Even then, Addie remained in disbelief and turned towards George for a reality check. Addie mouthed the question, "I'm right?"

George nodded yes with a smile and tears of joy were in his own eyes.

THE TRUTH AND PASSION, Chapter Ten

The morning sun abundantly came in through the parlor's windows. George went to get a box of tissues as Addie and Gabbie sat down on the sofa. They both were trying to dry their eyes between sniffles and after several unsuccessful attempts, George arrived with the tissue box.

"Thank you, Love," Gabbie said as she took enough tissues for her and Addie.

"For a while there..." Addie started to mention as she wiped her eyes. "I was trying to convince myself that there were three women with the same exact name. My Great Grandmother, this scientist in England, and you here at the lab. But, there is only one. I can't believe this."

"Yes, only me; the invisible family member. The top secret scientist kept under government protection."

"More like house arrest," George commented as he stood there with his arms behind his back and a smile from ear to ear. Animated about the truth finally known, George finally became a pacified man.

"Is that the reason we didn't know you were still alive? But, Grandma knew! Right?"

"My daughter always knew and she protected me all these years keeping my secret. Yes, your grandmother kept her mother's secret well." Gabbie took Addie's hands as they sat next to each other and proudly looked at her great granddaughter. Spent tissues were all about their laps.

"There is a great deal of catching up to be done by the two of you," George emphasized. I am going to get dressed and then make us all a delicious breakfast. After all, that is the only kind I make. I'll call the two of you when everything is done."

"Ooh thank you, Love," Gabbie said with a loving look and a proud smile as George left the room.

"So Gabbie... I mean Great Grandma...oh that sounds so strange." Addie saw Gabbie's face slowly start to cry again. "What did I say, I'm sorry, what's wrong?"

"There isn't anything wrong with what you said... You do not know how long I waited to hear those words. Nobody ever called me Grandma or Great Grandma in my life until now. Your mother is my granddaughter and she doesn't even know I'm alive." Gabbie took additional tissues from the box George left on the table in front of the sofa. "I have lived so long, but I hardly lived." Gabbie wiped her eyes again. "I could never have a dinner party with my family. Matter of fact, I could not even have dinner with my family. How I longed for the joy of watching my granddaughter open a birthday gift from me. To have only been there when she learned to walk, to hug her when she cried. My work in England stole my life away and I missed raising my own daughter, your grandmother. Then all the plans to protect my family made everything worse here in America. I missed my granddaughter's life and I had to steal glimpses of you in the hospital nursery after hours. Always watching from afar, however you winning that Science Fair told me that you were like me and this was a chance for me to get to know you...help you...live a life with you. What you have done for me these past months, I thank you with all my heart. I simply could not miss your life also. Your God knows how I missed everything else. And now...now all I want to do is be around for your graduation, your wedding...but this morning I woke up with a sick feeling that I will not even be here to see you graduate high school." Gabbie covered her face with both hands and now Addie had a turn to take her great grandmother's hands and hold them.

Gabbie had become so revealing for her own sanity. She had endured years of not being able to communicate her story, her life, and her love. At first, Addie had no confidence as what to say to her great grandmother. She had a hundred questions, but not a word to help console her great grandmother and that fact embarrassed her. Finally, Addie spoke from her heart.

"Great Grandma, I know you realize that I have questions galore...but I will not be able...it is just apparent to me that you have spent enough years shedding tears and carrying a heavy heart. I think today is a day for smiles and hugs and wiping the tears away."

Gabbie looked up at Addie with a simple smile.

"May I call you Grandma G?" asked Addie.

"Oh my," Gabbie said with a laugh. "Isn't that snappy! Why of course, dear. Is the 'G' for Great or Gabbie?"

"Its for Great," Addie said and they both smiled at each other. Subsequently, Addie tried to relax, but she became all too aware about her dismay with asking the first major question. She could no longer wait, she had to confirm her belief. "So you are that scientist from England?" Addie slowly shook her head still finding this hard to accept. "I would love to know how the V2 rocket that supposedly killed you, didn't kill you. Also, I read that you were sixty back then. I can calculate approximately how old you are, but I can't believe that. You aren't really that old. Are you?"

"Addie... I was born in eighteen seventy-nine, I am one hundred twenty-three years old."

Addie's eyes widened and she began to stare. "My God...with an excellent...sixty-something...year old body," Addie recited with a pseudo-hypnotic tone. Then shock turned into urgency for Addie. "Oh God, that's what they want! They'll murder for your secret! The FBI! Tell the FBI!"

"They know. They know, Addie, and so does the CIA. We are safe here," said a calm Gabbie who now had better control of her emotions. "I guess I should start from the beginning. I owe you at least that.

"When I was sixteen, and that was five years before the turn of the *last century*, most of my friends were done with school. They wanted to find the perfect suitor to marry. I on the other hand wanted to continue my education. I loved learning, but I had to work full time to help my family so we would have sufficient means for living. Back in those times, having food and a roof over your head was a blessing. The work offered to me was at the hospital-wing caring for elderly people. If I did not receive this job, my education would have been over. My family did not have the connections or money to send me to classes for a higher level of learning. Your Great, Great Grandfather was ill and I was the oldest of five children. In addition, I was a girl. Back then, women didn't attend universities."

Addie looked with commiseration toward Gabbie and slowly sat back on the sofa. Her eye contact with Gabbie did not yield for a second.

"Fortunately, I was noticed by the doctors at the hospital. You see, I was enthralled with everything around me, because everything was new to me. I never saw or heard about things such as wheelchairs and germs. I read everything I could find on Monsieur Louis Pasteur, who had just passed away that very year. The doctors were impressed when I implemented changes throughout the hospital-wing that Monsieur Pasteur would have recommended. The health of the patients immediately improved.

"Over the next five years the doctors helped me by teaching and contributing to my higher education whenever we had spare time. I started to save my money so that someday I would be able to attend a college. What I did not know was that the doctors were saving some money for me too. On my twenty-first birthday they presented me with the funds they collected and entrance to Lady Margaret Hall at Oxford University. This was a dream come true for me. The school was for women and the doctors at the hospital had the right connections.

"I still worked at the hospital part time to pay for school and to send money to my family. I also entered Oxford with the haunting knowledge that every elderly person I cared for at the hospital lived a life just like me, and I did not like the results. Old age brought them misery, pain, and sometimes complete loss of their life's memories. I found this unacceptable, for if old age were a disease, we would never accept that and we would search for a cure. I guess the reason I viewed old age this way was since most of my patients in the hospital were not old by today's standards. Most were in their fifties or sixties, but aged as if they were in their eighties. There was only one woman who was in her eighties or more. Nobody knew for sure. Her mind was still sharp, but her body was a mess. One day, just before I was to leave for Oxford University, she held me near and would not let me go. Her eyes were ablaze and she said to me, 'My body was once like yours. What did I do so wrong to get this way? I am trapped in this old body and in my mind, I am still like you, young and wanting to do things. Why is God punishing me so? Can you please help me get out of this broken body?' When I told her that I was sorry, I did not know how to help her, she cried out to God for help. She died in my very arms right then and there."

There came a brief pause in Gabbie's voice before she continued,

"Four years later I graduated with honors and went on to become a doctor. However, I did not go to work in a hospital. I went into research at Oxford University. The image of that woman in my arms still haunts me to this day. The reason for that is because a year after she died I found out I was related to her. A school assignment had me trace my family's medical history. She was my Great Grandmother on my father's side and I did not even know. She married and had children at a much younger age than me. We had lost all contact with my father's remaining family when he died."

Addie listened to Gabbie's every word and Addie's skin began to crawl about her arms and neck. At that moment, an interruption would not be appreciated. However, an interruption occurred anyway. George walked through the room as he announced breakfast would be ready in fifteen minutes. Gabbie acknowledged with gratitude and continued talking to an eager Addie.

"In nineteen ten, I was thirty-one and had started my own research on the side regarding aging. By nineteen-thirteen, I had already worked six years doing research at Oxford. The Titanic had sunk a year earlier and I was thirty-four years old. I was living alone and I had lost most of my family due to various illnesses. They never saw a doctor and they also refused to change their living habits. Washing by the basin in the kitchen once a week was fine and a bath once a month was a maybe. To bathe once a week was a waste of water. They did not cook their meats well enough and indoor plumbing was a future dream that added up to an unnecessary expense.

"That year, nineteen thirteen, I went to France to work at the Pasteur Institute. I fell in love with Paris, but the following year brought England into World War One. I came back home before I even started working there.

"I made considerable progress with my private work over the war years. Then in nineteen seventeen, I met your Great Grandfather. He was in England because America just entered the war. He was a doctor and seven years my junior. We worked together at the hospital with the wounded soldiers and on our time off he introduced me to a different world...a world outside the lab, a world where even a thirty-nine year old scientist could fall in love. The year was nineteen eighteen, the war ended and I was getting married. Ten months later your grandmother was born.

"For the next twenty years we continued to live in England and I worked in research again at Oxford. On the side, I continued with my own theories and work on aging.

"Nineteen thirty-eight changed everything. With my premise and what I theorized about aging, I started to take samples of my own cells to grow and preserve. My daughter turned twenty and my research now published... With hindsight, I would have never submitted my research for publishing. To this day, none of my recent findings or studies have been published. Neither the world's infrastructure or man's intelligence is ready to handle what my work will entail.

"I was first overjoyed by the attention my paper received, but then I didn't like who became the most interested party. Within months the British government, Scotland Yard, and the military knew Hitler was not only interested, Hitler wanted me.

"The first kidnap attempt we never knew about. Scotland Yard and the British government terminated the plot before they were able to implement. The second attempt targeted my daughter. My poor Brenda, what she went through when those damn Nazis took her. They wanted to use her to get to me. Your grandmother never gave them any information about my possible location. Happily, the plot failed, mostly due to the bravery of your Great Grandfather. What he did to get his daughter back was not anything less than heroic. No serious harm came to them, except some emotional turmoil for your grandmother.

"The next plan was from our side. The Americans and British governments set things up so we could move to the States. They established funding for my research and searched for a lab that met my needs. So in nineteen thirty-nine, I was sixty years old with a ton of gray hair and moving to America. My husband and daughter left ahead of me. The plan was to stage my death by an assassin the day before I was supposed to leave. This would make Hitler believe I was dead and thus so was my research. All my published work and every known file or copy was destroyed. At least that is what they told me. Apparently, that was not the case, because this past week I learned that a copy was still on file in the archives of Oxford University. Now, due to an over-productive historian who uncovered this copy of my published paper, my research has been on the Internet for over three years!

"I know that I cannot blame the poor woman, she was just doing her job. She had no idea about the torment this caused. Now, another group of psychopaths are after me and my secret."

After a few seconds of Gabbie looking at the floor, Addie sat forward and took Gabbie's hand. Again, Addie asked a simple question.

"Grandpa G and Grandma knew about the staged death?"

Gabbie looked up and smiled upon hearing Grandpa G, "Yes, they were privy of the plan. They sent my family by oceanliner to Washington D.C. where I was supposed to join them. Notwithstanding, plans changed at the last minute and I came here instead of going to Washington. I did not get to see them again for almost a year. In nineteen forty the government bought a house for them, not us, just my husband and daughter. I was to live at the lab and they were to live as if I was dead. They moved into a house located east of Cold Creek Harbor and I had to schedule our visits at either house.

"Addie, I hated every minute of my life. I was living alone in this big house and I had to get approval to schedule an appointment to see my husband and daughter. I knew my future was discouraging and embroiled. In the summer of forty-one I had to report to Washington. I asked how I would attend my daughter's wedding when she wed. They told me that I could attend as a friend of the family.

"Just when I wanted to put an end to everything, the Japanese bombed Pearl Harbor. Nobody in the government had time to listen to an old crabby scientist. I was all but forgotten, except by Hitler. I was sixty-two and I will never forget that night. George saved my life; in fact, he almost died that night. I had two Nazis dead here in my house. The commander died in the hallway; the other one was young and laid dead right over there. I can still picture his face. How sad, a young man brainwashed to die for a tyrant leader. Now again today, children made prejudice by decadent individuals who only care about themselves so they can rule the world."

"But, that is not good enough. They want to rule forever," Addie included.

"Sadly yes, and they are after me for that possibility once again."

"Who killed the Nazi soldiers?"

"A young Corporal and Private who were in charge of security that night. Since the bombing of Pearl Harbor, the United States Military Police have been protecting us here. The security Uniforms they wear today are just a cover."

"That explains a whole load of things," Addie replied with a comprehending nod of her head.

"I stayed in touch with those two men that saved our lives. Just a few years later, nineteen forty-five to be exact, I was informed that the Corporal was killed when stationed in Germany. The Private became ill and died in the fifties. All I have left of those two fine young men is a cracked vase on my piano. One bullet they fired hit the vase; I did the best repair job possible. We were all scared that night and yet those two young men saved us. I'll never forget them."

Gabbie took a tissue and Addie turned to look at the vase as if she found an old friend. She remembered seeing all the cracks the first day she stood in this room. Now she knew the significance of the vase's condition.

"Actually, I do have something else from them," Gabbie added after some thought. "Flying crab crap."

"What, you can't remember?" asked Addie.

"Can't remember what?"

"What else you have that reminds you of the..."

"Ooh no. That is what I have from them... Flying crab crap. That saying became popular that night amongst the military men."

"Ooh I see...and now that I think about that, I've heard my school bus driver say a short version a few times. Yeah...and he said he served in Vietnam and his father was in World War Two."

"What does he say?"

"Crab crap."

"Well, there you go. The saying still lingers on to this day."

"He also told me about a rumor. First, he obviously stands correct about this place being a lab and not just homes. Yet, now that I think back to what he said... Jake said that if..."

"And Jake is your school bus driver who served in Vietnam?"

"Oh yes, sorry. Yeah...he said that if Hitler won the war, this was his first stop in America because of the research going on here. Once Hitler realized he wasn't going to beat America he sent his bombers to blow up the lab. Luckily they missed and only blew up the harbor waters. The U.S. Navy had to clean out all the bombs that didn't go off."

Gabbie just sat there with a contemplating smile and George who came into the room to hear Addie talk about Jake, started to chuckle.

"I know what the rumor is based on, but events didn't happen that way," George said. "Please let's go inside and have some breakfast."

The time went by quickly as they sat around the breakfast table talking. The clock on the kitchen wall, obviously from the nineteen fifties, showed the time of eight fifty.

"Thank you very much for breakfast," Addie said politely and then asked for some clarification. "So because they came in on a sub, the U.S. Air Force bombed the harbor in hopes to sink it?"

"Oh they sank that sub all right," George accentuated. "The Navy took three weeks to clean up the mess and play down the event."

The two Doctors sat there silently slowly nodding their heads in thought. "They killed Captain Wayne," George verbally recalled. "Remember the old Captain?"

"Yes, such a proud man he was, right, Love?"

"Yes, and remember the fish he would bring over when he caught extra? He always caught extra for us and he would always say, 'How about George cooking us up some?' So I would end up cooking dinner for us all and he would tell us old stories of when he was Captain during the First World War."

"After Pearl Harbor they wouldn't allow him to dock at Land's End or anywhere on the property anymore," Gabbie looked at the floor when she said that.

Addie became tearful about what she heard. This had become a difficult morning as far as emotions go. Suddenly *God Bless America* music started to play.

"Holy cow, what is that?" George asked.

"It's my cell phone," Addie called out. "Excuse me, it's probably my mom..."

"Don't say anything to her yet," Gabbie called out.

"I won't. Hello?" A few seconds of silence and then, "Hi Mom, I'm at Gabbie and George's house. We just finished eating a healthy breakfast George made for us. You saw my note, right?"

Again, Addie listened to her mother talking on the other end of the telephone and looked over toward Gabbie so she could better comprehend what Gabbie started whispering.

"Ask your mom if you can stay the day," Gabbie relayed to Addie. "I would like you to stay for the day."

Addie nodded in agreement to what Gabbie requested and waited to talk. "Everything is all right, I visited Grandma already, but I didn't have breakfast with her. Something came up so I stopped by here and George was kind enough to make breakfast."

Again, a few seconds of silence before Addie continued, "No, just things, no biggie. Also Mom, Gabbie wants to know if I can stay for the rest of the day. Do you or Dad need the car?" A brief pause before, "I think she wants to show me some stuff." Again a brief pause before, "You know, just some science stuff."

Gabbie looked at George with a comical face regarding this conversation her great granddaughter conducted that contained such great intellectual verbiage.

"Okay Mom, thanks and I will. Bye." Addie clicked her cell phone off and slid the small phone back into the front pocket of her jeans. "Oh my God...what am I saying? Did I just tell my mother that this was a no biggie?"

"Yes, I believe you used those words," George reported.

"No biggie! Does anything get any bigger than this? I still cannot believe what we are talking about here this morning. How did you do this?"

"If you can stay the day, I'll not only tell you, I will also show you."

"Oh yes, yes I can stay, but I have to get home for dinner. My parents are going out and they want me to stay with my brother."

George stood up and started to collect dishes. "You two go back and sit in the parlor and I'll clean up here."

Gabbie took her cup of tea with her into the parlor and as they sat down Addie exhaled nervously. "Grandma G, before I ask anything else or before you tell me something else, I have to ask you this question."

"Okay, Love, you can ask me anything now."

"Do you believe...or at least, do you believe in the possibility of a God?"

"Do you really want to ask me that?"

"I have to ask. You have been alive for one hundred twenty-three years. You understand and know more than anyone in history. Yes, I really want to ask you that. Especially after what you said earlier."

"What did I say that has you so immersed in this topic?"

"You said to me and I quote, 'Your God knows how I missed out on everything else' unquote. So He is my God, not yours... You don't believe in God, do you?"

"I did believe in God once upon a time. Then so much started to happen and most things did not add up for a God to exist somewhere out there. That night, when I had that young boy dead in my house and even today when leaders maintain ascendancy over their followers by brainwashing them to commit murder. That's not God; so how can one believe in a God?"

Addie just looked at her great grandmother with the disillusioned eyes of a child when blatantly told that there is no Santa without a word of comfort about Saint Nicholas. Then like an innocent child, Addie put the responsibility back onto Gabbie by ingenuously saying, "I was hoping you would be able to tell me."

Gabbie snuffed a laugh short to just a 'humph' sound. "I should be able to tell you, shouldn't I? All right, let us look at this from a different point of view. Okay, everything you know about God is true."

Addie became eager about the prospects for this communion and at once contributed, "Okay great, everything is true except the part about God being a He. The need to describe God as a man in today's world is so inept. I understand how centuries ago that made things easier. Especially for people without an education to relate. I mean get real! God does not have a human body. If God was a He or even a She, then look out for a million questions. What color skin, how tall, how does God eat and on and on. I mean isn't it time we realized God doesn't have skin! God is an existence, an entity, or sum of all that is good and alive. Alive not just in body, but also in spirit."

"Oh this is going to be good," Gabbie said with a grin of pride. "I bet you asked all those questions when you were little."

"Of course I did." Addie said casually.

"Okay then how can a spirit be in us? Just give me half an explanation of what a spirit is."

George had quietly come into the room, neither Gabbie or Addie noticed him. Gradually he sat in the first chair before the fireplace as he fastidiously listened.

"Okay, we are told we have a soul, spirit or essence. Well, as a scientist I know we have a brain that is matter and decays after we are dead. I also know that I have a mind. My mind works my brain. I think and therefore I do. Without the thinking I would not do a single thing."

Addie became completely animated with her words. Her spoken beliefs and her gestures all flowed together in a production of passion. There were no pauses for thought, she completed the thought process before. She didn't hesitate or have any retrogression, all was solidified and she continued to convey in hopes to satisfy.

"Now Grandma G, what works my mind or what is my mind? I say energy. My energy is me...my body is not me. For example, our body is a glove. On the table, the glove doesn't do a thing. Now my hand is my spirit or energy, put my hand into the glove and the glove will move. My energy is my essence, spirit, or soul. Call it whatever you wish. When my body stops working and dies, my energy...the real me is what will live forever."

Gabbie sat there looking at her granddaughter with surprise and respect. "That is a potent way of viewing existence. I am impressed and I must say there is a seed there for me to dwell on. However, let us say for argument sake, that all that is true and we go to heaven. What is heaven and more important what in heaven do we all do there? Addie, remember when we went to the mall together. All those people running about, all those people made me dizzy. Am I to socialize with all those people in heaven? Am I to have nothing to do for all eternity that I would want to get to know all of them? Will I wish to do that? What else is there to do in quote, heaven, unquote? Supposedly I will not need to eat or sleep in heaven, so what are we to do?"

"Perhaps having knowledge of someone is habitual. Rather like your relationship between mind, body, and soul. However, I believe your mind is your soul. They are one in the same. My mind is energy and that energy signature is me, Addie Erickson. And our energy signature is how we are created in the image of God so we may commune, share, exist with others. Oh, I see a raised eyebrow."

"So I raised one eyebrow, no biggie."

"Grandma G, are you implying, that I shouldn't get cocky?"

"Yes, but I prefer malapert over cocky any day. Addie, can you offer me a comprehensive explanation of heaven?"

"Well, heaven isn't a place with clouds or angels running around with halos. In the past, that was the better way to describe something that is incommensurate so people could understand or relate. In reality heaven is not a place. Heaven is another dimension."

"I've heard that before and I even believed for a time, but I never had one permanence that even began to predicate your hypothesis."

"Really? You gave me one yourself when you assigned me to the Double MRI project."

"I did no such thing."

"Yes, you did. Grandma G, think of this for a second. When we die, is that all or do we enter a different rate of motion? Can living or existing forever then become understandable to us? Especially if there is no such thing as time."

"You are answering my question with questions. Oh I detest that. Nevertheless, you have presented me with a different outlook and this requires more thought. Don't smile yet, you have still only raised one eyebrow."

"Okay, so now when we fail to understand or separate ourselves from worldly anchors, we terminate our energy signature. For example, never having the foresight to acknowledge what you did that hurt others. Then, because of that fault, do you fail to enter a different rate of motion or perhaps as I say, enter the correct dimension? If yes, then we truly die, truly stop to exist?"

"Again? More answers with questions."

"Grandma G, I read the Introduction on NASA's Propulsion Physics Workshop to create a space drive that may someday enable interstellar travel. I also read about the Zero-Point Field concept of Haisch, Rueda and Puthoff."

Gabbie slowly sat back in the sofa and George, who remained sitting in his chair unnoticed by the two women, sat forward with both eyebrows raised as Addie proceeded with her discourse.

"Now while NASA explored the concepts of superluminal motion owing to the theory of space-time metric distortions within general relativity proposed by Alcubierre in nineteen ninety-four, Pfenning and Ford showed that to be physically unattainable in nineteen ninety-seven. So NASA's radically new propulsion units are out the window for now.

"Next I read about the Russian physicist Andrei Sakharov and I'm going off on a space drive tangent, I'm sorry. Anyhow, the point I wish to make is this. If we stop looking at the purely hypothetical and review the theoretical foundation of the zero-point field as the basis of inertia and gravitation, we can see that motion or movement through space is rather a space-time distortion. So what is the bottom line? The bottom line is that time does not exist, and thus the massive distances of space do not exist, but we do! Since we know that both gravity and speed warp time, does this scientific verbiage lend itself to the actuality of another dimension, another domain, or heaven if I may? I ask this because if reaching the speed of light causes time not to exist, then doesn't that answer how God always was and will be? How can we ignore that possibility?" Addie paused, thus offering Gabbie a chance to say something.

"Again you answered with questions," Gabbie mentioned as she continued contemplating. "You really read all those papers?"

"I'm using questions because I did say I was hoping you could tell me the answers and yes, I really read all those papers, theories, and concepts."

"Addie you know your answers already, you just want me to comprehend and confirm."

"That would be more than nice. That would be almost like irrefutable data."

"You offer me too much credit."

"Are you kidding? I probably don't offer you enough distinction in comparison to what you have lived through. I'm aware that our presence is in a linear conformity and approach. I know you cannot circle around to go back and change the past, but that fact should not take away from what you have achieved."

"Actually, that is one of the nicest things anyone has said to me."

"You are welcome," Addie reciprocated with a smile. A moment passed before Addie asked a solemn question. "Grandma G, when did Great Grandpa die?"

"Just four years after your mother was born and the year I started testing my work on myself. He died in nineteen fifty-four."

"One year after Watson and Crick determined the precise molecular structure of DNA," Addie thought aloud.

"Yes, that is true." Gabbie slowly continued, "I was seventy-five then and your Great Grandfather was sixty-eight. I tried to save him, but it was too late. Cigarette smoking had done too much damage. However, I have been at peace with failing to help him, because even today I would not be able to do anything. Too much damage to the body." Gabbie looked up at Addie with a smile, "George and I married in nineteen seventy-six. We were both doing well from the benefits of my work. I was in reality ninety-seven, but I had slowly transformed back to look like I do now, around fifty-nine, I would say. George is nine years younger than I am. He is one hundred and fourteen in reality, but looks around sixty I hope." Gabbie leaned forward and whispered to Addie, "Mum's the word, I want him to look older than me."

George heard, as he remained hidden in the first of the two chairs by the fireplace. He just shook his head with a smirk.

"Anyway, the government helped us with any legal entanglements so suspicions about us and our marriage were avoided. In nineteen eighty-three my granddaughter, your mother, at the age of thirty-three gave birth to my beautiful great granddaughter. The way you looked at me when George and I first visited. I was pretending a relationship to some other baby, but you looked at me as if to say, 'I know who you are, you're my Great Granny.' And yes, I know you really didn't see me, but I sensed that you were aware of me and all was very purposeful. You see, even with extra time to live, I spent very little or no time at all with my family. The more time you have, the faster time goes by. The extra time is never enough, I still want more. Getting old just sucks."

"That's a bit scary, because I sense from you right now, that especially today, you are so afraid of dying. Are you afraid to die?"

"Let us leave that question to be answered later," Gabbie almost pleaded.

"Grandma G, perhaps one more thought on the subject may help. Our human bodies are so complex; you of all people know that. Am I to believe that life has happened by chance, by luck, by the toss of an energy mass and amino acids? I saw the book, A Brief History Of Time, in one of the piles at your office. I heard a reporter once asked the author, Stephen Hawking, if he believed in God. Hawking said that he couldn't rule out the possible existence of a God. With everything that Dr. Hawking understands about Black Holes, the Big Bang theory and the universe, he could not rule out the possibility of a God. Why have you ruled out an Existence, Grandma G? Have you scientifically ruled out God or is this your self-defense mechanism causing a knee-jerk response to all your grief, to all your sustained guilt that your work could place you in a god-playing role? Does not believing in God make you obsess with finding a cure to your own mortality?"

Silence unexpectedly replaced voices, as Addie maintained firm eye contact with her great grandmother.

George slowly stood up and walked over to Addie. "Congratulations, Addie," he spoke softly.

"Oh Love, you startled me," Gabbie suddenly reacted. "How long have you been sitting there?"

"Long enough to hear a teenager do what I couldn't do all these years. Change the tide of your opinion toward the existence of a God or as Addie put it, an Existence."

George faced Addie with respect and acknowledged, "Addie, your faith serves you well. While a well educated scientist may be in tune with reality, the fact is, one needs to be truly unpretentious in order to righteously be in tune with surrounding nature, the Existence or as I like to say... God."

Next George respectfully told Gabbie, "I believe the time has come to show your young apprentice, your private lab. I'll cover your schedule at the office lab and I'll see you two back here for lunch."

Gabbie led Addie down the hall to the original basement door. As she turned the glass doorknob, a new fluorescent light fixture turned on automatically at the bottom of the stairs. The new steel staircase that led them down contrasted against the four old wine barrels that were still there. Just beyond the wine barrels stood a new stronger steel door with an ID card lock. Once Gabbie swung this new door open a massive well-refined laboratory came into view, illuminated by several fluorescent fixtures mounted to a decorative nine-foot high hung ceiling.

"Welcome to my private laboratory," Gabbie said. "I hope you don't think that I'm like one of those mad scientists in the movies."

Addie's engaged eyes assimilated everything and she admitted what she surmised. "On the contrary, you must be a genius to get the government to support all this."

"Perhaps you are right, but I'm not so sure. Let's sit down at my desk."

The lab encompassed up-to-date furniture, computers and lab equipment from electron microscopes to storage freezers. Compared to the way the lab looked in nineteen forty-one, one would not recognize a single thing. Gabbie sat in a lush high-back black leather chair behind an executive sized desk. Addie made herself comfortable on a similar, but smaller chair in front of the desk.

"Grandma G, how many people are involved with your research?"

"The number of involved people I know without a doubt. The total is three. George and I here at the lab and a scientist at a different location. That scientist who has to remain unnamed is my failsafe contact, just in case of an emergency. Only my research is known to this scientist, not the fact that George and I are benefiting from my work. This is my failsafe, the government doesn't know a thing. I established this contact before you were born to guarantee success. As far as the number of people who know about my work, I am not sure. I know about you and my daughter. With the government's people under top-secret clearance there could be a half dozen more."

"What about people you worked with over the years? How did you pull this off? Didn't they see that you were getting younger, not older?"

"People leave positions, move on to other projects, get married or just retire. New people come to the lab, not knowing when I started working here or how old I was or am. Also their research and work never mingled with mine to the point where they would know those details. For those in government from the start, well I only gave verbal reports. I never published my research again, thus the top secret Matron's Project is dead along with all the government officials from back then. Today, I cover my research under the other work done at the lab here."

"Are you still getting younger?"

"No, this is as young as I can get. Did you find and read my paper on self-chromosome growth?"

"No not yet. What's the reason for what age you can maintain?"

"There are many factors involved with aging, over the period you have been working here at the lab, I have been teaching you various contributing dynamics. Most deal with basic care and functionality of our bodies in everyday life. For example, it is best to eat up to six small meals and drink six glasses of water a day. What does that help? That supports your body's physical performances that developed over three million years with our ancestors living on this earth."

Gabbie swiveled in her chair left to right twice as she unlocked a bottom drawer to her desk. She took out a brown envelope the size of a catalog and placed the package on the side of her turquoise desk blotter. The aging pouch had been well stuffed and tied closed with a cord.

"I want you to have this. When you leave today take this with you and put it in a safe place. All of my original notes, published paper, and updated computer Zip disks are all in here. My life's work I am leaving for you."

Addie stared at the pouch that resembled items just removed from a time capsule. "Oh no, I can't take that responsibility...and what do you mean leaving your life's work to me. You are going nowhere, that should stay here."

"Well, wherever I go you still have to take this, because even if we work on this together in the future we may need to rent our own lab space." Gabbie scribbled out a note as she said that and stuffed the note into the pouch.

"Why, what do you mean?"

"My work has never been concluded and some bean counter in Washington uncovered this. So, this CPA with top secret clearance has recently informed me that my production of results has not justified the cost over all these years. Therefore, I should expect to be cut loose."

"What about you and George, both of you are living proof that you have been successful."

"Yes, and no, things are so much more complicated than that. Your grandmother is the only outside person to benefit somewhat from my research. Unfortunately, I only was able to get some cell samples from her starting about ten years ago. The best I can do is take five to ten years off her age. She does not mind and is happy with whatever I can do. I'm still her mother taking care of her, but most of her organs are still aging. I need to complete my sampling of cells from her. The problem is that some samples require a major operation and the older you are, the more complications you can have."

Addie's face now showed a realization, "So you never did volunteer work at Grandma's Nursing Home."

"No, I do volunteer. That was the only way I would be able to administer to my daughter without raising suspicions. That day your grandmother told me you would be stopping by after school, so I waited around to get a closer look at my great granddaughter."

Addie just stared at Gabbie, "I can't believe this, one hundred twenty-three years. Well, if they close you down, you come live with us."

"I would love to Addie, but I'm not sure how things would work out. I don't have a credit card, social security number, or a driver's license for a reason. I don't pay taxes and I am not paid. The government gets me everything I need. In return, I can do the work that I love..." Gabbie swallowed before continuing. "But, be dead to all those whom I love."

Addie reflected the pain Gabbie felt with a similar expression. Eventually, Gabbie carried through and completed what she wanted to convey.

"The government will give me a new identity so I can work with a private lab or university. However, I am afraid that my secret will catch up to me working out in the public. The only way to prevent that is for me to stop treating myself. I will grow old again at my normal rate."

"Then you live with us," repeated Addie. "We will rent lab space at a university."

"All right," a revitalized Gabbie said. "We'll see, but you'll realize sooner or later you will be using this envelope. Even with my treatment, I cannot stay alive forever. You have to take over. Presently, I believe that I could live until two hundred fifty years old. I don't have enough cell samples or supply to go beyond that. As for you, taking a complete sample of cells and growing a large supply, will allow you to live... Indefinitely?"

“Oooh my God! How in the world are you doing this?”

Gabbie led the way to the rear of the lab. As they walked across this large open lab, they passed a glass enclosed circular room in the center. Only two curtains hanging on the inside were open, clarifying a dark inside area with one operating table surrounded by stainless steel equipment reflecting the little light penetrating inward. A moveable arm holding an array of lights extended downward from the ceiling. The lights were not on, but ominously hovered over the operation table almost hidden amongst the shadows of the room. Only in appearance, this now portrayed a few features of a mad scientist’s lab.

A small sitting area occupied the rear of the lab. Four lounge chairs, each with virtual reality goggles hanging on them.

“You know, there is a drawback to living so long,” Gabbie said as she picked up a pair of VR goggles. “Your nose and ears continue to grow. Somebody should study that. Valuable lessons are there to learn.”

“Ookay,” Addie cautiously verbalized as she reviewed Gabbie’s ears. “What are the goggles for?” Addie inquisitively asked about her preferred interest.

“An introduction program that I put together with PowerPoint software. Here, put one of these headsets on and after you sit, pull down the screen over your eyes. I will turn on the program that runs just a few minutes. I don’t want anybody wearing these things too long because they bombard your eye balls with radiation.”

Addie followed the instructions stated by Gabbie. At the same time Gabbie gave a few clicks on a nearby computer and went to sit in the chair next to Addie.

“The program will start in a few seconds, lower the stereo ear pieces and you’ll hear my voice.”

“Okay I did, but I see blackness and hear nothing. Oh okay... I have you sitting at your desk here in the lab.”

“Very good, just enjoy the presentation.” Gabbie sat back in her chair and closed her eyes as Addie watched a full color exposition of Gabbie turning in her chair to face the camera. She wore her lab coat and held a clipboard.

"Thank you for joining me today. The following presentation was designed to offer you a summary that explains how I am in fine health at the age of one hundred and twenty-three years.

"What you are now looking at is a human chromosome slowly being magnified to show you what is at the very end or tip of every chromosome in your body.

"Here lies genetic material that is critical to our aging process. This part at the end of your chromosome is called a telomere by the scientific community. My unpublished name was Maidasite."

Once Addie heard the word 'telomere' she flashed back to that night in the shed. She immediately realized that the G and G carved inside the heart stood for Gabbie and George.

The image of the chromosome changed to a man and woman standing naked in the forefront of a field with trees in the background. A rapid progression of this couple from twenty years of age to ninety years was simulated not just on their bodies, but also through repetitive changes on the trees as all four seasons occurred for seventy years. In the background, Gabbie's voice-over continued to explain.

"As we age, our cells divide and with each division the telomeres become shorter and shorter. This only makes us older and older, because the genetic information about being young at twenty years of age is lost as the telomeres continue to breakdown. Before my research, aging was believed to be inevitable, but what if we could collect, grow, and save the chromosomes holding the genetic age data in the telomeres from the age of twenty years? That would be astounding, but that would also lead to many profound questions if this theory is proven."

Next Addie saw a series of pictures showing a man reclined on a doctor's bench. A nurse rolled up his right shirt's sleeve and started a procedure. Gabbie's voice continued to explain as Addie viewed the remaining images.

"Presently you are watching a nurse take a sample of this patient's skin cells. After disinfecting the skin, the nurse takes a sterilized cylinder with a diameter slightly larger than a straw. The incisive end of the cylinder dissects a circular pattern of the epidermis and captures the sample inside the hollow cylinder. This gentleman and his wife have one

healthy child, but also had two miscarriages. In the lab his skin cells will be grown so his chromosomes may be examined for any possible reason contributing to their situation."

Several images flashed before Addie's eyes showing cells growing in the lab. Next the images zoomed in to show the tip of each chromosome.

"However, at the end of each chromosome in all the newly grown skin cells you have the age data of the person the samples were collected from. The more cells you grow, the more data filled telomeres you have from the age the samples were taken."

Next, images slowly changed showing different human organs, blood samples, incubators, and freezer units.

"The more samples you take of cells from different parts of the body, the more customized data you collect. These cells with all the telomeres holding data from the age of twenty, for example, could now be grown and stored for later use."

The image of the couple at ninety years of age appeared again. Addie continued to watch as the old couple stood in the field with the trees in the background.

"Now when your own genetic telomeres' data from twenty years of age is returned to you at ninety years of age, your body's cells can again live and divide with the restored youthful information starting from when you were twenty."

Now the age process of the couple went in reverse and the trees showed only ten years of season changes, as the couple went from ninety backwards to twenty years of age.

"In just ten years time, this couple will again be twenty; thus having a major impact on age related diseases and our world."

The program ended and Addie pulled off the virtual reality headgear to shout, "This is awesome! Incredible!"

Gabbie jumped out of her chair screaming, literally screaming.

"Oh my God, what's the matter?" Addie yelled back as she also jumped out of her chair.

"Oh I'm awfully sorry," Gabbie started to profusely apologize. "I'm awfully sorry, I must have been dreaming and I heard you yell. I'm sorry, I thought they were killing you."

"Killing me? Who was killing me?"

"I'm sorry Addie, your great grandmother has a great deal of bad dreams lately. Let me catch myself for a second... I gather you saw the entire presentation?"

"Yes, definitely and I can now fully understand why you're having bad dreams. You're worried about those men being after you for your research."

"Yes, this is Hitler all over again. Like Hitler, they want to rule the world forever and they see me as the instrument for making that come true."

"So what has the FBI done about these men who are after you?"

"They are working with the CIA. Let us sit down... Please don't worry dear, we're safe here."

"If you say so..." Addie acquiesced as she sat down.

"So...what did you think of my presentation?"

"What did I think? You found a way to obtain mankind's most unreachable want! My God, what happens next?"

"Well, you can work with me or go work with the competition in California."

"What do you mean? What competition?"

"A lab has a great deal of private money supporting the same research. They are about where I was fifty years ago. The difference between us is that they are producing an enzyme and I am using cell samples to grow customized telomeres from each person, for each person. George and I gave our own younger genetic data back to ourselves. This company bio-engineered an enzyme that they call telomerase. In the lab, they proved how their enzyme rebuilds telomeres in human cells. So far, they have seen a fifty-percent extension in the lifespan of the cells. However, by manufacturing telomerase enzymes as a 'Carte Blanche' solution for all, you increase the number of risks. For example, rapid division in the cells may occur and cause diseases instead of preventing them."

"In the presentation I just saw, you said this would lead to many profound questions and change our world as we know it. How so?"

"Think about this for a minute. People will want to benefit from this in great numbers. However, my more accurate and customized approach would not be delivered to the masses at any reasonable cost. A customized program would create numerous jobs in the medical industry to handle all the requests, but the cost factor will be out of reach for the majority of the good people living on this earth.

"A paradox would be created one way or another. First, as we already have crazed leaders, then criminals, and rich fanatics doing anything to live longer. They would be able to afford or steal the procedures. Then they would live hundreds of years, only to make life for us all, hell on earth.

"The other scenario is that this becomes available at an affordable price. People start living longer and put a strain on our resources, both man-made and natural. Earth's infrastructures will collapse.

"In nineteen ninety-eight the average life-span in America was seventy-six years old. Sixty-four thousand people were one hundred years of age or older. In two thousand and twenty, they estimate that number will rise to two hundred and fourteen thousand people. Add my work into the equation and that would cause our economy, food supply, and etceteras to immediately falter.

"If NASA had Mars prepared for habitation or a space drive so we could travel and expand to other planets, then maybe, just maybe the human race would be able to handle my work. You have to realize, all of us will not be able to live here on Earth."

"I understand," Addie replied with thought in mind. "And then expanding to other planets also leaves us vulnerable to alien diseases. Our medical industry, would need to go to a planet first to evaluate every living and nonliving thing."

"That's true. We will be living longer, but we become extinct due to a microscopic organism. How ironic, but despite all that, my work must succeed. At least for my family... Oh my look at the time. Let us go upstairs and join George for lunch. George and I have one more thing to ask you."

As the two women walked out of the lab, Gabbie picked up the old stuffed envelope on her desk and handed the package to Addie.

* * * * *

"George, thank you. That was the best veggie burger I ever had," said Addie.

"You are very welcome. Amazing how a slice of organic beefsteak tomato and a sliver of organic Spanish onion on a whole wheat bun can replace ketchup, salt and special sauce?"

Addie's cell phone went off diverting everyone's attention with the music from *God Bless America*. "Excuse me while I answer this. It's probably my mom calling again. "Hi... Oh hi, Chris."

"Addie I've been calling you all morning. What's going on? You leave me that message and then you never answer your phone. I even called your house and your mom said you where at the lab. Are you all right?"

"I'm fine... Oh God, Chris, you didn't say anything about my message to my mother?"

"Noo, but Addie you've freaked me out here real good."

"Sorry... Was I that bad with the message?" wondered Addie.

"Let's just say you covered the full spectrum... But I am not complaining, I can't. Not when I have someone as beautiful as you for a girlfriend?"

"Oh Chris, thanks for putting up with all this. I really..." Addie just then noticed Gabbie and George staring at her with big smiles, their elbows on the table and teacups in hand.

“Aad, are you there?”

“Yeah, ooh you never...” Addie turned a little in her chair and whispered the rest. “You never called me that before.”

“I know... You don’t like it?” wondered Chris.

“No, I like it. I mean... How can I complain when I have the best looking guy in school for a boyfriend?”

Gabbie and George synchronized a silly look at each other upon hearing that whisper.

“Oh man, I don’t believe you said that. When are you coming home?”

“Hold on. Gabbie, what else did you want to ask me? Chris wants to meet me when I get home.”

“Well, if you say yes, we will need a few hours. Ah, you should be home by half past four the very latest.”

“Great, Chris, meet me at my house at four or so. I should be home by then and we’ll talk. Okay?”

“Okay, I’ll seen you then. Bye.”

“Bye... Okay where were we?” Addie said as she flipped her phone closed and slipped the device back into her pocket.

“Well, now I have two questions for you,” said Gabbie. “First, are you planning to tell Chris?”

Concern and deep thought went across Addie’s face before she answered, “No, I guess not. What am I going to tell him?”

“George and I worked out the best way to keep this amongst ourselves and how to deny in case of a leak or emergency. We will go over that after we hear your next answer.”

“Okay, what’s the question?”

“Will you give us permission to take samples from you over the next two hours or so?”

"You mean like in the presentation with the skin cells?"

"Yes, and a great deal more." Gabbie paused and the seriousness of what she said next dominated her voice, "Some cell samples will require us to apply local anesthetic so the pain can be somewhat bearable."

"You're kidding, right?"

"No, I'm afraid not. The cell samples that require an operation and us putting you under, we can do another time."

"Oooh, you got that right," Addie emphasized. "And the end result to all this?"

"When you are fifty, sixty or eighty, we will give you back your own grown telomeres with all the information to be eighteen again."

"Oh shit..." Addie froze in thought and shock.

George quickly injected as he threw his arms into the air, "No, you should say something more like... Flying crab crap!"

Addie smiled at George who still held his arms in the air. She nervously giggled before saying, "Yes, let's do this."

Addie found herself in the center circular room of the lab with the operating table. She shivered from the cold stainless steel table that touched her body through a thin paper robe she had put on. George and Gabbie were in full surgical scrubs with masks and gloves.

"All right, first I am going to take a sample of skin cells from your right arm," Gabbie said through the mask. "This will sting a little."

After five seconds of silence, Addie began to complain. "Aah Grandma G, that is more than a...a sting! Oh it's burning, it's burning!"

"All done, don't worry. I will dress the area with Neosporin and a Band-Aid."

Just twenty minutes later, Addie's skin had sweat building up from being under the lights and she looked worn out. Gabbie just replaced her mask with a new one and George finished labeling test tubes filled with Addie's blood. Addie could not believe how much blood they took, and at this point, she did not care. Slowly she counted with dreary eyes as George put one, two, three, four, five, six and seven test tubes filled with her blood into a holding rack.

"Are we almost done?" asked Addie. "I have Band-Aids on both arms and my ankle, you sucked enough blood out of me to feed a vampire family for a week and..."

Gabbie approached Addie with a large syringe, squirting out some clear liquid to make sure all the air bubbles were gone.

"Oh my God, what is that for?" protested Addie.

"You know you are pretty squeamish for a scientist to be," Gabbie said through the mask. "This is a local anesthetic to numb the pain."

"To numb the pain where?"

"Under your mammary glands."

"I was afraid you would say something like that. Oh noo, aaah! This hurts, you know."

"Well, the needle hurts now, but at least the probe will not hurt as much later."

"Oh no," Addie moaned as Gabbie finished injecting her under her left breast.

"Oh yes," George said as he worked in the background getting some equipment ready. "And your great grandmother here is failing to tell you that even with this local anesthetic you will feel the pain."

"George, don't tell her that! You are not helping, Doctor," Gabbie said firmly. Gabbie continued to inject under Addie's right breast with as much kindness as possible.

"Oh my God, we have to do both?" Addie continued to protest.

Gabbie stopped and pulled back with the needle as she looked at George.

"Why are you looking at me?" George complained. "I didn't say anything. I'm minding my own business down here by the floor checking on this fuse box."

"And stay down there until I'm done." Gabbie turned her attention back to Addie. "Yes, Addie, I have to do both to be sure. Unless you want to run the risk of walking around with one breast looking a perky eighteen and the other looking a droopy seventy-five."

"That's not going to happen." Addie established.

"You are probably right, but we are still in the learning stages here so it's important to be sure."

"According to George it's going to hurt!"

Gabbie gave George another dirty look and then ever so gently stuck Addie with the syringe.

"Oh crab crap, crab crap, more crab crap," Addie repeated as Gabbie injected her.

"Okay, all done," Gabbie said as she placed the syringe on a portable rolling tray table. "We now have to wait about ten minutes so the anesthetic can take full effect."

Exactly ten minutes later, Gabbie struggled with a probe that she inserted halfway up under Addie's left breast. At the same time, Addie struggled to deal with the discomfort and pain.

"I'm sorry... Grandma... G... I can't take this anymore. Please stop!"

George sat on the floor facing the fuse box for most of the equipment in the room. He scrunched his face in sympathy to the sounds Addie made for each pain she felt.

"Okay I'm done. George, please take this sample. All right Addie, we just have the other breast to do and a lower alimentary canal exam to get a cell sample of your colon. Then we are finished for today."

"Oh no! I don't wanna be young anymore. I want to grow old!"

THE RED ALERT, Chapter Eleven

A cool gentle breeze blew through Addie's sweaty hair when she stepped out onto Gabbie's front porch. Gabbie closed the front door behind her and delighted in the view of her little serene neighborhood.

"What a gorgeous day," Gabbie noted. "My, look at all the boats in the harbor. Almost everyone must have taken advantage of the beautiful weather and put their boat into the water today."

"I guess," said Addie with little attention to the boats or the weather. "I feel like one giant bruise. I was really looking forward to a nice evening with Chris and now I just want to go home and heal."

"I'm awfully sorry, Addie, I was just so excited to do this for you at such a young age... I'm sorry."

"That's okay. Walk me to the security booth so you can help me get into my car."

"Really? Do you hurt that much?"

"No, I'm okay, but walk with me anyway."

They slowly strolled along the grounds of the lab, while unknown to them, they were being watched. By traveling along the winding path, that passed in front of the Victorian houses, they kept themselves within view of a telescope watching from across Cold Creek Harbor. The lens protruded between the dirty blinds that covered the window in the Sales Office trailer. However, this time the gravel lot by the edge of the water stood barren, except for that spy trailer. All the used RV units and Trailers that were for sale on the parcel were now gone. The sign that once said **SALES OFFICE**; now stated **OUT OF BUSINESS**.

Addie gave her great grandmother a long hug at the front gate. "All right Grandma G, call me when you hear something from the FBI."

"I will, dear."

"I love you."

"Ooh and I love you," Gabbie squeezed out before they finished hugging.

"I'll give you a ring when I get home so you don't worry."

"Actually, you don't have to. I'll watch from downstairs in the security booth to see that you arrived home safely."

"What do you mean?"

"Come with me, I'll show you."

"Wait one second," Addie said as she went over to her minivan and unlocked the passenger's door. Addie placed the album on the front seat and her backpack on top. After tossing Gabbie's envelope on the floor in front of the seat she locked the car and joined Gabbie outside the entrance of the security booth.

Gabbie walked into the security booth and they saw Charlie on duty. "Good afternoon Doctor, Miss Erickson. How may I help you?"

"Hi, Charlie," Addie acknowledged.

"Addie is going home now. May I show her the surveillance system downstairs? I want her to see how I will know that she arrived home safely."

"Yes, Ma'am, whatever you say."

"Thank you," Gabbie replied and she led the way down the stairs.

They entered a meeting room immediately to the right of a long hallway. Only the two rear light fixtures were on in the room. The front left corner had a folding table holding a computer, small television, coffee maker, and an empty box of pizza. A pile of used paper plates, empty soda cans, boxes of donuts, wire, duct tape, and a phone company tool belt had been tossed about on an oak table in the center of the room. A gentleman in a suit and loose tie, glanced over his shoulder to see who came inside.

"Good afternoon, Doctor."

"Good afternoon. Addie, you remember Agent Epstein?"

"Oh yeah, he drove us to that FBI meeting. Hello."

"Good to see you again. I have been watching your house all day. So far your dad was teaching your brother how to cut the lawn, your mom planted some new petunias in the front yard and they ran a few errands."

"Oh my God, you can see all that from here?"

"Sure, come here I'll show you. This is a good way for us to keep watch on you and your family without sitting in a car across the street. Besides, sitting in a car would be the biggest tip off to those creeps in the SUV. If they ever drive by your house again, we'll know."

"How can you tell that my mom planted petunias?"

"Watch," Agent Epstein said as he moved the mouse to a drop down menu on the computer monitor and clicked the zoom-in feature. The view zoomed closer and closer, until the funnel-shaped corolla on one flower filled the screen.

"Wow, look at that power!" Addie expressed.

The view now slowly pulled back out as a car pulled up in front of Addie's house. Chris had the roof down and hopped out without opening the door. He wore black jeans, sneakers and the long sleeves of his unbuttoned plaid shirt were rolled up. His straight-back sunglasses matched the color of his blue tee shirt.

"Oh my, you do have a cool boyfriend," Gabbie said teasingly.

"He is, isn't he," agreed Addie as she stared at the television with a smile. "He's already there an hour early, it's not even three thirty. He can't wait to see me."

Noticing this, Agent Epstein butted in, "Oh boy, someone has it bad."

"What, what do I have bad?" asked Addie quizzically.

Gabbie and the FBI Agent just giggled. Then the agent threw his folding chair back and stood up as he gave the computer a command to zoom out faster. A black SUV came to a skidding stop right behind Chris' car. Chris had just rang the doorbell as he turned to investigate the sound. Two men wearing ski masks flew out of the SUV toward him. Agent Epstein started to command the camera to zoom back in.

"Oh my God! That's the SUV. Chris!" Addie screamed.

"What should we do?" Gabbie demanded.

Chris froze in fear, allowing the two men to slam him into the front door. As he fell, Chris managed a kick-out move sending one assailant to the ground. Chris pushed off the ground to land back on his feet and the other masked man rammed him into the door again.

"Oh no, he's hurt," Gabbie called out as the Agent typed on the computer as fast as he could.

"Do something!" Addie pleaded as she shook Epstein's arm. "You gotta do something!"

"I am!" Epstein yelled. "Stop shaking my arm!"

"Noo!" Addie screamed. "Phillip, close the door!"

Alas, Addie's screaming advise could not be heard by her younger brother who opened the front door that removed the barrier between them. Chris with the masked man fell inward and onto Phillip. Both men now dragged Phillip and Chris into the house. Just before slamming the door shut, one of the masked men looked directly at the camera and motioned with both hands to come and get him.

"Oh shit! They know about the camera." Agent Epstein cried.

* * * * *

"Remember me, karate kid? Inside or I break your nose and kill little brother," came the threats through the ski mask in broken English.

"Okay, lighten up. Come on Phillip, you okay?"

The assailants pushed Phillip and Chris into the family room. At the same time, they heard Phillip's mom running above on the second floor. In a panic, she rushed to the stairs wearing stockings and her dress with the zipper still down in the back.

"My God, what was that noise? Phillip!" Brielle Erickson called out as she hurried down the stairs.

One masked man stayed in the room with Chris and Phillip. He now pointed a gun at them. The other man went and grabbed Brielle Erickson before she reached the bottom of the stairs.

"Stu! 911..." Brielle yelled out before a gun went up to her face and a hand to her mouth. The gunman had black leather gloves on and his flannel shirt with the ski mask had him sweating profusely.

* * * * *

"What should we do?" Gabbie demanded to know again.

"I already dispatched agents to the house," said Epstein. "You go up and get that guard down here."

Gabbie turned to run up, but Addie flew by her through the meeting room door. She hit the stairs taking three steps at a time and yelling, "Charlie! Charlie!"

* * * * *

"No dial tone!" a frantic Stewart yelled from upstairs while shaking the cordless phone. Having no dial tone coupled with his wife screaming 911, Stewart entered a frenzied state of mind. "What happened?" he demanded to know while he spontaneously departed the bedroom.

Half dressed for an evening out with his wife, Stewart came barreling down the stairs with just a gray undershirt, socks, and black trousers on, while still holding the cordless phone.

"Who is hurt?" Stu yelled as he reached the lower steps and looked up.

"Stop there!" commanded the gunman.

"Oh Shit!"

In the second Stewart took to say those two words an amazing level of emotion raced through his body. Fear, constructed by a masked man with a gun in his house. He had no idea what this man did to his wife and son; thus, he began to fabricate possibilities and reactions. With the momentum of coming down the stairs, he acted on an impulse. Throwing the phone at the masked man caused him to reel backwards when the phone hit his head. Stewart instantaneously decided to grab the end of the railing to swing himself over, kicking the gunman squarely in the chest.

From the sofa in the family room, Chris and the Ericksons witnessed this through the room's entrance. Brielle screamed and Phillip stood up with Chris.

"Yeah, Dad!" Phillip yelled.

The gunman in the room with them swung around and clobbered Chris in the jaw with his gun. Chris fell back onto the sofa, Brielle screamed again, Phillip sat down to the floor, and a gunshot went off.

Upon hearing the gunshot, Stewart halted his attempt to grab the gun from the man he just knocked to the floor when he flew over the railing. Stewart looked up to see the gunman in the family room pointing his gun to the ceiling. Slowly Stewart raised his arms as the gunman he kicked, pointed his gun at him.

* * * * *

Addie and Charlie hustled into the meeting room. Gabbie grabbed Addie and hugged her.

“What’s the order, sir?” Charlie shouted as he came to a stop at attention.

“Call your Commander and call in all security shifts,” ordered Agent Epstein. “We didn’t see it going down like this.”

“Yes, sir.”

“Whoever is on duty with you now, tell them they’re doing overtime today. Nobody gets off duty at four o’clock.”

“Yes, sir.”

“Agents are on the way to Addie’s house. They’ll take too long to get there. Charlie, you and one of your partners are coming with me to Addie’s house. Leave the third guard here at the booth until he is backed-up by the evening and graveyard shifts.”

“Yes, sir.”

“I need Addie and you, Doctor, to get back to your house and stay there.”

“But, my family is in...” Addie started to say.

“No buts! These men didn’t drive by or stakeout your house. They attacked it! Move it! Soldier put this lab on Red Alert!”

“Yes, sir!”

* * * * *

Stewart, his wife, son and Chris were sitting on the sofa. The two gunmen stood watching over them. One gunman went over to the windows and pulled the shades down as the other offered an explanation.

“We make a diversion. We just want Ageless Matron’s secret at Cold Creek Harbor lab. So don’t move and don’t get hurt.”

“We have no idea what you’re talking about,” Stewart stated while slowly shaking his head and trying to understand the heavy accent.

"I don't care," the gunman squawked back.

Chris began to worry about Addie at the lab after realizing the Ageless Matron might be Gabbie. Both gunmen were now keeping watch through the side of the shades. Chris leaned back on the sofa as he nudged Mr. Erickson who sat next to him. When Stewart looked over, he saw Chris had his cell phone halfway out of his pocket.

* * * * *

Gabbie and Addie were running back to the house when Addie suddenly stopped.

"What's wrong, Addie?"

"I'm sorry, I can't run anymore," declared Addie as she bent over holding her breast. "I'm hurting bad after that procedure and I'm dizzy. We should've taken my van."

"All right, we don't have to run the rest of the way, we'll walk."

* * * * *

"Oh my gosh!" Stewart said. "I left the water running upstairs. We have to shut it."

"No! You go nowhere," said the gunman who clobbered Chris.

"You can come with me," begged Stewart. "The water will flood, set off alarms, trigger the alarm company to investigate." Stewart stood slowly and nervously.

"Follow him upstairs, I'll watch them down here."

Stewart put his arms up and walked out of the room with one gunman behind him. The gunman doing all the talking went to the base of the stairs and watched everyone else through the family room entrance.

* * * * *

"Oh, there is George in the doorway," noted Gabbie as she helped Addie walk as fast as she could.

“I was still in your lab,” said George as he rushed down to help Addie. “I was trying to fix that fuse box when the Red Alert emergency alarm went on. Come in. Come in! What’s wrong?”

* * * * *

The FBI’s car sped out through the front entrance of the lab, leaving one guard behind to close the gate. The hands on the telescope watching from across the harbor reached over and picked up a cell phone.

“Hell-low,” he said over the cell phone in broken English.

“Aged-less Matron’s secret at CCH. Act two.”

“Act two, understood.”

“Bye.”

“Wait! What if they can’t get back in time?”

“They are expendable. Hang up now!”

* * * * *

Chris moved to the end of the sofa and half out of sight of the gunman watching them. Leaning over the sofa, he operated his cell phone with one hand.

Addie sat down on Gabbie’s sofa while still holding her chest. “That’s my phone! Ooh, please be... Chris!” she hopefully expressed.

“It’s me!” Chris whispered as fast as he could. “Don’t come home. SUV guys are here! Call 911!” Chris flipped his phone closed.

“Chris, don’t hang up!” Addie pleaded to no avail.

Chris stuck the cell phone back in his pocket just as the gunman walked in.

“What are you doing?”

"Talking to myself, my head is pounding," mumbled Chris.

"Let me get him some ice from the freezer," said Brielle.

"No! Nobody got me ice when he broke my nose."

"Oh, poor deprived baby," Phillip mocked to the surprise of everyone in the room.

"Shut up, kid," the gunman ordered.

Upstairs, Stewart twisted the faucets to his bathroom sink. "Nope they are off, my mistake. I swore I left them on."

"Back downstairs idiot," commanded the gunman with Stewart.

* * * * *

Just past the lab, where Harbor View Road forked-off to a dirt road that dropped halfway down to sealevel, three men were fishing. They were sitting on the guard railing and fishing off the end of the road where Chris and Addie parked that disconcerting night. With a ten-foot drop to the water below, the men were perched high enough to have an excellent view of the harbor.

"My, oh my, look at that new boat pulling up below," said an elderly gentleman sitting at the end of the railing. "She's a beauty."

"Let's have a look, Pop," said Jake. Addie's bus driver always enjoyed some leisure time fishing with his father and friend, but he enjoyed boats more and he wanted a better view. "Yep, that's a fine looking craft. Looks like she wants to dock at the old pier on the end of the lab's property."

"That's mighty sweet son, now stop leaning on me and move back! You are tangling my fishing line," complained Jake's father.

* * * * *

George paced the floor in the parlor; Gabbie and Addie sat nervously on the sofa.

“What should I do, Gabbie? Chris said to call 911.”

“George, what do you think?”

“I don’t know, Gabbie, I don’t know. The FBI should be at the house by now.”

“What if they aren’t?” insisted a fearful Addie.

“True,” agreed George. “Yes, all right, call 911! Tell them to send police to your house.”

Addie had her cell phone still in hand and started dialing before George finished his sentence.

* * * * *

A beautiful Saturday afternoon in spring always brought crowds to the delightful shops and restaurants on Main Street. Pedestrians were everywhere, American flags were blowing in the breeze, parking was at a premium, and cars crawled along as people window-shopped from their car windows. This would be blissful to just about anyone, except for Agent Epstein at this time.

Epstein put his window down and reached out to slam a siren light on the roof of his car. Only half a mile from Addie’s house and at this rate he would take fifteen minutes to get there. The light went on, the car horn blew, and he tried to drive down the middle of a two-way street that barely had room for two cars. Parked cars, flagpoles, and pedestrians prevented Epstein from driving onto the sidewalk. His patience grew thin and out the window he screamed, “FBI damn it! Get out of my way!”

Charlie and the other security guard jumped from the car and started directing drivers so Epstein could get through. They finally stifled the chaos and the guards jumped back in as their vehicle went through most traffic.

* * * * *

Stewart sat back on the sofa with everyone else. Once the gunmen looked out the windows again, Stewart turned to Chris and whispered,

"You called?"

Chris gave Stewart a 'thumbs up' and cringed when he tried to smile through his swollen, pummeled jaw.

"Mom, I have no room," complained Phillip as he squirmed about on the sofa.

"Don't worry," consoled Brielle. "Please, that is the least of our problems."

"You listen to your mother," said the talkative gunman as he walked toward the sofa. "Do you understand?"

"I understand," shouted Phillip with watery eyes. "That you don't understand basic hygiene, you stink from here to high heaven! Take a bath."

Phillip shocked everyone with his verbal revolt. Brielle started tapping him on the arm as he talked, but she did not say anything to him due to fear. Her eyes remained fixed on the gun.

"Smart mouth kid," said the gunman by the window as the other gunman moved closer to Phillip.

"What do you know about heaven, little man?"

"More than you. Buy some deodorant!"

The gunman pointed his gun at Phillip's nose. Stewart's right fist tightened and then relaxed as the gunman burst out laughing. "Good one...little man!" The gunman walked back to the windows and with his back to his prisoners, he lifted the ski mask for a second. Quickly he raised his other arm to wipe some sweat from his face.

"Police car!" shouted the gunman looking out the window.

"No," said the other gunman as he pulled his mask back down and faced the Ericksons. "Who called police? Who?"

"Not us, the phones are dead." Stewart snapped back. "Didn't you cut the wires?"

"Oh, that is correct."

"Nincompoop," said Phillip.

"I don't even want to know what that means," said a now agitated gunman.

"Err...a woman police," groaned the gunman by the window. "She saw SUV and is on radio...wait I now see FBI car. Three men I see. One agent and two...security."

"Yes," Chris quietly exclaimed.

"Let me look," ordered the gunman by the sofa. "Our plan is working. Get them ready to leave."

"All you up and go slowly to front door."

* * * * *

The sole guard in the security booth never knew what happened. Two masked men stood over his body in the booth. One held a sniper's rifle and the other held a cell phone. The taking of Cold Creek Harbor lab had commenced.

* * * * *

"George, please stop walking all about and sit down."

"I cannot sit down Gabbie, this is very troublesome."

"Could we call the guard at the front gate to see if he can tell us what's going on?" suggested Addie.

"Yes, that is correct!" George realized and went off into the kitchen.

"No matter what happens, Addie, you stay with me." Gabbie said as she held Addie's hand and looked her in the eyes. "I will never let anyone harm my great granddaughter."

"I know..." Addie started to say, but stopped because she became concerned that George entered the room so soon.

"The phone line is dead, Gabbie." George said as he swallowed hard. "They are on the property."

"I can call security with my cell phone," reassured Addie with her offer of hope.

Just then, the sound of an upstairs bedroom window smashing open ripped through the house, followed by two thuds.

"Gabbie, they are in the house!" George yelled and he put his hand over his mouth.

"I'll call security..." Addie rushed to say. "What's the number?"

"We have no time," shouted Gabbie as she led Addie off the sofa by her hand and started running to the hall. "To my lab, George."

"Yeah, the lab."

All three ran down the hall, as two pairs of footsteps pounded about on the second floor.

"Grandma G!" Addie screamed as they ran down the metal flight of stairs and two pairs of feet ran down the second floor staircase. "What about the tunnels to the other houses you told me about at breakfast?"

"Oh Addie, they were hastily made in forty-one. They filled them all up in ninety-five."

"They are long gone!" shouted George. "Keep running!"

* * * * *

The front door to Addie's house slowly opened. The brief conversation the law enforcers were having ended abruptly when Chris and Phillip appeared in the doorway. Officer, Donna Rampey, took cover behind her patrol car and drew her gun. Both security guards remained standing behind Agent Epstein as he waited to see what would go down.

* * * * *

Gabbie had the entrance door to her lab opened in no time flat with her ID card, but just as she turned to shut and lock the steel door, two masked men bounded toward her. George saw this and threw his body against the door. Both him and Gabbie had the door an inch away from closing, but the two men were stronger. However, just before they could get the upper hand, Addie screamed and did a Front Ball kick into the door between George and Gabbie. Thus offering enough assistance to slam the door shut. Gabbie locked the door and they all stepped away. The three of them stood there listening to the two men pounding on the door from the other side.

"Some kick, Addie," said an impressed George.

"Those lessons are worth every penny," acknowledged Gabbie.

"I'll call security," said Addie as she pulled out her cell phone.

"That won't work down here," George sadly stated and walked over to Gabbie's desk.

"Oh no, you're right, I have no signal, why doesn't it work?"

"For the same reasons cell phones don't work in any lab underground here," concluded Gabbie.

"That's right," said Addie depressingly. "Jim told me about that."

"These phones are dead also, they killed the entire lab." George hung up Gabbie's desk telephone as he noticed the banging on the door had stopped.

"What do we do now?" Addie asked with immense concern.

"We wait Addie, we wait until help comes," said George who slowly walked over to where Gabbie sat down. Her arms folded across her chest and eyes filled with tears, Gabbie looked at George for comfort.

* * * * *

Stewart and Brielle were being dragged out of their house backwards by the two gunmen who stood in the middle of their selfmade human shield. Chris and Phillip were in front and the situation did not offer too many options.

"Stand down!" the gunman yelled. "We leave now in our car. Not try anything or we kill smart mouth kid!"

Brielle started crying, Stewart clenched his right fist again while breathing rapidly, Chris kept walking forward with Phillip as they both felt the nudge of a gun barrel.

"Listen!" Agent Epstein yelled. "Tell us what you want and we may work a deal."

"No deals! Back off! Get behind your cars. Allow us to leave!"

"Officer," Agent Epstein called out. "Can you get a police helicopter over here to follow them?"

"No problem," said Officer Rampey as she clicked the microphone hooked to her shirt. "Backup should be here any minute."

"Not if they are coming the same way my backup is coming on Main Street."

* * * * *

Up the hill on Route 5A, a car parked on the side of the road against the fence going around the lab's property. The car faced the opposite direction of traffic and Tommy used his binoculars to look down the hill at the security booth. Just above him, on a wooden pole and at the edge of the woods, a large red light blinked on and off alerting all those approaching the perimeter of the red alert situation. A Ford pick up truck came speeding over the hill with Tommy's partners.

"Lance, look!" said the female security guard from the passenger's seat. "There's Tommy. The lab is definitely on Red Alert."

"I see him, hold on, muffin!" replied Lance who hit the truck's brakes causing them to screech for a second. Then the truck immediately went across the oncoming lane of traffic, causing the horn of a motorist to sound off. Lance pulled behind Tommy who stood at the edge of the road.

"What can you make out?" The female security guard spit her question out as she slammed her door closed.

"Not much, Charisse, that's what has me worried," said Tommy calmly.

All three security guards were in their street clothes. Normal procedure had them arrive early and inconspicuously. The security uniforms were in the locker room below the security booth and worn as a cover when on duty at the lab. At all other locations and assignments, these soldiers wore their Military Police uniforms.

"Let me have a look," requested Lance as he came alongside Tommy.

"I tried calling Charlie back at the booth, but the lines are down," Tommy said as he passed the binoculars off to Lance.

"Shit, if they knew how to take out our phones lines, then we're dealing with some serious dudes," Commented Lance as he continued looking through the binoculars. "What do we do next?"

"We wait until the graveyard shift gets here with Hennington," answered Tommy. "He's in command, so he'll give the orders."

* * * * *

"George do you hear anything?" Gabbie asked as she stood with Addie at a safe distance from her lab's door.

"Something is going on," whispered George as he put his ear to the door. "I can't tell what... Aaah get down!"

Slightly muffled gunshots blasted off the other side of the door. George dived from the door while the women took cover behind the desk. George stuck his head up and came crawling around the desk as fast as he could.

"Love, are you all right?" asked Gabbie.

"Yes, yes. They are trying to shoot the lock off."

"Will the door open?" asked Addie fearfully.

"I hope...no. No, the door won't open," affirmed George.

"They're going to kill us for your secret," declared Addie as the bullet shots stopped.

"Now don't talk that way, Addie. I am no good to them dead. They are not killing me if they want my secrets."

"Yeah, but Grandma G, they'll kill me and George."

Spoken words that were a horrifying realization for Gabbie as she looked into Addie's fear-filled eyes. Finally, after several seconds, Gabbie spoke with confidence, "Well then, I will just have to hide you both."

* * * * *

The doors slammed shut on the black SUV. The gunmen had Brielle behind the wheel and Phillip stood on his knees in front of the passenger's seat that one gunman occupied. The second gunman sat in the backseat with Chris on one side and Stewart on the other.

"Drive very slow woman or your son and the teenager will be punished." Acutely aware of that fact, Brielle put the SUV into reverse and slowly backed up so she could drive around Chris' car.

Agent Epstein stood there with the others as the shaded windows of the SUV went by and offered no view of the interior. A neighbor two houses down came out onto his driveway and started sweeping. Through the SUV's front window he saw Brielle and waved hello. Only when he saw the masked man in the passenger seat and the petrified faces on Brielle and Phillip did he start to understand what just transpired. As the SUV drove to the corner of the block the neighbor turned back to see the police and security personnel scrambling to get into their cars. The broom dropped to the driveway and he went running into the house.

Once Brielle made a left turn, the gunman ordered her to stop the SUV. Two cars that came up from behind had to stop also.

"Get out now and stay standing in middle of street or we kill you!" threatened the gunman. One second of hesitation by the Ericksons brought a scream, "Get out now!"

The doors started banging shut as the gunman in the front jumped over to the driver's seat. The horn of the car from behind them tooted as the driver raised the palm side of his hands upward as if to ask, 'what's going on.'

The SUV sped away leaving dazed people standing in the median of the road. The police car with the siren roaring came around the corner only to skid to a stop when the Ericksons came into view. The FBI car went up and onto the grass to pass by the police car. Agent Epstein continued after the SUV. Charlie sat in the front passenger seat and turned his head to see if the Ericksons were all okay as they went by.

Officer Rampey jumped out of her car and ran over to help the Ericksons off the road.

* * * * *

"Epstein, come in," a woman's voice came into the car.

"Epstein here," the agent answered after picking up the handheld radio.

"Where the hell are you? This is Rigano, I've been calling you for ten minutes."

"Been a little busy outside the car without the radio."

"I'm stuck with Cooper on Main Street! We're at the parking lot entrance."

"Stay there! I repeat, stay there. The black SUV is coming your way. I'm in pursuit with two lab security guards."

"Affirmative, we will set up a road block. What's the status at the lab?"

"All shifts called in and they are on Red Alert. Did you drive by?"

"Negative, we came down from the turnpike and Pond Lake Road. We didn't pass the lab."

* * * * *

An unmarked car with a light stuck to the roof now pulled up behind Officer Rampey. Detective Rodriguez stepped out and at once closed his eyes in sympathy after seeing Chris standing on the side of the road.

Traffic started to back up when the sound of the police helicopter came overhead. Officer Rampey continued talking with the Ericksons, who were sitting on the side of the road when she looked up to see the helicopter.

"All right," consoled Rampey. "I know you are all shaken up. Detective Rodriguez will stay with you while I talk to this chopper overhead and direct some traffic."

* * * * *

"Aspetta un momento Gabbie, I'm sorry, this is not going to work," said George as he struggled to slide back out of a square air vent by the floor.

"This must work," insisted Gabbie.

"Wait a moment! Listen to me. The ductwork doesn't go back far enough. We cannot both fit in there. Just let Addie get in. They are not getting through that door, but just in case, let's get Addie in and the metal grate back up."

"All right," said Gabbie reluctantly. "Addie please get in. I have to at least hide you."

Addie, also reluctant, bent down and started to crawl in backwards. "Be careful you two," said Addie with a glance up from the floor.

"Yes, yes and you be quiet in there," instructed George. "Everything echoes inside that thing."

* * * * *

The police chopper stopped hovering and dispatched further down Main Street. Officer Rampey directed traffic to make a 'U' turn and go back.

Detective Rodriguez had on a new suit and wrote some notes after speaking with Stewart.

"Just make sure our daughter is safe," Stewart concluded as he held his wife's hand tightly.

Rodriguez then turned to Chris sitting on the curb, "How you doing, kid? I'm sorry about all this."

"Yes, sir," said Chris without looking up.

"It looks like you have another shiner on your face."

"Yes, sir... Detective, can you tell me what's going on at the lab?"

"I really don't know Chris. Why?"

"I was trying to call Addie who's there and all I get is the recording saying her cell isn't in service and to leave a message."

"I don't know what to tell you, kid. Look, let's get everyone off the street first, then I'll radio in for you."

* * * * *

"Addie are you sure that you are okay in there?" asked Gabbie with doubt.

"Yes, now please don't worry. Go see what George is doing by the door. I can watch all the way from here."

"All right, Love," said Gabbie.

George had his ear to the door again, but much lower to the floor this time.

"What do you hear?" Gabbie asked as she knelt down next to George.

"Shush," George sounded. "I believe I hear duct tape."

"What?"

"Duct tape. I hear them ripping off pieces of duct tape."

George and Gabbie looked at each other with dread. They both stood up and ran from the door.

"Here, help me push my desk up against the door," said Gabbie as she grabbed her monitor and tower to place both of them on the floor.

George had already begun to push the desk towards the door. When Gabbie added her assistance, the distance the desk traveled promptly increased. The force pulled the wires attached to the telephone and keyboard on the desk. Both items went crashing to the floor. Addie watched from her unobstructed view as Gabbie and George fortified the door.

* * * * *

"Epstein, come in," called Rigano.

"Go ahead," answered Epstein over the radio.

"We have a black SUV that entered the public parking lot through the exit, east of me. They parked in the second row and dead center."

"How many rows of parking are in that lot?"

"Four, but we wait for backup. The police are coming to close down the street and clear everybody out."

"Roger, I'm twenty feet away from the parking lot exit. I'll hold my position here."

Charlie looked at Epstein, "All due respect sir, they are not going to sit in their SUV while the police close down the town."

"Tell me about it," agreed Epstein.

* * * * *

Three more parked cars cluttered the side of the road by the lab's property. A map of the property covered the hood of one car. Charisse and her husband Lance were standing in front of the car with Hennington, who had command. The midnight crew consisted of José Gonzalez, Steve Bougiamas, and Frank the Hawk Shenandoah.

"Hawk and Tommy should be back in a few minutes with answers for why the phones are down and why nobody is manning the security booth," said Hennington who then paused and turned to look down the hill. "My biggest concern is how we are going to get to our gear below the security booth unnoticed."

* * * * *

"Hey, Rodriguez," Officer Rampey yelled. "We have to go. They have the SUV blocked off in the parking lot on Main Street. We have to close down the street. They need all the help they can get."

Detective Rodriguez yelled back, "Go! I'll catch up. I'm bringing the Ericksons back to their house."

"All right..." said Rampey as she approached Rodriguez. "Hey what happened to the other kid?"

"He already started walking back to the Erickson's place to get his car."

"Fine, see you later," stated Rampey while she went toward her vehicle.

* * * * *

"Sir," José called out. "Here comes Hawk up the hill. Man is he peddling fast."

They all ran to meet Hawk as his bicycle reached the parked cars. Charisse grabbed the bike as Hawk let go so he could bend over to get some more oxygen into his lungs.

"Hawk, you'll have to breathe later," ordered Hennington. "Give us your report."

"Yes, sir. Drove past entrance saw no one." Hawk took in some more air. "Parked my truck at Firehouse, took my bike and rode back past the entrance." Again another deep gasp for some air. "I went slowly past the entrance and I saw two men moving about with semiautomatics. Next I saw them going down below." His breathing gradually became normal again. "They were not our guys. They were wearing ski masks."

"Shit," said Lance.

"What the hell happened?" asked José.

"All right, all right," Hennington repeated to keep order. "We wait for Tommy to get back and report in."

"Damn shit. Sir, Tommy is coming out of the woods now!" Charisse reported as she stopped her slow preoccupied drift toward the fence after hearing Hawk's report.

A clump of leaves and dirt started to come over the fence. Only after Tommy shed some branches and leaves did his mud-covered face become clear. He jogged up the slight embankment to the side of the road with Charisse joining him at his side.

"Sir, I observed one man jogging from Land's End into the lab neighborhood. He was wearing a short, white lab coat..." Tommy paused to catch his breath. "Not a long one like the standard here at the lab. He was carrying a duffel bag and ran into Doctor Maida's house through the back door. I also noticed a broken second floor window on the rear of Doctor Maida's house above the carport roof. Next, I proceeded slowly to Land's End and observed two men on a boat docked at the old pier wearing the same short lab coats. On the way back, I didn't see any security personnel on the property. I regret to report that terrorists have the lab."

"All right, our worst concern has been confirmed," Hennington said. "I'll notify the CIA and the local police, because we can't do much without our firearms."

* * * * *

Three loud bangs came from the door in Gabbie's lab. George and Gabbie were standing about six feet away.

"Knock, knock! Doctor scientist people in there! Move away from your door! We are going to blow your door open in five minutes!"

* * * * *

Detective Rodriguez pulled into the Erickson's driveway after passing Chris still walking back. Brielle and Stewart stepped out of the car after shaking the Detective's hand in gratitude. Phillip jumped out of the car first and saw several neighbors running over to ask if they were all right. Detective Rodriguez backed out of the driveway leaving the Ericksons to talk with their friends. Chris jumped into his car and at the same time called Addie on his cell phone. Once Chris started his engine, his car's stereo came on playing the song, *Hole in the World Tonight*. Chris looked at his stereo with eyes of dismay before he noticed that Detective Rodriguez had stopped his car right in front of him. After Rodriguez did some talking on the radio, the Detective put his car into Park and walked over to Chris.

"Listen kid," Rodriguez said as he leaned on the corner of Chris' front windshield. "I need your help. Word has just been passed along that terrorists took the lab."

Chris' face went into shock as the Detective continued talking. "They have a boat at the end of the lab's property, so the Coast Guard has been notified and I'm heading down to Main Street because it's been closed off since they trapped the SUV in the parking lot. Do me a favor; stay here with the Ericksons. I'll call when I know more. Thanks, kid, and get some ice for your face."

The siren light stuck on top of Rodriguez's car snapped on and he raced to the corner. Chris watched the vehicle make a left turn toward town as he closed his cell phone and turned up the stereo's volume.

Stewart excused himself from his family and friends to go over and ask Chris what the Detective said to him. However, Chris didn't wait around. Especially since Addie still didn't answer her cell phone. He threw his car into gear and peeled out to the corner, leaving Stewart waving after him in vain.

Skidding to a stop at the corner, Chris made a right turn. He had to go the long way around and the pulsating determination on his face proved not one thing would stop him.

* * * * *

"Listen Addie, no matter what, you stay in there. George and I are going to hide in the center operating room with the curtains closed."

"I don't think they can blow the door open," George added. "However, just in case they do and they take us away, I have all the screws very loose holding the grate. I did just one half of a turn. You should be able to bang this grate open."

"Okay go hide!" Addie could not see the center operating room from her position, but she could see the entrance door.

Gabbie and George closed all the curtains and just as they took cover behind the operating table an explosion ripped through the lab. Addie saw the entire door come out of the doorframe with a flash of light and smoke. She covered her head with her arms as the sound vibrated throughout the ductwork. The door smashed into Gabbie's desk so fast and hard that the steel door bent. The wooden desk flipped over and broke into two. Pulsating smoke alarms were sounding in tandem with a white strobe light. Inside the center operating room, all the glass walls facing the entrance shattered. Fortunately, the closed curtains prevented the broken glass from showering the room.

* * * * *

Police cars were behind Agent Epstein's car as they started to move people off the street and away from the parking lot. Traffic had to be turned around when detective Rodriguez showed up.

Suddenly, a beautiful afternoon on Main Street changed into an ugly one. The SUV gunmen were overheated, nervous, and running out of time. The police helicopter adjusted first to the event occurring. The SUV had peeled out of its parking space and the police chopper moved to follow the vehicle. The lot became void of people since the police stopped everyone from entering either by foot or by car. The SUV headed for the entrance to the parking lot unobstructed.

Showing no mercy, the SUV came around and went up onto the sidewalk between the police car and Rigano's car. A garbage can and one of the American flags on a pole collided against the car before hitting the ground. Into the middle of the street still pushing the garbage can went the SUV. Rigano and Cooper who were standing outside their car, spun around and fired off six rounds as the SUV turned left and sped toward the harbor. The people still moving off the sidewalks started to run in all directions. The garbage can continued to fly from the front of the SUV and into a parked car. The decorative, metal garbage container flipped over the top of the parked car's hood and hit several people running down the sidewalk. One woman fell to her knees with a gash on her forehead and a couple fell over their baby stroller as they took a ricochet hit from the container. The rear window of the SUV shattered and the rear panel took four bullets from Rigano and Cooper. Screams filled the air and horror surrounded this little town. A police officer directing traffic, turned to see the SUV heading for him. Immediately he tried to pull his revolver and remained blocking the only way clear for the SUV to escape. They drove their SUV right into him. The police officer flipped over and hit the ground as the SUV muscled its way between cars facing both directions. Only the helicopter above could follow now. The law enforcers made calls for an ambulance and some jockeyed their vehicles into position eventually to go in pursuit. Broken car mirrors, glass, garbage, and blood now littered Main Street.

THE PASSAGE, Chapter Twelve

One gunman stepped through the broken glass panel of the center operating room and threw the curtain to the side. Outside lights and sounds now filtered into the dark room. The crunching of glass under foot made each step the gunman took very audible. Gabbie and George remained seated on the floor behind the operating table as they listened and waited.

"Where are you, Doctor? We just want your secret lab formula!" The voice that entered the lab had a thick and uninvited accent.

The two masked gunmen slowly walked around. Debris from the explosion filled the floor and smoke alarms continued to blast on and off despite the clearing air.

Addie, however, suffered the most from the smoke created by the explosion. By hiding in the ductwork that returned air to the venting system, a strong flow of smoke and dirt came in the vent. Placing her head within her arms didn't help, she gasped for air and her eyes were burning.

The lights came on inside the center operating room and within a few seconds, the intruders would walk around to find their victims hiding behind the operating table. However, a distant cough echoed between the sounds of the smoke alarm.

One of the gunman outside the operating room turned, What was that? Did you hear that?"

Gabbie fixed her apprehensive eyes onto George and mouthed, "Addie."

"Sounds like from inside something, look around!" shouted the gunman in the operating room.

Gabbie's expression became the manifestation of panic. George tried to stop her, but to no avail. Her instinctive reaction is inevitable and understandable for any parent.

"I'm coughing down here!" Gabbie called out as she stood up with George clinging to her. "The smoke is affecting my lungs."

The gunman swung back around to see Gabbie and George standing up from behind the operating table. "I have them here!" The gunman called to his accomplice.

Addie scarcely heard this inside the vent where she hid. She shook her head in turmoil and guilt, knowing that her coughing caused her great grandmother's capture.

* * * * *

"Sir, I just spoke with the police," Charisse said with her cell phone still in hand. "We won't see any help for some time. The FBI and the CIA agents along with the entire Cold Creek Harbor Police force are at Main Street. The black SUV has wreaked havoc and a police chopper is in pursuit."

"Do you mean that chopper?" Hennington yelled as he pointed across the harbor to airspace above the opposite hillside.

"Binoculars!" yelled Charisse.

Her husband Lance came running over with them. She grabbed the binoculars and spied down the chopper to confirm if the police were operating the bird.

"Yes, sir! That's a police chopper," reported Charisse.

"What about State Troopers helping?" Hennington inquired.

"At best, one or two in fifteen to twenty minutes, sir." Tommy responded. Mud still covered his face from his previous camouflage surveillance.

"Crap," Hennington complained as he ran his hand over his short blonde hair. "The National Guard will take too long to mobilize." He thought aloud. "Damn it! These bullshit policies with uniforms and side-arms are killing us. Everything we need is stored below the security booth. I'm calling in our brothers and sisters. Call the police back and remind them that Main Street is not our only problem. I already informed them that these S. O. B.s are more than a half dozen strong and they have the lab!"

* * * * *

"My oh my, look at that chopper on the other side of the harbor. She is a beauty."

"Let's have a look, Pop," Jake said as he leaned over for a better view. "Hayden, what can you make of it?"

Hayden and Jake were best friend for decades. The boat had docked at the old pier below them and they were out of sight because of the bluff.

"Must be some trouble over there," Hayden answered while maintaining the majority of his attention on his fishing line.

* * * * *

The black SUV blew by all the cars in the opposite lane that were stuck in traffic. Before the right turn where Main Street becomes Route 5A heading toward the lab, the SUV had turned right into the lot with the trailer hosting the **Out Of Business** sign. The SUV came to a skidding stop on the gravel just before the water's edge. The police chopper hovered right overhead. Two other masked men came running out of the trailer with semiautomatic guns and backpacks. The two in the SUV leaped out and tossed everything into the back. The gunman who had his nose broke by Chris ran back into the trailer as another backed the SUV up. The last two masked men started hooking up the trailer to the SUV.

* * * * *

"I don't ask you again, Doctors!"

"And I will answer you for the last time," Gabbie nervously said. "I have no notes to give you, because you blew up my computer."

"You have backups, get them!"

"Backups of what?"

"How you are still young, we know how old you are."

"I'm fifty-nine thank you."

"No, you are older. Much older."

"You have the wrong person."

"Then we should just shoot you both."

The other gunman looked over all the equipment in the center operating room and decided to start turning everything on. "Let her show us how she stays young."

"Oh no, do not turn all that on," George objected. "The fuses are not going to handle everything..."

"Shut up! Show us procedures."

"Sure, sure..." Gabbie said as the gunman pushed her to the countertop on the side.

Addie now struggled to hear the spoken words from the center operating room. Smudged filth covered her face, hair, and her clothes. The ringing echoing in her ears reached her maximum tolerance level. Finally, the pulsating smoke alarm stopped.

* * * * *

Detective Rodriguez and Officer Rampey were at her patrol car with Agent Epstein. The car doors were open and Charlie with his partner Derrick Brown stood nearby in their security uniforms.

"With all due respect, sir," Charlie said to Epstein. "We have to get back to the lab. Especially with word that the enemy has control of the facility with a boat and the nearest Coast Guard station is half an hour away."

"I hear you, but unless you want to walk, we are not getting through with cars just yet. Once the ambulance takes Officer Olsen to..." A siren from another ambulance came speeding up behind them. "Look here's another one. All right let them through!"

As the ambulance went by to help the people on the sidewalk, the siren shut off and the patrol car's radio came alive.

"Air to car this is Chopper One. They loaded their vehicle with weapons and backpacks. However, I can't see them getting far." Everyone by the patrol car now listened to the voice of the pilot as the chopper came into view high in the sky on the horizon. "They are hooking up a trailer to the back of the SUV," reported the pilot over the radio. "Oh my God!"

The gunman that went into the trailer came back out. He shouldered his weapon and fired. Everyone who watched from Main Street, saw the helicopter veer off, but that maneuver wasn't enough. The ground to air munition created a cloud trail and an explosion upon reaching the chopper. Smoke, flame, and debris fell straight down and out of view.

Everybody stopped to contemplate what just happened, everyone except Charlie and Derrick. They were running across the street, across the parking lot, up the hill and through the woods. They were taking a shortcut over the hillside to the lab in military double time.

* * * * *

Jake, his father, and Hayden froze. Every person on a boat in the harbor stopped. People on Main Street stopped. People in their cars and stuck in traffic just outside the gravel lot jumped from their cars to see what happened. Every law enforcer on Main Street raced to his or her car and all their sirens started. Everyone moved out of their way, even the two ambulances. This would be the second time, in less than a year, that evil sent its soldiers to bring hell to the front yard of these people.

Those in their cars by the entrance of the gravel lot found out that they were in need of cover. One of the chopper blades came swirling through the treetops with a horrifying howl. The sides of two cars took the hit leaving one elderly driver injured and trapped inside.

Debris from the helicopter also slammed into a neighboring house of the gravel lot. Several drivers stuck on the road were using their cell phones to call 911. Some were trying to help the injured driver trapped under the chopper's blade. People were shouting and asking one another what to do. Intuitively they all knew what to do at the same time, run! They had to run for their lives. The SUV dragged the trailer out of the lot and the gunman in the passenger seat started spraying bullets out of his window and onto the congested street with his semiautomatic.

They brought the trailer into the middle of the street and up against the car with the trapped driver. The SUV turned sharply to face away from the police and towards Route 5A that went to the lab. Four masked men jumped from the SUV fully armed. All the law enforcers started to arrive with their cars on the opposite side of the trailer, which completely blocked their passage and view. The elderly injured man still trapped inside his car, next to the trailer, reached up for help. He immediately withdrew his request when he saw the masked gunman looking in his window. With his semiautomatic tapping the smashed in car door, the gunman slowly rolled up his ski mask just over his mouth and spit onto the injured driver. He casually walked away as one by one each police siren shut off.

The police with Epstein, Rigano, and Cooper hurried the people behind their cars. While two gunman took positions on opposite corners of the trailer, the other two started to disconnect the SUV from its burden.

On the harbor waters, people with their boats were slowly moving close to the downed police helicopter. They could not offer any help for the pilot. His lifeless body floated among the wreckage.

* * * * *

Hennington and the entire security crew saw the chopper go down. Upon noticing that cars were turning around at the bottom of the hill to come back up, Hennington gave a different order.

"Listen up! Let's move our vehicles to the very top of the hill and block any more traffic from coming over. Move it! Move it!"

* * * * *

Two additional police cars now came down from Main Street to join forces with those already stopped before the trailer.

"I don't care, we cannot make a move until we know what is in that trailer!" yelled Cooper the CIA agent to the Police Chief. "I'm calling in the military, we need serious help."

"Get your HAZMAT team down here!" Rigano ordered the Police Chief.

The Police Chief looked at Agent Rigano, "You'll have to call the County for any hazard team or equipment. Right now all I can get here is the town's volunteer fire department."

"Every move we make from here on has to consider that these guys didn't shoot that chopper out of the sky with a bullet," Detective Rodriguez announced just before they all had to take cover behind their cars. The two gunmen on opposite corners of the trailer fired over their heads for two full seconds before the bullets stopped flying.

"Back off! We are leaving and don't try to stop us or the guy stuck in the car here eats bullets!" Only a minor accent could be heard in this yelling voice.

* * * * *

"Stop delaying! Stop!" yelled the gunman and he punished Gabbie with a backhand slap. George tried to intervene, but could not. The other gunman held George's arms behind his back.

"How do you expect me to explain everything to you in just a few minutes?" Gabbie slowly drilled the words home to the masked gunman. "You have been lied to, you have been used, and you don't even realize..."

"Shut up woman, we have no time left. We are leaving."

Snapping sounds and sparks spewed out from the fuse box that George knew could not handle the load. Unfortunately, he could not do anything about that now.

"Whoa, fire," said the gunman holding George.

"Oh no, George, what happened?" Gabbie asked as she stumbled backwards with the gunman who continued to pull her towards the door.

"Oh, Gabbie," George cried out. "The fuse box and curtains are on fire!"

"All right I'll get the fire extinguisher."

"You'll get nothing. You give and tell us nothing, now the two of you come with us." Both Gabbie and George were being hustled out of the lab.

"Noo!" Gabbie yelled. "Addie, the lab is on fire! Get out!"

"We are going to let your lab burn to the ground!" The gunman yelled at the same time Gabbie cried out to Addie, thus not hearing what she said.

Addie heard everything loud and clear as they all moved into her view. Addie placed her fingertips onto the grating covering the vent as she watched in horror and everything became surreal.

"I'm not going anywhere with you!" protested Gabbie.

The gunman swung Gabbie around and hit her square in the face with his gun. She fell to the floor with her left eyebrow bleeding.

George broke loose and charged her attacker, who turned and shot him twice. As George slowly fell to the floor in disbelief, Gabbie screamed his name and her whole body shook with trauma. The smoke alarms started again and Addie cried out in anguish.

Both gunmen grabbed Gabbie, who struggled toward the back of the lab. Addie watched Gabbie reaching for her in vain as the gunmen literally carried Gabbie out of the burning lab.

"George! Addie!" Gabbie's voice started to fade as they carried her up the stairs. "I love you both!"

Somehow through the horror and fear, Addie knew she had to get out. She started banging on the vent's grate until the top right and lower left screws popped out. The other two screws in opposite corners held the grate in place. Now Addie could only rock the grating from corner to corner and she slowly began to panic.

* * * * *

Charlie and Derrick hopped over the backyard fence of a house to see a sharp drop to the intersection of Route 5A and Pond Lake Road below.

"That's a big first step," Derrick gasped. "We're going down, right Charlie?"

"Damn straight."

Without another moment of hesitation both men started down the slope. First, they did some sliding, followed by a jump or two on the way down. However, when they bumped into each other they had to grab the only vegetation available to maintain balance. Only one-third the way down and holding a small tree growing out the side of the slope, Charlie and Derrick reevaluated their situation.

"Look up the road," Derrick called out. "The entire unit is at the top of the road."

"I see them," Charlie answered. "And I see a new boat that isn't supposed to be there. Look, out at Land's End."

"I see it, now what about our next giant step beneath us?"

"All right, look down this way. This will offer us the safest way down." Charlie surmised.

"Damn, if that's the safest, what does the dangerous one look like?" Derrick complained because the drop would give anyone vertigo.

* * * * *

They dragged Gabbie up to her back door as she kicked and screamed for help. They threw her to the floor and held down her arms as they duct taped her ankles together.

"Oh God, please God," Gabbie called out as the masked gunman ripped off a small piece of duct tape. God, I beg you, please save my great granddau..." The small piece of duct tape slammed down over her mouth and they quickly carried her away.

George opened his eyes wide and fast. He saw smoke crawling all along the ceiling and he heard Addie banging on the grate. George slowly rolled over and stood up with an inanimate appearance. Fire began to spread swiftly, and through the smoke emphasized by the alarm's strobe light, Addie thought she saw an apparition.

"My God, George is that you?" Addie started coughing again. "Oh George, thank God you're okay. Please help me out. Some screws are stuck."

George slowly went to his knees and crawled to the vent. Slowly he laid down right in front for a second.

"George, are you all right?" Addie asked as she coughed some more.

George's hand reached up and turned the screw that he put in earlier. The screw and his hand dropped to the floor. Addie continued coughing, but the smoke did not bother George.

"Sorry, Addie," mumbled George. "That screw was in too much."

"George!" Addie called out after he put his head to the floor. "George, please there is one more."

Addie banged and forced a big enough opening so she could bend the grate open until that last screw popped out. The grate dropped on top of George. Addie quickly scurried out of the vent and threw the grate off to the side so she could shake George.

"George, let's get out of here."

"She called God, Addie."

"What? George, please let's get up." The combined elements of smoke in Addie's lungs, alarms going off, and the sight of blood covering George's shirt caused confusion to set in. All this snarled Addie's judgement and movements.

"Gabbie asked God to save you." George said his last words and turned to Addie with a smile.

"Oh no, God, why?" asked Addie. She tried dragging George's body as ceiling tiles started to crash down in the operating room and by the exit. The noise made as the flaming tiles fell spurred Addie to realize she had to leave. She kissed George softly on the cheek and closed his eyes. "Thank you, Doctor... Thank you George...and goodbye," she said before getting up and running out. At the door, she felt an immense amount of heat from the burning fragments of debris. Addie lowered herself to the floor and started crawling out the door, but this offered little relief. Coughing and crawling she passed the wooden barrels and made her way up the metal stairs.

* * * * *

Chris came speeding down Pond Lake Road in his car after going the long way around. His car's radio played the song, *Hero*, by Enrique Iglesias. The long gradual decline toward the harbor had him passing two elongated ponds on his left and steep hillsides on his right. Chris started to rapidly catch up with a police car that had its emergency lights and siren going. The police car stopped and turned to block Pond Lake Road about one-fourth of a mile from Route 5A. Chris hit his brakes and came to an abrupt stop. The patrol car also blocked off Hollow Hill Road, the only road that came down from the hillside to intersect with Pond Lake Road. However, making a right turn there would be no help to Chris. A brown minivan now came down from Hollow Hill Road and the police officer waved the vehicle to a stop. Chris saw the officer telling the driver that he could not turn right toward Route 5A. He also saw an opportunity to get by the police car. He slammed his gas pedal to the floor. Before the officer could get off a yell for Chris to stop, he zoomed pass with the left tires on the dirt and one layer of paint shy of hitting the patrol car on the right.

Meanwhile on the opposite side of the trailer, sirens were blaring again. Fire trucks came down from the Firehouse that stood around the bend and not far from the storefronts on Main Street. They joined all the police vehicles and officers taking cover before the trailer.

Chris came to a skidding stop at Route 5A and Pond Lake for several reasons. He had a red light, heard fire truck sirens, saw the black SUV with gunmen in front of a trailer just fifty yards beyond the intersection, and two security guards dropped off the hillside. They both hit the blacktop of the intersection with a cloud of dust.

“Oh sweet!” Charlie yelled half out of breath as he slammed his hands covered with dirt on the hood of Chris’ car. “Kid, are we glad to see you.”

“Are you guys crazy?” Chris said as he grabbed the top of his front windshield with both hands to lift himself to see over. “I almost killed you both!”

“Back off! Back off!” Chris heard from across the intersection. Charlie and Derrick turned to view the SUV with the trailer in heavy shade from the hillside and blooming roadside trees. However, harsh sunlight from a lowering sun hit the intersection and impaired their vision. Chris shut off his car’s stereo to hear better, but before any of them could confirm who did the yelling, several bullets rained upon them. Charlie and Derrick ran over the hood of Chris’ car and dove over the windshield into the rear section behind the front seats. A multitude of bullets hit the ground about twenty-five feet in front of the car.

“Back it up, kid!” Charlie yelled as Chris threw the car into reverse and sped back up the hill.

* * * * *

“What the hell are they shooting at now?” demanded Cooper as the fire trucks that pulled up behind them shut off their sirens.

“The two gunmen left the corners of the trailer,” reported Epstein.

“Yo!” shouted a teenage volunteer firefighter at the top of the Bucket truck. “They shot at some convertible on the other side of the intersection.”

“Ssshit!” yelled Detective Rodriguez who sat with his back against his unmarked car.

“What’s wrong?” Officer Rampey asked.

“Yo, Smokey!” Rodriguez called out to the firefighter on top of the truck. “Would that convertible be a black Mazda sports car?”

“You got it, gumshoe!”

“That kid is going to get himself killed,” mumbled Rodriguez.

"Rigano, cover me. I'm getting a look in that trailer's open window while they're preoccupied." With that said, Cooper ran around his car to sneak up closer to the trailer. He jumped up to grab the ledge of the open window and hoisted himself to look in.

* * * * *

"Stop shooting at them!" yelled an impatient masked man. "They are leaving. Help us disconnect the SUV that is stuck! We are turned too sharp there."

Chris had brought his car to a turning stop, causing the two security guards to bounce around in the small rear space.

"Shit that was close, are you guys all right back there?"

"I think coming down that slope was safer," Derrick sarcastically commented.

Next all three men in the car were startled by a triple pounded sound on the back of Chris' car.

"Are you guys crazy?" demanded the police officer who just ran down the hill with his gun drawn. "I have a roadblock back there for a reason! These guys are shooting real bullets and they blew our chopper out of the sky!"

"Yes, Officer, we know," Charlie pointed out. "We're with security at the Cold Creek Harbor lab and we could use your help right now."

"You think?" said the tense riddled officer sarcastically. "All of you get out of the car and take cover behind it."

* * * * *

Charisse and Lance were running back up the street to the top of the hill. A police car now arrived at the barricade of private cars after passing the vehicles turned around by Hennington, Steve, and José. Only the siren shut down after the officer parked his car sideways in the middle of the road.

“All right,” the officer said while getting out of his car. “Everyone has to clear the area.”

“Sir,” Charisse called out. “Hawk and Tommy are on their way back to report on the security booth surveillance.”

“Sir? Surveillance? What’s going on here?” A bewildered police officer demanded. Next, the officer saw two men camouflaged with mud on their faces and leaves all over their clothes. “Holy shit! Who are you guys?”

“Sir, reporting in.” Hawk called out as he and Tommy paused to inhale additional oxygen.

“Officer,” said Hennington. “The laboratory here is a government facility. We are the Military Police unit assigned to protect it. I’m in command of this unit.”

* * * * *

With a rush and panic Cooper ran back toward his car. He jumped over one corner of his car’s hood and landed on the other side where Rigano had taking cover. The Police Chief, Epstein and Rodriguez crawled over to listen to Cooper’s findings.

“Chief, I think things will be best if we move everyone back and evacuate any residents still in their homes.”

“Move back?” the Chief quizzically asked. “How far?”

“I would say about one mile.”

“What! What the hell is in that trailer?”

“Half of the trailer is stuffed to the ceiling with explosives and it looked wired to go.”

Just then, the SUV pulled free of the trailer and the front end dropped to the ground with a loud thud. Every public servant who heard Cooper and that thud sound, jumped out of their skin.

"All right everyone we are pulling back!" shouted the Police Chief without hesitation.

* * * * *

Addie now found herself outside on Gabbie's front porch on her hands and knees. Still dizzy, coughing badly, and after a minor spit up, her cell phone started to ring. She crawled into the corner of the porch and pulled the phone out of her pocket.

Addie's mother only heard coughing and once she heard a pause, she called out over the phone, "Addie, Addie is that you?"

"M...om," came Addie's broken verbalization of the word.

"Oh my God, Addie what's wrong? I've been calling you for the longest time."

"They killed George..." Addie coughed again.

"What! Who? Addie, where are you?" shear hysteria echoed in Brielle's voice.

"They have... Oh my God, the house is on fire up here now."

"Fire! Addie, please dear where are you?"

"I'm outside... Gabbie's house. I'm go...going to security."

"Oh yes, go there..." Brielle drew in air and literally screamed at the top of her lungs from her bedroom. "My God Stu! Stu we have to get to the lab!" She then placed the cell phone back to her mouth and with tears in her eyes shouted to her daughter. "Addie, get to security we'll be right there!"

"Yeah, I'm going." Addie hung up before standing and climbing over the porch's railing to get a golf cart from under Gabbie's carport. Scurrying into the only golf cart available, Addie began a frantic search for the keys. Alas, she could not find keys anywhere and that realization along with George's blood all over her hands caused Addie to breakdown. She dropped her head into her arms across the steering wheel and started sobbing.

* * * * *

Police chatter started over the officer's radio with Chris and the two security guards, Charlie and Derrick. They were moving up on the intersection through the trees by the pond.

"This is Officer Popovich," cracked over the radios for all police to hear. "I am south of the trailer and I count four gunmen inside the black SUV."

Everyone near a police officer started to listen. Popovich disengaged his radio on his shirt and turned to Chris, Charlie, and Derrick. "The three of you stay here."

The SUV started to peel out just as Popovich ran toward the intersection. "They are making a break for it," he yelled over his radio. "They are heading toward the lab. I have a shot!"

The SUV sped through the intersection and Popovich unloaded his revolver as he came to a running stop in the intersection. Half the bullets missed and headed out over the waters of the harbor. Two bullets hit the left rear tire; causing a blowout. With a splatter of sparks the SUV's tire rim contacted with the road once the majority of the rubber tire stripped away. The driver slowed to preserve control of the vehicle.

"Get going, get back!" the Police Chief commanded.

"We have to get that trailer into the drink," Cooper thought aloud in front of Rigano, Epstein, and Rodriguez.

"The bucket fire truck!" Rodriguez yelled out. "Hey kid, hold up with the fire truck!"

Several firefighters using a fire hose and rope were attaching the fire truck's bucket to the front end of the trailer.

"All clear!" yelled one of the firefighters. "Go, go...lift it up!"

Just as the bucket cleared the roof of the trailer, the front end came up off the ground. Immediately, the teenage firefighter at the controls swung toward the gravel filled lot causing the trailer to roll backwards from which it came. Other firefighters raced with the Jaws of Life to the driver stuck in his car. The Fire Chief ran down to the water with his bullhorn. Cooper, Rigano, Epstein, and Rodriguez ran along both sides of the trailer yelling out helpful directions to speed up the launching of the trailer into the harbor. The fire truck continued to back up and push the trailer toward the water.

"Evacuate the area!" yelled the Fire Chief through his bullhorn at all the boats by the crash site of the helicopter and the shoreline. "All boats leave at top speed now! Pass the word to other boats out of my range. The trailer has a bomb inside, go, go, go!"

"Oh my God," the elderly driver stuck in his car said to the firefighter trying to free him. "They're going to blow us up."

"No, they are not!" insisted the firefighter. "We'll have you out of there in no time." The Jaws of Life started its job.

Two men in a small rowboat were not going anywhere fast. Both men frantically tried to wave another boat down for a tow instead of rowing. Two sisters on a sailboat were already getting a tow and one of them in that sailboat saw the men waving.

Four men in a dinghy from a larger boat were now pulling the pilot's body from the water. Never did these four citizens think that this day would call upon them to save the dignity of a fallen police officer as the risk of a bomb going off increased with each passing second.

The SUV grind to a stop at the security gate and the four gunmen celebrated meeting the other two in the security booth with hugs and laughter. They were happy to be alive, because in the back of their minds they knew this diversion made them expendable. As they unscrupulously celebrated their corrupt reunion, the men and women of Cold Creek Harbor's volunteer fire department were rolling the bomb filled trailer to the edge of the empty lot. Every firefighter rushed to disconnect the rope and hoses used to attach the trailer's hitch to the fire truck.

"Drop your sail!" yelled the Skipper of the boat towing the sailboat toward the two stranded men. Immediately after the sail fell, their speed doubled.

The four men already brought the deceased pilot aboard the larger boat. They tied off the dinghy, as the two engines built up to full power to rip away.

"Go, go, go!" The Fire Chief yelled through his bullhorn at everyone in the lot. They all started running back up to the street dragging the rope and fire hose. The driver of the fire truck backed her truck into the trailer. The large wheels spun on the gravel, but slowly pushed the threat into the harbor.

Waves from the fleeing boats pounded the small boat with the two stranded men as the rescue craft came along side.

"Jump aboard," the Skipper ordered. "Leave your boat, we don't have time!"

Upon hearing that, the two sisters dove off their sailboat and feverishly swam to the Skipper's boat. They climbed aboard and untied their vessel.

"Go!" yelled the older sister of the two women.

The fire truck now sped out of the lot as common sense told the firefighters to drop the hose they were dragging and run.

Across the harbor one of the six gunmen noticed the trailer went over the edge and started shouting. He literally had to start hitting the others who were still laughing to get their attention.

The injured driver, free of his crushed car, had several firefighters place him inside an ambulance that rushed back up to the firehouse without closing the rear doors.

Chris drove his car with the two security guards at eighty miles an hour, blowing by the security booth. A few of the six gunmen noticed while the rest went through the SUV, tossing out backpacks, fast food litter and blood covered rags. Sirens were now blasting as the cars of Rodriguez, Rampey, Epstein, Rigano with Cooper, and the Police Chief raced toward the lab's entrance.

The radio control rested on the floor of the SUV. Without hesitation, the gunman pushed the button as he reached across the rear seat. However, nothing happened, thus causing the gunman with the radio control to sit up with anger. Only the top fourth of the trailer stuck out of the water. The police sirens were getting closer and this time he pointed the radio control across the harbor before pushing the button.

Chris' car did a spin out stop at the top of the hill by the rest of the security team. Charlie and Derrick literally rolled out of Chris' car. Plenty of questions would have started for all the Military Police just reunited, if the hillsides did not start to shudder. The harbor's water swelled, and the air permutated with a percussion sound that bellowed.

The rear of the fire truck slammed into trees on the edge of the road. Windows on each house by the water blew in and the two abandoned boats capsized. Addie's head leaped up. With tear-filled eyes and a face smudged with soot she looked across the harbor.

Each police car came to a skidding stop just before the lab's entrance and witnessed a geyser of water cascade sixty feet straight up. Forthwith, forty feet of land from the gravel lot disintegrated into the harbor. Only twenty feet or so remained of the parcel.

Firefighters took cover behind other fire trucks and held their ears. Simultaneously they dispatched an ambulance down to the brave firefighter still in her truck that sent the trailer to an impuissant explosion.

* * * * *

"Oh my Lord," Jake's father cried out. The three of them had stopped fishing to watch what happened across the harbor. "Jake, my boy, what is going on here?"

"I don't know, Pop, but I sure don't like any of this one bit."

* * * * *

Water began to rain down on the ambulance. Firefighters raced to the aid of the woman firefighter driving the truck. Upon reaching the damaged vehicle, they saw an arm swing over the door from the inside.

"Some weather we're having, huh boys?" said the driver as she popped her head up to look out the window. "I see that it's raining, but I can't hear a thing."

* * * * *

The police, FBI, and CIA now engaged the six gunmen at the security booth. However, they all had to take serious cover when several semiautomatics began shooting back.

“They don’t have enough fire power,” Hennington said as they watched from the top of the street.

“These guys are going to head to their boat for an escape,” stated Tommy.

“I’m getting in my car and adding one more revolver to our fire power.” With that said, Officer O’Connor ran to his patrol car.

“We need our brothers and sisters here now,” Hennington wished aloud. Unfortunately, that could no longer happen. The First Air Force at Mitchell field closed down in the early nineteen-sixties. Help would arrive much later as compared to that first morning in nineteen forty-two.

“Clear the way, here he comes,” Chris yelled to everyone as the patrol car zoomed by them. Chris immediately jumped into his own car and went in the direction the police car just came from.

“Hey, where are you going?” Charlie yelled out.

“To find my girlfriend!” Chris rushed to answer.

The tires on Chris’ car screeched as he made the right turn onto Harbor View Road. Once he came upon the break in the guard railing, he instantly took the dirt road that dropped halfway down to sea level. Chris stopped his car about forty yards from the end of the dirt road and the three men who were no longer fishing.

“My God, is that Chris Wilkins?” Jake asked himself.

“Chris who?” Jake’s father wanted to know.

“That’s Chris,” Jake accepted. That’s his car... Oh Pop, he’s a kid that I have on one of my school bus routes for the district.”

"He looks awful distraught to me," Jake's father noticed. "Let's find out what's going down."

"Right, Pop, let's go Hayden."

The two younger men started up the dirt slope toward Chris in a full sprint. Once the father started jogging up, his son and his friend already slowed to a jog. About twenty yards up, Jake's father went by them.

"Look at this... And the WW Two Vet of eighty-three years takes the lead over the two younger Vietnam Vets! You gotta stop eating those burgers, son."

Nonetheless, all three arrived at Chris' car at the same time. Completely winded, all of them had to lean on the car for support.

"This is embarrassing," mumbled Hayden.

"Yo, Chris..." called Jake. "What are you looking at?"

Chris hugged low to the ground while looking down on the boat just below the bluff. With the first sound of Jake's voice, Chris spun his head to see who shouted his name. Then he put his finger to his lips, signaling the three men to be quiet.

Jake went down low and crawled up next to Chris. Once he looked over the edge and saw below he grabbed Chris and dragged him back to the car.

"Shit man! Are you crazy?" demanded Jake of Chris.

"What son? What's the problem?" Jake's father asked his son.

"Shit, Pop, there are two men on that boat we saw down there and they are carrying semiautomatics and wearing ski masks!"

"Son, what's going on?" Jake's father first asked of Chris before adding, "Your jaw is swollen, son."

"I know... I know and they have Addie down there! This is real bad."

"Where the hell are all those security guards?" Jake wanted to know.

"They're all pinned-down at the front security booth by six more guys with the same guns. So I gotta do something," Chris rushed to verbalize.

"Jake," said Hayden. "If you listen carefully you'll hear the sound of gunfire in the distance."

"You're right," agreed Jake. "Let's drive up the road for a look."

* * * * *

The six gunmen started to fall back toward the garage, leaving their black SUV behind. The police moved their cars in front of the entrance gate and continued to return fire. Hennington wasted no time leading his people under the gunfire and into the security booth. Charlie arrived first inside the booth and started yelling, "Man down in here! Pete? Pete?"

Hennington crouched down just outside the security booth while yelling orders. "Keep moving Charlie! Downstairs now with Derrick, Steve, Lance, Hawk and José! Get your real uniforms on with full gear! Charlie, bring up my gear! Charisse see to Pete's condition. Tommy get on the control panel. I want a status report on the whole lab."

"Yes, sir!" yelled Tommy as everyone else flew downstairs.

"I have a pulse, sir," said Charisse. "It's weak, but he's alive."

"Tommy we need an ambulance what's the status?" Hennington demanded as he took shelter just inside the booth's door.

Tommy stood next to a small console built into one of the counters of the booth. "All systems have been shut down sir. Phones are dead."

"Charisse?" yelled Hennington.

"Yes, sir, calling for ambulance on my cell phone now."

"Sir, I'm bringing the system back online now."

"Charisse, get below and get ready while on the phone. I'll watch Pete."

"Yes, sir," said Charisse as she went down the stairs.

"Sir! System is back up! We have a fire alarm in the Private Lab and for Victorian Seventeen!"

"Crap. All right, get below and tell Charisse to call the fire department and get them here also!"

"Yes, sir!"

"And move it people!" Hennington yelled down the stairs. "Those cops are going to be out of bullets any second!"

* * * * *

Smoke poured out of Gabbie's house and two gunmen continued to move back through the woods in that direction. The other four gunmen held the police and agents back by the gate.

All this time Addie remained hiding in Gabbie's carport by the golf cart. Chris, Hayden, Jake, and his father had a new view. They had slowly driven halfway down the road back toward the front of the lab's property. Through several trees and down the hill in the distance stood the security booth, that now became crowded with helmets. Each soldier awaited orders on one knee.

"Okay, everyone ready?" asked Hennington.

"Yes, sir!" shouted out in unison.

"Charisse, wait here with Pete until the ambulance arrives. Direct the fire trucks when appropriate."

"Yes, sir," she replied.

"Everyone else. Let's move out!" Hennington yelled as he finished dressing.

Upon seeing the MPs move out from the security booth, Cooper held his arm up yelling, "Hold your fire! Hold your fire!"

With precision and alternating turns, the MPs moved out in full uniform and gear. They protected each other's back as they took turns getting into position against available cover such as Addie's minivan. They spread out systematically and deliberately before they started to return fire with calm accuracy. One gunman fell wounded and another fell dead. Each MP used his side arm far more efficiently than the enemy used their semiautomatics.

"Look down there, Pop!" an excited Jake, yelled out. "I told ya who those guys were! Hayden that there is the United States Military Police. Right, Pop?"

"I can't see well that far away son."

"I see them now," said Chris. "Look here through these trees."

"Damn, well look at that," said Jake's father.

"I tell you that's America down there," Jake proudly announced. "Look who is below us defending; brothers from all around the world. We're all people; that's America."

Sirens were in the distance again as the ambulance and fire trucks headed down Route 5A to the lab's entrance.

"Jake," said Hayden as he tapped his friend's back. "Look, that house is starting to burn up pretty bad."

"Look!" Chris called out. "Two of them are under that carport. Oh God! Oh God! They have Addie!"

"Okay, okay Chris, don't panic," reassured Jake. "They're holding her hostage to keep the MPs off their tail."

"This is going to be a stalemate son," said Jake's dad with concern.

"Not if I can help it, Pop," said Jake. "Chris, let me have your car keys."

"What?"

"I live right down from here on Old Ocean Street. I'm going to get my rifle." Jake caught the car keys tossed to him by Chris.

Addie screamed as they dragged her away against her will. All this sounded upward to the top of the overlook. Hearing Addie's screams sent emotions raging in Chris.

"They're hurting her," Chris said with clenched fist. "I'll..."

"Okay, okay, now just wait a minute." Jake told Chris as he shook him with one hand. "We can't lose our heads or we'll all get killed. You guys follow them from up here as they make their way to the boat. I'll be right back."

The MPs now moved forward tediously while they held their fire. Three of the militants were now using Addie as a shield. They slowly and methodically dragged her backwards toward their boat, allowing enough time for their wounded partner to get there first.

The police, ambulance, and the government agents stayed at the security booth. They removed Pete and placed him in the ambulance as Charisse looked on. Once the ambulance pulled away, a police station wagon pulled up.

"We have more munitions arriving," shouted the Police Chief. Cooper, Rigano, Epstein, and the Chief took immediate advantage.

"Charisse, do you read?" Hennington called over his radio.

"Yes, sir," Charisse answered just outside the security booth with her own portable radio.

"They're moving back toward their boat at Land's end. They have that young assistant Addie Erickson as hostage."

Upon overhearing that, Detective Rodriguez turned away with a wrenching feeling and serious concern slashed across Officer Rampey's face.

"We're beyond Victorian Seventeen that's on fire. Send the fire trucks in and have the police give them cover."

"Yes, sir, consider it done." Within seconds, Charisse spread the word.

“Come on, Epstein,” Cooper called out.

Let’s go!” Rigano yelled over the sirens as she ran to catch up to the fire truck.

Chris, Jake’s dad and Hayden now found themselves back on the bluff looking down on the boat. The same area Chris and Addie went down that night in December. The old shack still stood there, as well as the torn tarpaulin over the dry rot wooden barrels. The barrels were stacked high enough to provide coverage for a man to stand. The three men spied down on the forty foot long boat and watched the wounded gunman assisted aboard by two others in masks and short lab coats. A short distance from the boat, Addie fought against being dragged backwards down the last dirt slope and onto the old wooden deck.

“They’re going use that boat as their getaway,” mentioned Jake’s dad.

Just then, Jake pulled onto the dirt road with Chris’ car. “Get away from the edge! Don’t let them see you!” Jake yelled as he grabbed his rifle before getting out of Chris’ car.

Chris went running toward Jake, “Leave it running! Don’t shut off my car!”

Jake stepped out of Chris’ way as Chris reached in the car and took a key off the keychain. Chris ran around and unlocked his car’s trunk. Immediately he tossed a crate filled with car care supplies out of the trunk. His red baseball bag followed.

“What are you doing?” Jake’s dad questioned as he and Hayden jogged up to the car.

“Stopping that boat...” Chris slammed the trunk shut. “From being their get away.” Chris pulled his aluminum baseball bat out of the bag and jumped into his car. He adjusted the direction his car faced. After putting the car into park, he jumped out and ran to look over the bluff. The gunmen had Addie between the wooden barrels and shed now. Chris turned and looked back at his car with one eye closed, then ran back to his car to move the driver’s seat all the way forward.

“What my Pop means is, what are you thinking?” a slightly nervous

Jake asked as he and his dad stood there with Hayden.

Chris reached for his bat that he left on the passenger's seat and placed the top end on the gas pedal. Once he wedged the bat's handle into the driver's seat, the engine roared. Chris slammed his driver side door shut for the last time. He reached in and threw the car into Drive.

"Dear Lord, what are you doing child!" Jake's father yelled as Jake grabbed Chris by the arm and pulled him away from his car that ripped across the dirt road.

They all watched as the car rammed through some dry underbrush and saplings before plunging over the bluff. After a count of two, the atmosphere in front of them crashed upward in noise, water, and a gust of smoke.

"Don't run to the edge to look just yet!" Jake yelled. "They'll be looking up to see who sent that car over."

Gabbie had been taken prisoner below deck of the boat. There she experienced a forward and backward rocking motion. The two gunmen watching her ran above deck to investigate. They left behind the wounded gunman who rolled off his bench seat. Gabbie saw that he died. She frantically searched through the litter of items all around for something to cut the duct tape off her ankles. In a used fast food bag she found a plastic knife and went to work posthaste.

The chaos continued on deck over the car just missing the boat by five feet. Chris now ran straight up to the bluff before the other men and looked down on the scene.

"Chris, get low!" Jake yelled out.

"Chris!" Addie screamed as she looked up between the gunmen. Four gunmen were standing around Addie behind the wooden barrels spraying bullets at the Military Police who had taken cover behind boulders, large trees, and mounds of dirt. One gunman saw Addie looking up from where the car came from and this time when he looked up again, he saw Chris standing there in defiance with his right hand raised just above the level of his head. The back of his hand faced the gunman and Chris held up his middle finger. Bullets left the gunman's semiautomatic. Addie screamed as dirt flew up from the hillside just below Chris' feet.

Each burst of dirt into the air moved higher and higher toward Chris. The gun paused and several more rounds went over Chris' shoulder. However, the last bullet sent him falling backwards. Addie buried her face in her knees and started screaming as she held her ears.

Chris fell back into Jake's arms, "Shit Pop, he's been hit." Cloth, flesh, blood, and bone chips flew into the air and unto Jake's face.

The three men all began to suffer from flashbacks. Those words Jake yelled and the sight of a young man falling triggered the subconscious of each man. The amount of years that had passed since the last war they had each experienced did not matter. Everything became surreal and seemed to move in slow motion. Jake's dad flashed back sixty years to World War II. The all African American army unit took heavy casualties. Jake and Hayden were back in Vietnam, only thirty-four years ago. Smoke filled air, swamps, and rain haunted Jake. Wounded brothers were all around Hayden no matter where he looked.

"I'm okay..." Chris mumbled three times, pulling the three men back to reality. "I think I'm okay," Chris concluded.

Jake dragged Chris away from the bluff from under his arms and saw the blood building on top of Chris' left shoulder.

"Don't worry, Chris," Jake said as he gasped for some air and did a shake off of memories. "Hayden here was a Medic in Nam. Right Hayden? Hayden?"

"That's right," Hayden finally said. "You just stay put here and let me take a look. I need some bandages to apply pressure."

"Pop, get some of those rags Chris threw out of his trunk before," Jake said after looking away from Chris' wound.

"Yes, sir. Right away son!"

The front right side of Chris' car went through the edge of the old wooden deck. The other half went in the water and remained stuck in the mud. The back tires rested on the sharp incline of the bluff and the entire underside of the car caught fire. The convertible roof broke off on impact and landed on the rear deck of the boat. Somehow flames from the car ignited the cloth roof. The four gunmen in short lab coats were trying to put out the fire. Two were on deck dealing successfully with the convertible roof and the other two were half in the water trying in vain to control the fire under the car to avoid an explosion.

"Sir, that was Chris' car," Charlie said to Hennington.

"Give the kid a damn medal, because two more minutes they would have all been off and away in that boat. Let's get some people to go back around and join him up there."

"That's going to be difficult, they have us pinned down since we are not returning fire," concluded Charlie.

"We can't risk hitting the girl. Get on my radio to Charisse, tell her to get up there on the double!"

"Yes, sir!"

* * * * *

Gabbie had cut through the duct tape around her ankles and painfully removed just a section of the tape from her mouth. Leaving the tape with just one corner partly pulled down; Gabbie went to investigate the intermittent gunfire she heard. Slowly she went up the steps to look out on deck. On the top step, she saw two masked men throwing the burning convertible car roof over the side and into the water.

* * * * *

Charisse started going through the black SUV abandoned at the security entrance, when she heard Charlie on the radio.

"Charisse, this is Charlie. Come in, over."

"This is Charisse, go ahead."

"These guys are going to get away on this boat because they are holding Addie Erickson hostage and... Shit! That's Doctor Maida running off the boat! Don't let them get her!"

Gabbie had made a dash off the boat as the four gunmen were preoccupied with the burning car. However, Gabbie didn't know about the other four gunmen between the shack and wooden barrels. Two gunmen on the deck of the boat saw Gabbie jump onto the dock so they fired upon the MPs. In doing so, they offered cover for two gunmen behind the barrels to reach out and grab Gabbie.

"You are not going anywhere, Doctor!" laughed the tallest gunman who spoke perfect English.

Addie threw her arms around her great grandmother who could only express her feelings with her eyes. Blood continued flowing out of her left eyebrow and she thanked God for Addie's deliverance out of the burning lab by looking upward.

"Oh my God," prayed Addie. "Please help us."

"Do you wish to say something," said the tall gunman. Without warning he gripped the loose corner of tape and yanked until the tape ripped completely off. He did this with a hideous laugh, while the others continued firing on the MPs still holding their positions.

Both Gabbie and Addie held their screams. Splotches of skin were missing about Gabbie's top lip and blood began to ooze.

"Charlie, answer me!" Charisse called over the radio. "Did you get Doctor Maida?"

"Negative," came back the depressed voice of Charlie. "She's a hostage. Charisse get to the bluff overlooking Land's End and see if you can tell us the positions of the hostages behind the tarp covered barrels."

"Roger that," Charisse said as she lifted a blanket out of the SUV's rear compartment. She froze for a second before saying, "Damn it, a Stinger. Ah, Charlie, do you read?"

"Go ahead."

"I may have a better idea."

There in the back of the SUV laid the Stinger used to shoot down the police helicopter. Charisse shouldered the weapon, grabbed its munitions, and jumped into the first vehicle with keys.

* * * * *

"Hennington!" Epstein called out. "We're coming up to join you."

Epstein, along with Rigano and Cooper, scrambled through the brush and trees to join the MPs.

"The police have everything under control with the firefighters," reported Cooper. "That house is a goner."

* * * * *

"Grandma G, George saved me...and he's dead...and they shot Chris!" cried Addie with tears.

"Ooh George...and not Chris too?" Gabbie said between the shooting and began to cry.

"Yeah, I saw him fall." Addie held her head down with Gabbie as they both sat on the deck holding their ears with each burst of gunfire. "He was with some other men up on the bluff."

* * * * *

"Okay kid, you can sit up now," Hayden said. Chris' left shoulder had a professionally made sling to hold his left arm.

"You are lucky," said Jake's father.

"Yep," said Hayden. "Mostly skin lost, a little bone. Heck, all you have is a deep gash. A real 'bad-ass' scar. That bullet was just high enough to avoid major damage."

"It hurts bad, but thanks," said Chris.

Jake crawled back from the edge of the bluff and reported back to everyone. "They started the boat's engines and moved the damn boat just enough to cause Chris' car to fall over into the water. The fire is out. One or two shots from my gun now isn't going to do much. They're going to be out of here soon enough."

They all turned to hear and see a patrol car come skidding to a stop.

Charisse stepped out with the Stinger and placed the weapon on her right shoulder as she marched toward the bluff.

"Oh my Lord," Jake's father said and immediately stood to salute.

"Do any of you boys think I can get a clean shot at the boat from here?"

"Yes, Ma'am!" Jake and Hayden both yelled at the same time.

* * * * *

"We are all leaving now," roared the gunman who ripped the tape off Gabbie's mouth. His furious anger came from not calculating someone like Chris and his car, into the plan's equation. "You two join the others on deck and provide me cover from up there. I will slowly back onto boat with Doctor in front of me."

Gabbie became terribly fearful of that last statement as the gunman forced her to her feet leaving Addie still sitting against the tarp covered barrels.

* * * * *

Jake, Chris, Charisse, Pop, and Hayden were all on their stomachs looking off the bluff from a different location. The boat came into Charisse's sights as she waited for most gunmen to be onboard.

* * * * *

The gunman pulled Gabbie closer to him and instinctively she knew what would happen next. "You...kill the girl and get on the boat," said the gunman holding Gabbie.

Gabbie did not wait until the gunman finished speaking his words. She broke free by spinning away and stopped just in front of the other gunman, only a second after the word 'boat' had been spoken.

Five bullets came from the semiautomatic. Gabbie took two bullets across the back. The gunman pulled up trying to avoid hitting her; thus sending the last three shots into the air. Gabbie fell to the deck and into Addie's lap.

"You fool!" the gunman that held Gabbie screamed as he stood behind the barrels.

"Oh Doc..." said Charisse with a sunken heart at the top of the bluff.

"I'll get the S. O. B.," cried Jake as he aimed his rifle, but Jake immediately taken aback as they witnessed the tall gunman unload his semiautomatic into the gunman who mistakenly shot Gabbie.

Addie screamed while her hands were again over her ears. The gunman quickly pulled Addie to her feet.

"You are my protection now young woman." The gunman said right into Addie's ear as she wept.

"Hold your fire, son!" directed Jake's father. "The girl is in the way."

"I need a diversion, Pop." Jake quickly wiped the sweat from around his eyes.

"You got it!" Chris yelled and pulled his cell phone out of his pocket. "Speed dial...it's ringing!"

"Where is that music!" The gunman demanded to know as *God Bless America* echoed between the shack and the wooden barrels. While the gunman held Addie's left arm and his position, Addie pulled her cell phone out with her right hand. She hit the speaker button as the gunman signaled the boat for more coverage.

"Chris?" Addie instinctively called out to her cell phone.

"Addie, do a Slap Out! Slap Out!"

Addie spun around pulling her arm free and threw herself to the ground. Slapping both arms outward and down as her back hit the ground was a basic move taught at her Dojo. The cell phone smashed to pieces when Addie let go to slap the ground with her open palm. Instantaneously from the top of the bluff, Jake took the shot. He only needed one. Charisse then stood and fired the Stinger sending the missile through the hatch opening to the lower deck of the boat.

* * * * *

Four military Blackhawk choppers fractured the distant air. The MPs converged upon the deck and burning remains of the boat. Hennington gave orders to search the water for any gunmen. Parts of the boat were in the shack and that shack protected Addie and Gabbie from further injuries.

Jake slowly stood up and looked at Charisse. They both wore the same expression on their faces as they looked at each other. They never wanted to do what they had to, even with the responsibility of their actions completely on those who provoked and forced them. Still, they both dorpped their weapons to the ground at the same time.

Addie crawled to Gabbie and rested Gabbie's head in her arms. Between crying, Addie spoke by saying, "Grandma G, it's over... Security blew up the boat... Chris called me... He's all right." Addie continued weeping copiously.

Addie did not know just yet, but Chris along with Charisse were sliding their way down the bluff to the deck.

"I guess... I won't make your graduation and wedding," Gabbie said with much difficulty.

"Don't say that. Please don't. You can't die, you haven't hugged my mom or brother yet...your granddaughter and...great grandson."

"You'll have to...hug them for me. You and Chris...he is admirable. That was...his car."

"I know, I know," Addie agreed between the tears. "Grandma G, those bullets were meant for me."

Gabbie had serious pain and she struggled to talk. "No...don't live with that. They were mine. Live with... Addie the pain...."

The Blackhawk helicopters were getting louder. Charlie, Tommy, and Steve were now kneeling by Gabbie.

"We have an ambulance on the way, Miss Erickson... I mean Addie." Charlie bit his lower lip after saying that.

"You boys..." Gabbie said as she looked up. "Thank you, take care of Addie, my great granddaughter."

"Hang on, Doc," said Steve. "Help is on the way."

"Did she say great granddaughter?" Tommy asked of Charlie.

"Addie... I am tired of playing god. I'm not afraid to die...so I hope that answers everything...it's your project now... I have to meet our Existence."

"Grandma G, please hold on."

"Addie, stop the pain..." Gabbie wrenched.

"I can't Grandma G, I don't know how."

"Oh God, please stop the pain!" Gabbie called out, then passed on.

The repetitive pounding of all the Blackhawk chopper blades echoed in the air as each helicopter hovered in a four-corner pattern around the harbor. Chris came to Addie's side as she wept. Chris fell to his knees and hugged Addie with his one good arm as if they would never be able to hug again.

Soldiers equipped for conventional warfare, as well as chemical, poured out of each chopper by way of rope. They landed in front of the Firehouse, at the intersection of Route 5A and Pond Lake Road, and the security booth. The dock at Land's End became the fourth location where troops came down by rope.

It was over. Gabbie's private lab and her wood frame Victorian house would be consumed by fire within the hour, but her life's work rested safely on the floor by the passenger seat in Addie's bullet-ridden mini-van.

EPILOGUE

Three years have passed since that terrible Saturday afternoon. The lab never closed down nor did the government sell the houses for a profit. In fact, just the opposite happened. Since the Top Secret research conducted at the lab ended, the government increased the working budget. Within thirty-six months, they built new commercially designed buildings; one large building is now by the water. Gabbie's house, as well as a few others, are gone. There is no longer any security booth or gate. That area was cleared of trees and is now a parking lot. The dirt road by Land's End and the bluff collapsed during a northeast rainstorm that brought awful flooding. The landslide crushed the small pier and created a 'spit' of land going halfway out into the harbor. The property now looks more like a small university than a small town neighborhood. Road signs are now up by the original front entrance clearly stating the new name of the road and that a lab is on the property. The town even installed a turning lane and traffic light for the lab's entrance.

Addie's grandmother is aging again, gracefully. She is living with the Ericksons at their new house in another state. Jake now has much more than a rumor to tell the young kids on his school bus, each time he drives by the lab. After all, Jake became a genuine hometown hero and Chris is forever grateful that he saved Addie's life.

The CIA spared Addie of all investigations and Addie graduated from high school with honors. She is still dating Chris and they are seeing a great deal of each other. Due to everything they went through together, plans changed. Chris and Addie are attending the same university.

Addie did not make any promises to her great grandmother, but she holds the promise of Gabbie's gift to humankind in her mind and soul. What the future will bring, nobody knows. In the meantime, Gabbie's life work stays stuffed in a brown aging pouch the size of a catalog and tied closed with a cord. Addie will open that envelope soon enough.

In the end, this is not so much a story about individuals, as this is a story about humanity. A story where despair goes against hope, evil against good, stupidity against intelligence, and hatred against love. For people cannot comprehend their existence and purpose by a single source of information. If they do, then they have prejudiced themselves against the meaning of life.

About the Author:

L. J. Williams is an enigma. No photographs are available and the only reported information is that the author is a scientist. At least three novels have been penned by L. J. Williams, but only two are accessible as of 2012.

Gender is unknown, as well as age.

BBV
PUBLISHING

www.ingramcontent.com/pod-product-compliance
Lightning Source LLC
LaVergne TN
LVHW020705110826
845149LV00012B/2116

* 9 7 8 0 9 8 4 4 7 9 7 0 2 *